BACK FROM THE RIVER

At first all I saw was stacks of logs. On both sides of the Schuylkill there were miles of storage yards for lumber, ice, and coal. A refinery was not far off. I could smell the kerosene. And I liked that smell. It was better than a porterhouse steak or a steamed batch of linen.

I came out on Spruce and headed toward Rittenhouse Square. A white car with red lights was pulling up to the stop at Twenty-third. The horses were getting ready to move. I shouted to the conductor to wait. When I got on, dripping wet, he gave me a look. After I showed him the star that was miraculously still in my pocket, he ignored me and went to the back of the car. He lit a segar and kept busy aiming spit into the cuspidor.

A horsecar had never seemed so beautiful. The motion over the cobbles, the team's harnesses ringing against each other, the profane song of the driver—all were like some childhood memory—fresh and pure.

From the stop to my house was no more than a few blocks. I walked the rest of the way, feeling the water still clinging to me. It gave me chills, and each chill had a different reason for being there.

I went inside without lighting a lamp, removed my wet clothes, and collapsed in the bed. I don't remember saying any prayers that night, like I usually did. I'd given enough thanks when I pulled myself out of the drink.

Other Avon Books by
Mark Graham

THE RESURRECTIONIST
THE BLACK MARIAS

THE KILLING BREED

BREED

A MYSTERY OF OLD PHILADELPHIA

MARK GRAHAM

AVON BOOKS

An Imprint of HarperCollinsPublishers

AVON BOOKS
An Imprint of HarperCollins*Publishers*
10 East 53rd Street
New York, New York 10022-5299

Copyright © 1998 by Mark Graham
Library of Congress Catalog Card Number: 98-92570
ISBN: 0-380-80066-7
www.avonbooks.com

First Avon Books printing: December 1998

Avon Trademark Reg. U.S. Pat. Off. and in Other Countries, Marca Registrada, Hecho en U.S.A.
HarperCollins® is a trademark of HarperCollins Publishers Inc.

Printed in the U.S.A.

10 9 8 7 6 5 4 3

To Fauzia Nouristani Graham,
my wife, my world

IT WAS THE first night of July 1874, the kind of humid night that brings out all the smells you don't notice during the day. And all the creatures, too.

I was at a lot near the Schuylkill River. I wasn't the only one there. I could hear the rats squeaking and shambling beneath the cover of tall grass and broken barrels.

The place was familiar to me. When I was a roundsman it used to be the end of my beat. It was just the place to take a breather, pull out a bag of nuts, and have my midnight supper.

I remembered another humid July night, a year ago, when I'd been at this same lot. That night I stopped at the same place I usually did, near the remnants of a beached schooner nearly overgrown with grass, weeds, and assorted refuse from the row houses across the way. Like I said, there were all kinds of smells. Enough to turn your stomach inside out.

One of the smells that night was coming from inside the schooner. I don't know what made me kick that plank aside. Maybe it was the scurrying sound I heard underneath. Maybe it was the unsettling stench in my feasting place. I rapped my club against the wood, as a warning. A few rats creeped out from under it. They were the river variety, about the size of a small cat and five times as ferocious.

When I lifted the plank I cried out with surprise and disgust. I kicked three or four rats off the tiny thing and knew what the smell came from. There was little room for doubt.

The nuts I was chewing hardened in my stomach like lead balls. I backed away from the thing and ran through the field of garbage and weeds until I got to the street.

As I recall, I did not return to that lot for several weeks. I found somewhere else to enjoy my cashews.

Now, to-night, I was back. It hadn't changed much. As desolate and filth ridden as ever. There was one consolation, however. A breeze was wafting in the sound and smell of the Schuylkill. I could hear its waters lapping against the docks and beached boats. It was a pleasant sound. But I did not like the Schuylkill, especially at night. The water looked like tar with a few dim lights reflected on its surface, like men trapped beneath a thick sheet of ice.

Ugly things happened on the river, long after the scullers had locked up the boathouses. Predators came out of their holes and prowled the banks. I was waiting for some of them to show up.

These predators, strangely enough, weren't the kind that fed on humans. They fed on the vermin that were scurrying all around me unseen. They were two twelve-year-old boys named Ned and Basil Edgerton.

I'd found out about them from Joe Bunker. He told me I should talk to them about where his dog had disappeared to. "Disappeared" wasn't really the right word for it. Maybe they could tell me, he said, who had kidnapped his dog Jocko, the greatest ratting dog in the Commonwealth of Pennsylvania.

This was the Edgerton boys' favorite haunt. It was a fine hunting ground. With all the garbage dumped in the lot by the neighboring homes, the rats had a feast just about every night. There were all kinds of things for them to sink their teeth into—melon rinds, moldy bread, rotten heads of cabbage, bottles of milk as solid as a hunk of cheese, you name it. Not to mention the usual assortment of dumpings from chamber pots—or from people who hadn't bothered to use them.

From what I heard, Ned and Basil prowled through this cesspool every week looking for rats. It was a good quiet out-of-the-way place to corner them and ask them exactly what they'd seen at Bunker's stable five days ago.

A train whistled in the distance, probably crossing over the Market Street Bridge. I felt for my club at my waist and realized it wasn't there. Dicks didn't carry the standard billy clubs. It was hard to believe I was a detective. Me, Wilton McCleary.

And this was the beginning of my auspicious career, tracking down the kidnappers of a fox terrier in a garbage dump by the river.

It was as good a place to start as any. I had no doubt that the two rat catchers would appear that night. It was simply a matter of ignoring the various stenches and waiting.

About half an hour passed with me just sitting where I was. I saw a couple of steamers pass by on the river, the deck lights aglow. There must have been a frolic going on, because the music reached me on the shore. The fiddle playing and singing took me far away from the lot and back to the War, to our campfires. That was one of the few good memories of the War that I had.

I thought I recognized the melody. Maybe the music came from inside me. I started to hum along, and then I sang that old song:

> *All quiet along the Potomac to-night*
> *Except here and there a stray picket*
> *Is shot as he walks on his beat to and fro*
> *By a rifleman hid in the thicket.*
> *'Tis nothing! a private or two now and then*
> *Will not count in the news of the battle.*
> *Not an officer lost! Only one of the men*
> *Moaning out all alone the death rattle.*
> *All quiet along the Potomac to-night!*

Something got in my eye. Then it trickled away. I let it go.

By the time the steamer was out of sight I got my first glimpse of the Edgerton boys. They didn't care who heard or saw them. This wasn't like hunting bucks in grassville. The rats weren't scared by a little noise, or by creatures ten times their size.

The boys' voices came to me crystal clear, but for a while all I could see of them were two silhouettes against the opposite side of the Schuylkill. A tad of moonlight ringed their curly heads like a shoddy halo. Their black skins blended with the night.

"Well, lookee here, Basil. There's a whole mess of 'em."

"Where? I don't see nothin'."

"Underneath this ol' boat."

"I don't see nothin'."

"Why don't you stick your face in that hole there, nigguh? Yeah, right there. You see what I'm talkin' about?"

"Oh yeah! A whole nest of 'em!"

"I figger there must be about nine or ten, whatta you think?"

Making as little noise as I could, I edged my way closer to the boat that the boys were looking under. I had to watch where my boots stepped so I didn't kick over a broken bottle. Or step on something that wasn't quite dead yet.

Finally I made it to a large rusty anchor that was half buried in the muck. From there I could see the two boys quite clearly. They had a lantern lit by now. The smaller boy was holding it in front of him like it would ward off a horde of spooks. The tiny kerosene flame illuminated them only from the waist up, making them look like disemboweled ghosts wandering around a cemetery of junk.

"Gimme them tongs, Ned! C'mon, 'fore they get!"

"I don't wanna hold the bag this time, Basil! You said I could grab 'em to-night, dint ya?"

"What you talkin' about? I said no such thing! You's always the one who holds the bag and I's the one who grabs 'em, you got it?"

"Aw, c'mon! Just one time?"

"Gimme them tongs so I can catch these critters and then beat your ass! I gave 'em to you so you could get to hold 'em. Ain't that enough for you?"

The older boy glowered at his brother and waited. After a few more seconds of whining, I saw something metallic glimmer in the light.

Basil took the tongs and began poking around at their feet. The metal ends snapped together like hungry jaws.

"There's one, Basil!"

"I sees it!"

Basil darted back and forth with his elbows sticking out, his hands gripping the tongs like they were a divining rod leading him to the mother lode. Ned followed him around holding the lantern and a burlap sack. Suddenly Basil cried out with glee, "I got you now!"

I saw him bring the tongs up and over toward his brother. There was something in the jaws now. Something black with a long naked tail.

"Get the bag open! Hurry it up, fool!"

"I'm tryin', I'm tryin', damn it!"

"C'mon!"

"Got it! Okay? In he goes!"

Basil loosened the tongs' grip. The rat fell into the bag, squeaking with fear.

"One down!" Ned said.

"Yeah, and we got a sack more to go before we call it a night!"

That was when I got up from behind the anchor and said, "Hold it a minute, boys. I want to talk to you."

Their screams were high-pitched. The lantern fell with a clatter, extinguishing the flame. They were about ready to run when I said, "Hold your horses, Ned. You too, Basil."

Now they were curious. Ned said, "How you know who we are?"

"Cause I'm a friend of one of your pals. Reddy the Blacksmith."

"You a white man. Reddy don't have no white friends, 'cept Mistuh Bunker."

"Okay," I said, edging a little closer to them. My hands were out and nothing was in them. I was as harmless looking as I could be. "I'm not exactly a pal of Reddy's. But I know him and he knows you. And now I want to talk to you."

"We didn't do nothin'!" Ned said to me. His lips curled down and pouted. He wasn't so good as his older brother at controlling his fear.

"I didn't say you did anything. All I said was I wanted to talk with you. And I want to have that talk where no one else can hear us."

Silence.

"Don't worry. You got nothing to fear from me. I just wanted to make sure no one would be around to hear you peach on them when you do."

"Whatta ya mean, peach? You a policeman?"

"That's right. See this star here? Can you read those words? It says I'm a detective."

Now they started to moan with fright.

"Don't take us to jail, Mister, please!"

"I'm not taking you to any jail. All I wanna do is ask you some questions."

"You gonna make us peach on our friends?"

"All depends. Did your friends happen to be around Alderman Bunker's house last week?"

"You ain't shakin' the bag, fool!"

Basil slugged his brother in the arm. His eyes never left me while he did it.

The little boy sniffed from the pain and the fear. He jerked the bag up and down.

"What are you doing that for?" I asked them.

"Only way to keep the rat from biting his way out," Basil said, as if I were a half-wit.

"Just got one to-night, huh?"

"Yeah," the little one said, "but we aims to get

more.'' He gave me a cowering look that asked me if
they'd get the chance now.

I said, ''How much one of these critters fetch?''

Basil said, ''Depends. Sometimes we only gets five
cents. Other times we gets twelve. Depends on how fat
they come.''

''We catched forty-seven in one night,'' his brother
said.

''Oh yeah,'' I said. ''How much money did you
make?''

''Almost three dollars!'' Basil said proudly.

''We make lots of money, Mister. We got all kinds
of gentlemen buys their rats from us.''

''You don't say. You sell to Reddy, right?''

''Sure we do. Reddy's one of our regular customers,''
Basil said.

''Yeah, he don't mind these here critters. Some folks
don't want none of these here 'cause they stink so bad,''
Ned said, making a face and smiling.

''And they infects the dog's mouf when he bites
'em,'' Basil added.

''I'd sure like to get a barn rat,'' Ned told me. ''They
get you the most money. Two bits! Man, I'd like to get
me some o' them someday.''

''Listen, Basil, Ned. How'd you like to make a dollar
to-night?''

Their mouths opened a little bit wider.

''All you have to do,'' I said to them, ''is tell me
where Jocko is.''

I was close enough to see their faces. The expressions
on them changed from hope to despair in the wink of
an eye. I had a feeling they didn't know. Well, that was
all right. I kind of expected that they weren't the ones
who stole the dog. But they might have seen something.

''You don't know who stole Jocko from Mr. Bunker?''

They didn't say anything but just stared, probably seeing that dollar go up in smoke.

''Didn't Reddy tell you about it?''

"Reddy didn't tell us nothin', Mister," Basil said.

"We ain't seen Reddy since he made us these new tongs," Ned said, "and that was over a week ago."

"Well, now, that's not what Reddy told me. He said he saw you not more than five days ago when you paid him for the tongs."

"That liar! He never asks us for no money. We ain't got hardly any money either way. He's fibbin', Mister." The older boy turned to his brother and said, "Shake that bag, fool!"

"Look, don't play games with me. I don't think Reddy's fibbin'. He told me you were around the day Jocko got taken. So how about it?"

Both boys were quiet for a spell. I decided I might have to get rough with them. So I said, "All right, I've had it with the two o' you. We're takin' a walk to the station house."

They both cracked in an instant.

"No! Please, Mister? Please? We didn't do nothin'! All we did was promise Reddy we wouldn't go tellin' no one what he done."

This was what I wanted to hear. "Whatta ya mean, what he done?"

"He was . . . well, when we come up for our tongs we saw he was drinkin' this big bottle of likker. There was no one around but the three o' us so's he gave us a snip or two. That's all we done."

"Then you went home, right after that?"

"Naw, he made us help him for just a bit."

"Oh yeah? What did you help him with?"

The boys didn't get the chance to answer me. They saw something before I did. All they did was whisper, "Oh shit."

I took a look over my shoulder. Then I felt my stomach sink down into my groin. I wished I had a barker on me.

We were surrounded by five plug-uglies with broad brim hats and some of those new derby ones, covering their faces in deep shadows. White handkerchiefs dangled from their thick necks. Every single one had something in his hand, from a broken base-ball bat to a brick. Not sophisticated weapons, but they would cause pain plenty enough. One was smoking a segar. Another began to whistle. What the tune was I couldn't tell. He was tone-deaf. Another snickered. I wasn't laughing. I knew who they were, even if I couldn't see their faces.

River rats. Scum that prowled the waterfronts. They climbed onboard ships in the night and stole whatever they could. If they had to kill to get what they wanted, that was A1 with them.

No guns that I could see. That meant the most I could expect was a beating to death.

There was no sense in trying to reason with them or buy my way out of it. I didn't have any money on me except my streetcar fare.

After a few seconds I got tired of waiting for something to happen. I looked at the mug who was the leader of this mangy crew and said a few things about his mother. They weren't too complimentary. I didn't know his mother. But it was a fair bet she was at least half the things I called her, if this was the kind of son she'd raised.

He didn't take too well to my comments. He got a little closer, until he was about ten feet away from me. Now I could see him pretty well. I could smell him, too. He blended in with the lot, nice and rancid. There was half a jaw of teeth missing when he smiled and said, "I wasn't gonna do nothin' to you, pal, except beat you within an inch of yer life and steal every cent on ya. But now," he paused and spat on my shoes, "I'm gonna have a ball beating that last inch out of you."

The others laughed but didn't crowd us. I'd made it personal for their two-bit chief.

Without taking my eyes off him I whispered to the boys, "You fellas better dust out of here. I think we're gonna have some fireworks before Independence Day."

All in one movement I stepped forward, picked up the

lantern Ned had dropped on a rubbish heap, and swung it like a slung shot at the mug.

It caught him right in the nob. He fell back, crying out. That was when the other four rushed at us.

The two boys were in such a hurry to get out of there they dropped their bag and tongs. By the time the gang was on me I'd picked up both. I felt like one of those gladiators from Roman times, the kind who went into the arena with nothing but a pitchfork and a net. Gladiators usually didn't last long. I wasn't feeling optimistic myself. But I wanted to go down as hard as I could.

My back was against the old boat where the boys had been catching rats. The one in the bag was moving around. I could feel it jerking. When one of the four men got close enough, I swung the bag to deflect a blow from his base-ball bat. The bat got caught in the burlap. I gave it a big yank and sent his head crashing into the side of the boat. He fell down with a groan.

The other three had a chance to grab me while I was taking care of the base-ball player. After I smacked his head they were on me, dragging me down to the filthy layer of garbage that covered the lot. I landed right next to the boat, where the crawl space for the rat nest was.

As I fell down I felt something hit my back, small and flat. The next time the brick would be in my face.

Desperation and panic gave me some extra strength. There were only two on me now, but they were doing a bit of damage to my kidneys. I swung on my back with a jerk and planted a boot heel in one's Adam's apple. He fell back gagging, the brick dropping from his hand. The other had a broken bottle ready to carve me up with. It was coming down on me mighty fast. I had to get out of its way.

The only place to go was under the boat. Where the rats were.

Some were nice enough to make way for me when I rolled into their nest. Others weren't so polite. Tails slithered across my hands. I started screaming.

Then I saw the boat was moving. The gang was picking up the boat to get to me. There was something moving against my ear now. Any moment and I would feel the teeth sink into it.

I brought my knees up to my chin and my heels against the boat. When I saw it lift a little more, I gave the hardest kick I ever gave, crying out with anger and disgust.

The boat flew up and over. Whoever was lifting it hadn't been ready for that. They shouted and got out of its way, stumbling.

I rolled from the nest of rats down to the river. Broken cans and bottles bit into my clothing, but I kept rolling. I was laughing by then. Just like a little shaver. Like I was somersaulting down a hill with my playmates. I laughed and laughed. That was better than screaming about having those things crawl all over me.

The Schuylkill hit me like a slap in the face. The water was cold, even though the night was stinking hot and humid.

I started swimming then. Not across. With the current, letting it take me downstream. The Market Street Bridge loomed in front of me and then passed by. In the river it felt like I was standing still and the rest of the world was moving. The water felt wonderful. I let it crawl where the rats had been and more, into my ears, across my eyes, into my mouth, even. It was fresh, clean, pure.

Then I started thinking about how dark the water was, and deep. There were all kinds of things swimming around me. I could feel the emptiness beneath me. It felt very cold on that hot, humid night.

Next to the river, I was nothing. Just another human body that could get swallowed and then fished out a few days later. No one would miss me that much, I guess. Which, I have to say, was mostly my fault. Not that the river cared.

Fear was gnawing away at me. It put all kinds of pictures in my head. Mostly I saw rats. I felt them swimming around my legs in the drink. For all I knew, the river might be infested with them.

All I could do to stop the fear from taking over completely was to close my eyes. Somehow that made the water less frightful. The rats weren't so real then.

I could hear the sounds of the city, the clang of machines in the mills, and knew which direction I had to swim to get to shore. I swam blindly, too afraid to think anymore about what I might see.

For a few minutes that worked pretty well. Then a little wave rose up and drenched me. I must have swallowed half of it. My eyes came open in a reflex action, while I gagged on the water.

That was when I saw the steamer. It was advancing downstream at a moderate pace. Not that it mattered how fast it was going. All I cared about was the fact that it was only about two yards from me. The prow was ready to cleave through my head. If it didn't kill me outright, I'd be drowned for sure. The rest of me would be dragged under the hull and churned up in the paddle wheel.

I couldn't move out of its way quickly enough. It was coming too fast.

The steamer's whistle tooted. An echo rang underneath the Market Street Bridge.

In a few more seconds it would hit me and I'd be just another floater in the Schuylkill. I felt like one of the rats in the pincers.

There was the whistle again. Usually such a gay sound. Now it was cruel, mocking.

I closed my eyes and waited. I hoped it would be over quickly.

Then I felt the coldness beneath my feet—the empty deeps of the river. Like a gentle hand they pulled me under and I went with them.

I understood. My hands joined over my head like I was praying. Before I went under completely, I blew all the air out of my lungs. Then I went down into an incredible darkness, how deep I don't know. All I remember was the cold and the fear that I would never see light again, that light didn't even exist. I wanted to scream.

But that would have meant sucking water into my lungs, that would have meant staying down there forever.

It was so dark it didn't matter if my eyes were open or not. That part scared me the most.

For as long as I could hold my breath I stayed where I was, with the river. It kept me down there, in a pit as deep and horrible as any grave, and it saved me. Just when I thought I could breathe no longer, I felt my arms and legs move without any sign from me. The water seemed to be moving them. My limbs flailed through the water, toward a surface. But I had no idea how far away it was. There were no lights I could see.

My lungs were burning, my whole body shaking. Yet I felt no closer to the air. It was like the nightmare where you're trying to run away from something but you can't move, something's holding you back.

Just when the thing would have pounced on me, at the part when you wake up or die, I felt my hands break through. My head came next and I sucked the air into me in gasps.

The boat was passing under the Chestnut Street Bridge, well away from me. For the moment, I was safe, but still too weak to fight against the river. It was drawing me toward the bridge, toward the stone pier that held the arch over the water.

When I reached the bridge, I almost got flattened against the pier. Swinging myself to the side, I curled up as best I could to absorb the impact. When I hit it I felt my shoulder go numb against the slimy stone and mortar. I tried grabbing onto it but couldn't get a grip. With my back against the pier I floated for a few moments to get my strength back. Then I swam to shore. Philadelphia was nothing but an orange-and-black blur. I tried not to think about how deep the water was, or of how many bodies we'd fished out of it. I just made for shore, alight with chimneys and smokestacks puffing an endless barrage of steam and ash into the air.

I don't know how long it took me to splash my way to the riverbank. How many times had I walked across the bridge or ridden a streetcar on it, not giving so much as a thought to the water beneath? Now I would never forget it.

When I washed ashore I crawled in the mud, digging my hands deep into the earth to claw my way up the bank. Then I collapsed on my back and stared at the sky. My chest heaved. The warm, humid air stung my nostrils and mouth as I sucked it in. My heart was pumping like a locomotive. I wasn't aware of any pain just then. That would come later. For now I was aware of one thing. I was alive. That's all that mattered to me.

It took me awhile to get up and walk back toward the city. It took me even longer to open my eyes. What made me open them was the feeling that I was back under that boat with those rats crawling over me.

At first all I saw were stacks of logs. On both sides of the Schuylkill there were miles of storage yards for lumber, ice, and coal. A refinery was not far off. I could smell the kerosene. And I liked that smell. It was better than a porterhouse steak or a steamed batch of linen.

Once I started walking, I came out on Spruce and headed toward Rittenhouse Square. A white car with red lights was pulling up to the stop at Twenty-Third. The horses were getting ready to move. I shouted to the conductor to wait. When I got on, dripping wet, he gave me a look. After I showed him the star that miraculously was still in my pocket, he ignored me and went to the back of the car. He lit a segar and kept busy aiming spit into the cuspidor.

A horsecar had never seemed so beautiful. The motion over the cobbles, the team's harnesses ringing against each other, the profane song of the driver—all were like some childhood memory, fresh and pure.

From the stop to my house was no more than a few squares. I walked the rest of the way, feeling the water still clinging to me. It gave me chills, and each chill had a different reason for being there.

I went inside without lighting a lamp, removed my wet clothes, and collapsed in the bed. I don't remember saying any prayers that night, like I usually did. I'd given enough thanks when I'd pulled myself out of the drink.

Maybe I should have added a few extra prayers. They might have come in handy. But I didn't know what was going to happen. I hadn't yet heard anything about a child named Eddie Munroe.

But even if they had told me that he would change my life, I wouldn't have cared. All I wanted to do was sleep and dream of things other than darkness.

THE DAY BEFORE Cap Heins had showed me the ransom letter for the first time. I laughed out loud.

"You want me to take care of this?" I asked him.

"You bet your ass I do, McCleary."

Cap and Bunker were pals. It was a favor to Cap. And I couldn't say no to my first assignment, even if it was to find a runaway dog.

When Bunker came in to the Central Office to talk to us, I finally began to realize it was a serious situation.

The three of us were in Cap's office. Bunker was smoking a segar the size of a small cannon and fiddling with his prodigious salt-and-pepper moustache. The day was stinking hot and we were all mopping sweat off our brows. Cap introduced us. The first thing Bunker said to me was, "You a sportsman, McCleary?"

"I knock a ball around now and then. I lose some money on the Athletics when I can spare it."

"What about pugilism?"

"I can take it or leave it."

"He's been known to indulge in it on the job," Cap said with a grin.

"Strictly an amateur, sir," I said, returning his grin. "I picked it up beneath the Mason–Dixon line a few years ago."

16

"Hmm. A warrior and a patriot, no less. This is certainly the right man, William."

"I told you so," Cap said.

"Would you mind telling me what this is about? Begging your pardon?"

Cap started to open his mouth but Bunker beat him to it.

"There ain't too many things in this world I give a damn about other than politics, McCleary. Let me make that clear straight off. First in my heart is the Twenty-Fifth Ward. Then it's the Quaker City, and after that it's my wife, bless her. And last, but just barely a notch below any of the others, are my dogs."

"Mr. Bunker," Cap said, "breeds and pits ratting terriers, McCleary."

"Precisely," Bunker said. "Now hush and lemme tell my story. You see, McCleary, some people think ratting's bloody savage. Well, bloody it sure is. But what kind of sport is it where no blood gets let, I ask you? Where's the sport without it, eh? Pitting a dog is the same as pitting a chicken, and we all know cocking's a sport of kings from the medieval ages and all that. My wife read that to me from *Harper's* the other week. I don't suppose you've ever seen a ratting match?"

I told him I hadn't. But I sure knew about them. Ratting was *the* spectator sport of the day. It consisted of pitting a dog, usually a fox terrier, against a sack full of hungry rats. The dives where the event took place were usually saloons or political clubs. It was only after the audience was at a feverish stage of drunkenness that the owners began the match. The trick was seeing how long the dog would take to kill all the rats in the pit. Sometimes the dog would have to be rescued. The rats had teeth, too.

From what I'd heard, there was a lot of money passed around at matches like this. There were always the low-class matches, where the admission was fifty cents. But then there was the other level, for the high rollers. Most of the politicians in the city spent some time at the pits. And most of them had ratting terriers.

I had no interest in ratting. Killing rats was something I had had to do plenty of times. I doubted if I'd get a thrill watching a dog kill them. And I didn't like the idea of torturing dogs for money.

After I ran down what I knew about ratting, Bunker said to me, "But do you have any idea how much money you can win at a match?"

I told him I didn't.

Bunker went to Cap's desk to get his top hat. He pulled out a wad of currency from it, like a magician.

"I always keep important papers and such in my top hat. My wife told me our late president, Lincoln, God rest his soul, used to do the same. Now take this roll and count it for me."

The total came to five thousand dollars.

It was the most money I'd ever held in my hands. Enough to buy a house with a few dozen acres around it and a brand new carriage and a team to get you from one end to the other.

"What you got there," Bunker said, "are my profits from three ratting matches. This ain't no penny-ante stuff, McCleary. We play for keeps. The little matches you read about at so-and-so's saloon are for mechanics and masons. The ones I take my dogs to are for the big bugs. The sky's the limit for the bets there. Look here."

He went back to the top hat and pulled out a daguerreotype. I gave him back the money and took the photograph.

It was of Bunker in younger days, without jowls and with a little more hair. His "imperial" beard had no gray in it. In his arms was a fox terrier. Its eyes looked glazed from the flash. The dog must have moved a little bit because it was slightly out of focus.

"That there's Cindy, Jocko's ma. There's quite a resemblance. Same black head and white body. I don't got a picture of Jocko, actually. But I thought this would do. See the way her ears pop up like that and them sad-lookin' eyes? Jocko got them right from his ma.''

I must have looked bewildered. I had no idea what the hell Bunker and myself were doing here. Cap said, ''Jocko's been kidnapped.''

''Hunh?''

I didn't know what else to say. I had hoped my new assignment would involve a spectacular bank robbery or a ring of green goods operators.

''I know this sounds foolish, McCleary. You think I want to bother the Philadelphia police about a dog? Hell, around this time you got enough to worry about shooting the stray mad ones. But this ain't just about a dog.''

''It's about money, Mack,'' Cap said from behind his massive oaken desk. ''The dog wasn't just stolen. It was kidnapped. Read him the letter, Joe.''

Bunker accepted a piece of paper from Cap's burly hand.

''It's addressed to me at the Republican Club. I got it yesterday, two days after Jocko disappeared. I thought he run off or something. But then I got this and . . .''

''Read him the damn letter,'' Cap said.

''Awright! Christ, yer impatient.'' Bunker read the letter very carefully and stumbled over a few words.

We got yer dog, Jocko. He be in a safe hiding place and no harm will come to him if you pay us promptly the sum of ten thousand dollars. We know you can get the money, Bunker. We know you need Jocko next week. You cannot get the dog back without paying. If you do not pay us we will kill him. If you agree to pay us what we ask, place an advertisement in the Ledger *that runs as follows: Dear L.E., Goose hangs high, J.B. Then we will send you details about an exchange. Remember, Bunker, we will kill the dog if we have to.*

''Whatta you think, McCleary?''

He handed me the letter. There was nothing noticeable about the paper itself. I looked at the childish scrawl on it and said, "Is this some kind of prank, Cap?"

"McCleary, listen up," Bunker said. "Now, maybe I didn't explain this too good. I breed dogs for ratting. Jocko's my prize terrier. He is the champion dog not just in this state but in the whole Union. He's got the record for most rats killed in five minutes. Forty-eight! If he's pitted, the pot can come to one or two grand each time. A lot of money gets passed around. So if anything happens to Jocko I lose my prize cow, see? And I lose the chance of breedin' him and chargin' a mighty hefty sum for the privilege.

"I think I can trust you two fellers with this information. Jocko financed my last campaign. Don't laugh! I pitted him in one classic in Camden and made enough to rent out a dancing hall for a ward-wide party. Not one single person missed out on all that free liquor and music. Don't think that ain't what got me half them votes!

"So you see, this ain't about peanuts or some mangy mutt that I hold onto for old time's sake. I need Jocko, McCleary. I need him bad. Cause there's a classic comin' up right here in the Quaker City. It's the biggest one of the decade. The pot's gonna come to five grand, we think. And Jocko was the one who'd get me a piece of that. Now, I gotta get him back, and I don't care how much it takes!"

"Joe came to us because he knows our Ds have songbirds in every crib and dive in the city. You know the nigger scamps better than anybody. We got an idea that a nigger might be the one who stole the dog. Two of 'em were seen around Bunker's house the day of the kidnapping. I'm putting you on this full time, Mack."

Bunker slapped a hand against my shoulder and said, "I know you can help me, boy. And believe me, Joe Bunker never forgets those who lend him a helping hand. You get my drift?"

I could see there was no way I could back out of it, so I said, "Did you put the advertisement in the paper?"

"Sure did. That was this morning. I haven't heard from them yet."

"Whatta ya make of the letter?" Cap asked me.

"Well, the handwriting's peculiar. Like a kid scratched it out."

"That's good!" Bunker said, "I told you I saw them two nigger kids around!"

"Maybe," I said, "but I'll tell you what, Mr. Bunker. Why don't I just go on over to your place and talk to some people? Start like that, all right?"

"I'll take you over in my two-in-hand. You need to say anything to him, William?"

"Naw," Cap said, "He knows what to do. Take it easy, Joe."

"Likewise."

When Bunker and I left the office there were a few of the Ds milling around outside, waiting to see Cap. Some of the older ones gave me dirty looks. My friendship with Cap caused a lot of jealousy.

"Well, well," one of them said as we walked out. "Junior's got himself a case."

"That's right. A kidnapping."

"No kiddin'? The ratting dog? Yeah, I heard about that. The rest of us thought it was a job for a creampuff. We reckon Heins is afraid you might hurt yourself on a real job. We all know how he takes an interest in your welfare."

"Oh yeah?"

"That's right. Creampuff."

I thought about slugging him. Then I said, "Diefenderfer, you're a real tough guy. One hell of a dick. Guys like me can only try to be like you. Hey," I hollered at everyone in the room, "you hear about Diefenderfer getting clobbered by that bludget on Race Street? A colored one, too! I guess you must have been questioning her . . . or something. I guess your wife knows all about that, huh? Your kids, too?"

"Why, you piece of shit . . ."

He made a move at me, but his buddies held him back.

"Anytime you want, I'm here," I told him.

Bunker laughed. Some of the others dicks laughed, too.

We got out of there and headed for the Northern Liberties.

Joseph Bunker's diggings were modest, considering the money he had. It didn't look good to the rest of the Twenty-Fifth Ward if their boss lived in a mansion while they all lived in row houses and respectable but humble twins. He chose a small single house for himself and his family. While it didn't look much different from the others in the neighborhood, it had a lot more land behind it. There used to be some wooden shacks in his back alley that he'd had demolished. It was there that he built the kennels and stable for his two-in-hand.

Even when you stepped inside the Bunker house it was hard to see where the money was. The furniture was fashionable but not overly expensive. I could afford one or two pieces of it myself. His wife's fancy was Persian carpets and dogs, which was no surprise. The floors looked like something out of a Turkish harem. Dogs made out of plaster, marble, wood, or metal stood in every nook and cranny.

The most bizarre piece of her collection was the stuffed remains of their old dog Feisty in the parlor. A glass-blowing Swede who lived down the street had made the eyes for them. They were better than the usual marbles you saw. These eyes actually seemed alive. Wet-like. I don't know how he did it.

On the walls were the usual landscape paintings and sentimental prints. Mrs. Bunker liked to buy ones with dogs in them whenever possible. There was a large painting of Greyfriar's Bobby by a local artist in a huge gilded frame. That was the first thing she showed me when I called on them. She recounted the whole story for me, with tears in her eyes.

A nice lady. The kind of woman a certain kind of man likes to have around the house. Sentimental, docile, and thoroughly insipid. After Bunker almost apologetically introduced us, we ignored her.

Bunker had shown me where some of his money went to when he took me down to the basement. Like some schoolboy showing off his collection of segar bands, he gave me a tour of his weapons collection. I couldn't believe all the guns he had down there. Enough to start another war of rebellion. Except that none of them were loaded. Bunker told me he was extra careful about that. Didn't want any accidents to happen, was his explanation.

There were about a hundred guns, all in separate boxes lined with red velvet. He let me hold an old-style musket the size of a small cannon. There were hunting scenes engraved on the huge handle. He told me it was made in 1667 in Silesia.

As he polished a gilded revolver, he said to me, "I love firing these toys. I got a capital little cottage just for shootin' whenever I want. But shootin' these things at a target is no substitute for the real thing, eh?"

I merely nodded. I took no pleasure in talking about my experience in the War. But it wasn't long before the inevitable question came.

"Say, McCleary, how many Rebs did you put a pill into? D'ya ever have occasion to use one of these beauties?" He withdrew a gleaming bayonet from a velvet bag.

I closed my eyes and saw all the death that Bunker wanted to see. But most of it had been far from the field of battle—where my real war had taken place. In prison.

I remembered the first man I'd killed. He wasn't a Reb. Just a prisoner like me. If I hadn't killed him, he would've killed me. For my hardtack.

For a moment some old wounds opened, and their pus rose up in my throat. Then I said to Bunker, "Put that damn thing away."

His eyes narrowed into slits, as if he were looking at

me for the first time. Then he began to banter again as if nothing had happened.

Bunker told me the guns were just a fancy. His real passion was ratting. When he wasn't holding court at the barbershop down the street or at the Republican Club, he was at the kennel with Reddy the Blacksmith. The two of them had bred and trained a dynasty of champions, since before the war. The Mexican War, I mean.

I don't think it even occured to Bunker to suspect Reddy. Or if it did, he quickly buried the impulse. He was too close to the old negro.

That day there had been just enough time for me to interview Reddy and Bunker's colored cook. Then I had to go and almost get myself killed on the Schuylkill.

The cook, Ben Devers, was a young man of twenty-three, the hardworking, diligent type of negro. I knew his family. They were good church-going folk who lived near the Negro cemetery back in my old district. The father and mother both worked as servants in Spring Garden. Their son was following in their footsteps. It was one of the few jobs open to that race. Devers was lucky to have the situation, even if Bunker didn't pay him a king's ransom. Cooking the alderman's meals kept him out of the slums on South Street.

Devers didn't know much; I was pretty sure about that. He had no access to the kennels and very little contact with anyone outside the house. I'd known him for years, anyway. He was too smart to do something dumb like steal the prize pooch from his boss's kennel.

Reddy the Blacksmith was a different story. Nobody knew exactly how old Reddy was. Some said he was old enough to remember Lafayette's last tour of America. His crinkly white hair circled his head like a partial dome. It gave him an aura of wisdom.

Much of that wisdom had dissipated due to liquor. Reddy drank through most of the day, whenever he wasn't working at the forge, making doodads for Bunker's team of horses, or taking care of the dogs. Despite his dipsomania, Reddy would never be fired by Bunker. He'd been the favorite slave of Joseph Bunker, Senior, down in North Carolina and Bunker had honored his father's memory by tolerating the old drunk. It wasn't such a sacrifice. Reddy made awfully good horseshoes and tools that he sold throughout the neighborhood. He always kicked a portion of his profits to Bunker.

That was why Reddy was trusted with the dogs—that, and the fact that he was one of the best dog trainers Bunker had ever seen. Everything the alderman knew, he'd learned from his dead father's slave.

But after last night I wasn't going to trust Reddy anymore. Either he was lying, or the Edgerton boys were. Maybe both. I had to do something about that situation.

I remembered reading about the Spanish Inquisition. They had all kinds of ways to get confessions. Thumb screws, strappado, the rack.

I didn't like pain too much. But there was one thing I did like.

Fear.

I was going to put fear to work on Reddy the Blacksmith. I wanted to see if he was playing games with me or not. Maybe the boys were lying and maybe they weren't. That didn't matter. Reddy was the one who most likely had something to do with it. He was a suspect, guilty until proved innocent.

The morning after my night at the river I woke up to the sound of stray dogs barking in the alley behind my house. I lived in a new row house in the south of the city, near the Girard estate. It was still pretty early in the morning. When I stood up and looked out the window, I saw the milk wagon making its final rounds.

I got out of bed with a groan and stumbled over to the commode. My morning ablutions took about fifteen minutes.

It was impossible for me to start the day without bathing. No question where I picked up that habit. Andersonville. In all the months there I don't think I ever bathed. The creek was full of filth, anyway. Our water supply and our privy were one and the same. Everyday I remembered that and was thankful for what I had now.

I donned a new suit from Wanamaker's. They were about ten dollars, a little pricy. But I could afford them now with my detective's pay. I made about a thousand a year.

On my nightstand was a paper Bunker had given me. It said in large, boldface type:

RATTING CLASSIC!

Sporting gentlemen who staunchly support the destruction of these VERMIN will offer a pot of several THOUSANDS of dollars to be killed for by dogs under 13 and 3/4 pounds weight. The RATS will be killed in a large pit constructed to usual specifications. Any man touching dogs or rats or acting in any way unfair will have his dog disqualified. The match will take place on the night of Independence Day onboard the steamer *General Hooker*. Competitors will go to scale at half-past eleven.

If I got nothing else out of this case, I would get to see my first ratting match.

I wrapped a clean collar around my neck and buttoned my necktie, then headed for the door.

I had breakfast on the way to the streetcar stop. I bought apples from the same boy every morning. He and his father owned a stand on the corner. A little further down there was a bakery where I bought rolls. After that was a stand to buy coffee. Three stops and my breakfast was complete. I got on the car when it pulled up, showed my star to the conductor, and rode for free up to the Northern Liberties.

I had to see Joe Bunker. Before he paid the ten thousand dollars for Jocko, I wanted to see if he could tell me more. Especially about Reddy the Blacksmith.

* * *

After last night, I wasn't in the mood to go easy with Reddy—or with anyone else, for that matter. I wanted to settle the matter quickly and get the dog back, if it was still alive. I had a personal stake in the matter too. Bunker had promised me a part of the pot if Jocko got back in time to win the Independence Day Classic. Five hundred dollars. I could do a lot of things with that.

I went around the front of the house to the alley, where the kennels and the smith were. I heard a hammer clanging on an anvil. Reddy was at work. Bunker was getting a shave at the barbershop. The cook was out buying bread. It was a good time to have a talk with the old blacksmith, just the two of us.

The forge was throwing off a wave of heat that didn't mix too well with the humid and already warm air that morning. It was probably the only time he could use the forge without sweating every drop of water in him.

Reddy's back was turned to me. He was wearing a faded red cotton shirt and baggy, clay-stained trousers held up by suspenders. The smoke from his corncob pipe hung in the air like a long blue finger.

I watched him pick up the smoldering horse shoe and dip it in a nearby bucket. The shoe hissed going in and threw off a bunch of steam. That was when I stepped behind him and said, "Good morning, Reddy."

The old negro turned his head slowly, squinting at me.

"I don't recollect your name, suh."

His eyes were pretty bloodshot and it wasn't even eight in the morning. I was surprised the forge hadn't ignited his gin breath.

"Wilton McCleary. We met yesterday."

Wrinkles appeared around his eyes. The yellowish beard curled up with a smile.

"Sho' we did. That's right. Ol' Reddy don't remember so good no mo'. You the gennilmun from the police, ain't ya?"

"Uh-huh."

"Well, what can I do fo' ya? Told ya everything I know yestiddy."

A bluetail fly landed on his black cheek. He let it crawl there for a while, moving his hand slowly toward it. Then his hand blurred through the air and slapped his cheek. The insect fell dead to the dirt floor.

"Son of a bitch," Reddy said.

"You're pretty quick with your hands, Reddy," I said.

He snickered and spat a big gob after the fly.

"I hate them sons of bitches. Bloodsuckahs."

The way he looked at me when he said that made me think he wasn't just talking about flies.

"You go 'head and talk, 'cause I gots to make dese shoes fo' Joey's team fo' he gets back."

He turned his back to me and went over to the forge.

"I saw the Edgerton boys last night," I said to him.

For a moment he stopped where he was, like he was about to step on a snake.

"Did ya, now?"

"Uh-huh," I said, moving behind him. "And they told me an interesting story."

The old man was silent. His back was hunched. His hands were in front of him, where I couldn't see them. It didn't bother me at the time.

"They told me all about what went on between the three of you on Saturday. About the liquor you gave them. I'm surprised you'd share something that precious to you."

"So I gave 'em some likker. That ain't no crime."

"No, I guess not. But then there's what you did after."

"What they tell you?"

"Oh, not much. Just about how they helped you afterward . . ."

I was deliberately vague. The river rats had jumped us before I could get the specifics from the boys. As long as I pretended like I knew it all, he might believe I actually did.

"Back at the kennels."

It was a guess. A hit or a miss. They could have helped him with a sack of manure at the stables.

It turned out to be a hit. The old man swung around. A white-hot poker was in his hand. He took a swipe at me with it. The tip came close enough to singe my moustache.

I'd had enough of Reddy's games. His age was no longer a consideration.

My hand lashed out and grabbed the poker right above where he held it. Lucky for me it was just warm there. With another hand that turned into a fist I boxed him in the ear. He cried out and let go of the weapon.

Throwing it out of reach, I took hold of Reddy's frowsy collar and tightened my grip. After what happened last night, my tolerance for funny business was mighty low.

"Listen, you old juicehead," I whispered to him. "I could haul your ass downtown right now for assaulting a police officer. The bulls love old darkies like you. They got all kinds o' toys to try on you in the back room."

His red eyes turned into slits. Yellow teeth poked through his pursed lips.

"Joey Bunker isn't here to help you, Reddy. It's just me and you."

He was looking at me, but he wasn't seeing me. There was all this hate in him. You could feel it steaming off his black head.

"I ain't seen nothin' that day."

The words were spat at me. My grip on his collar got tighter. I shouted at him again, told him he was lying. I was morally certain he knew something he wasn't telling. By now his hate had dumbed him up. There was only one other way to get something out of him.

No, I wasn't going to hit him. Thrashing old men isn't in my line.

"All right, Reddy. If that's the way you want to play it."

I let go of his collar and backed away from him, slowly.

"I know how to get to you, Reddy. One way or the other."

I turned my back on him then and headed across the alley, toward the kennels.

"Where you goin'?" he stammered.

There was a barker beneath my jacket to-day. Should have been there the night before. It was one of the old Colt New Model Army revolvers. Forty-four calibre. A real beaut.

I took out the gun and let him see it.

"How many in that bitch's litter? The one you were tellin' me about the other day? What's her name, Sissy?"

It took him a while before he put it all together. Meanwhile, I was in the kennel. I made my way to a part that was sectioned off. A terrier bitch was nursing five puppies. They were barely old enough to have their eyes open. Most of them were sleeping. I aimed my revolver carefully and shot.

Reddy was screaming before I pulled the trigger. The sound of his clambering feet reached me just as I fired a second time. The dogs were yelping with fear from the thunderous noise.

I met Reddy at the door to the kennel.

"Three to go, Reddy."

Tears leaked down his cheeks and got soaked up in his beard. In between sobs he called me a whole bunch of things I didn't take personally.

After a minute of abuse I turned back toward the kennel. I made sure he could hear me pulling back the hammer of the gun.

"No, no, please! Please don't!"

The old man's gnarled hands grabbed my arm. His whole body trembled with emotion.

"Sissy's my baby. Please, I'll tell you. I'll tell you, God damn it!"

I turned around, pushed the hammer back in and drew him toward the entrance.

"Make it quick," I told him.

Reddy's head drooped over his red shirt like a willow branch. The words came in whispers and sobs.

"I dint mean ta do it, man. I swear. I dint mean ta do nothin'. If I'da known what was gonna happen, I woulda killed myself instead."

"You killed the dog?"

After a sigh, he said yes.

This made no sense to me and I told him so.

"Why go through the whole rigmarole of the letter? What were you were trying to do? Make it look like Jocko wasn't dead so you could collect the ransom and dust out of here?"

His head was shaking. Now it was his turn to look at me like I was an idiot.

"I ain't talkin' about Jocko, boy. I be talkin' 'bout Runt."

"Runt?"

"Yeah." Reddy started crying again. "He was one of Joey's favorites. Not so flashy as Jocko or nothin' but . . . man, he could tear them little bastards up in the pit. Yessuh."

I was lost. Reddy kept talking. I let him go on with his stuttering confession.

"See, I was feedin' the dogs that day. A-and, there was these two fellas around sellin' this stuff what kills rats dead. Poison, you unnerstand? I thought we could use some, 'specially with the puppies. I seen rats bite some of them ta death, once. Well, I bought some o' the powder from these peddler fellas after they was done talkin' with the boy in the kitchen. Then I went back to the kennel with Sissy.

"That's when everything went bad. C-cause I was drinkin'. I'd been drinkin' that whole mornin'. I musta fell asleep pettin' Runt, or somethin'. Anyways, I'd never put that powder away. It came in a box and I musta spilled it when I fell down. And . . ." He burst into tears. "I wake up and there's Runt, right next to me like he be sleepin'. But he ain't sleepin'. He's dead. Some of that poison was still on his nose. He musta been eatin' all the stuff I spilled."

Poor Reddy sank to the floor and hid his face behind his rough hands. It made me feel bad, watching him cry. I had never gotten used to that, even after all the confessions I'd witnessed. I put my hand on his shoulder and said, "So you kept mum about it."

" 'Sright. I cleaned the poison up. When Joey came home, I pretended to find him like that when I went to feed him. Runt wasn't old, but he wasn't young. Happens from time to time. Joey took it hard, but he didn't think it was unnatural or nothin'."

"And the Edgerton boys . . . they helped you clean up the poison?"

"Yeah. I had ta give 'em a pair of pincers fo' free to keep their mouths shut. Now it don't matter no mo'."

He looked at me for the first time since he began his story and said, "You gonna tell on me ta Joey?"

There was nothing to be gained from that. That story of his smelled like the truth. There was just the right amount of tears. Reddy must have been passed out while the kidnappers had made off with Jocko. He couldn't tell me anything more.

I had caused the old man enough pain for a morning.

"I won't say anything to anybody. Now, c'mere."

I led him over to Sissy. The five puppies were awake now, and whining.

The two balls had gone into the rafters. If you looked closely you could see the holes they'd made.

Reddy fell down next to Sissy and caressed her furry head. I patted him on the shoulder once. Then I walked out of the barn and into the alley.

The sound of weeping followed me. It was with me as I rode downtown.

I told myself that they'd been necessary, all the things I'd done. But the sound of his crying stung me like a bluetail fly. I remembered that I'd even wanted to hit him, just for an instant when he took a swing at me with the poker.

That's what did it. Not what I'd done, but what I'd wanted to do. Thinking about that made the sweat come out on my hands and brow. I hated who I was then.

As the car pulled up in front of the State House I bowed my head and asked for forgiveness. And a chance to redeem myself.

JUST A FEW feet from the steps of the Central Office I saw Sammy, the local shoeshiner. He was doing a brisk business. That was a good thing, because it had cost him a pretty penny to get the concession to operate in front of the State House. If you wanted to shine shoes in front of any station house, especially the big one, you had to pay for the privilege.

Walking past Sammy I noticed how closely he resembled Reddy. Both were old negroes, their hands hard and twisted like the bough of a tree. I said good morning to Sammy and when he wasn't looking I slipped a dollar into his segar box. Doing that made me feel just a little better.

Cap would have something for us. He always did. Maybe there was a parade to guard. Every year around this time the Orangemen paraded to celebrate the anniversary of England's victory over the Irish in the Battle of the Boyne. My daddy had done the same back in Troy, New York. Irish Catholics always turned out to hurl rotten potatoes and the like. One year I joined the lodge myself and got to hold the banner with my father.

Either a parade or the mayor had a bee in his bonnet about tramps again. Every few months the citizens got tired of all the tramps lounging about the depots. So we detectives would have to go and roust them out. It wasn't terribly dangerous. Neither was it glorious. I wasn't interested in these kinds of jobs. I wanted challenges. The kind that used to go with my old beat in the Seventh Ward.

When I walked inside, I made my way to the toilet room. A swell was in the water closet, coughing up something unpleasant. I checked my moustache in the mirror, smoothing it out. The cuts on my face didn't look too bad now. My tie was straight. I looked good enough for Cap and the detectives.

I climbed the marble stairs to the second floor, where the detectives' office was. All seven of them were in there waiting to be called in.

Philadelphia's finest.

All of them were older than me. Some of the boys remembered the anti-Catholic riots of the forties. One was proud of his involvement in them. He was relieved to know that I was an Orange mick.

They knew and I knew the only reason I was there was because I'd taken care of a very delicate matter for my captain, concerning an election. I never talked about it but people inferred things just the same. When he moved into City Hall I moved with him, right into the detective's office. I had a lot to prove. The papers had made a fuss about my new position, even though I'd been a special officer for four years. I was accused of bribing my way to Chestnut Street. That was nothing extraordinary. Plenty of patrolmen and roundsmen were walking their beats because they'd paid their local aldermen for the privilege or because they'd collected votes for them in the last election. But I hadn't done either. I got where I was by not being afraid and by doing favors for people. I was a good friend to some powerful men—like the captain. Good friends take care of each other.

We didn't have a horde of Ds back then. Eight was just enough to take care of the few serious crimes we had. Despite that, most of the time the dicks were doing nothing but pinching dips and rousting tramps. That was what the citizens wanted. They wanted their property protected and the streets clean of refuse. Human refuse, that is. Burglary was about as serious as murder.

We didn't spend too much time on murder cases. It didn't take long to find who'd killed whom. More than half the time if there was a death we knew who did it in about five minutes. Most of our homicides resulted from saloon brawls. The tougher cases didn't take long, either. All eight of us had a sack of connections in the underworld. One or two visits to a flash drum and we had an answer, if the right amount of money was exchanged or favors given.

Dicks liked big, flashy arrests. The bank sneak rings, the second-story artists, the banco and flim flam confidence men. Occasionally when the mood of the public suited it, we shut down gambling hells and bawdy houses. But only if they hadn't paid their month's rent.

There weren't many rewards for finding the killers of drunken mechanics and stevedores. But if there was a robbery at a Chestnut shop or a Spring Garden swell's crib, then the Ds would stick to it like flies on horse manure. Most of us detectives lived pretty well on the rewards we collected when we retrieved stolen property. Sometimes I felt like we weren't anything but city-subsidized bounty hunters. Or Labrador retrievers. Life wasn't retrievable. So we didn't bother with murders unless we had to.

Not that it mattered much in the end. Juries didn't like to convict men of things like first-degree murder. In all my years as a copper in the Quaker City I'd heard of only a handful of solid convictions. Most of the time the killers went to the chokey on a manslaughter sentence. There was a city-wide squeamishness about handing out life sentences or executions. Prison was supposed to be about rehabilitation. That was what Eastern State had been all about. Put them in a cell with a Bible and in a few years they'll come out monks ready to pound the Good Book.

I like to think I'm a good Christian, but I knew what

it was like to live in prison, too. And I still felt no sympathy for the convicts. In fact I enjoyed bagging the ones who really belonged inside. It was like getting back at the scum who'd put me in Andersonville. I looked at all the scamps and sneaks like they were the secesh. I had all of my life to fight the war I never got a chance to fight. I wanted to put them in prison and let them rot there, just like I'd done. I wanted to put the bad ones where they belonged. I'd seen too many good ones die in Georgia. The scales needed to be balanced.

I was a queer kind of copper. I had my own ax to grind and it didn't have to do with making money or cadging drinks or a piece of muslin from the fancy houses on my beat.

It all went back to the war. The war that I never got to fight.

The rest of the barrel-boarder Ds in that room weren't used to fighting. They were older men, mostly, and political appointees. They were detectives because they'd done some ward-heeling for the mayor or for some other politician. Well, that's not quite true. I'll say half of them were like that. The rest were like me.

Hugh Nolan was one of the latter. He was my only pal so far among the dicks. Nolan was a middle-aged man, short and stout. His huge gray moustache covered his lips almost completely. The only way you could tell if he was frowning or smiling was by watching his gray eyes. He was a man of song, always humming some ditty or another, and had a harmonica in his desk drawer which he frequently played, like he was then. The tune he hummed that particular day was "Home Sweet Home." That was one of his favorites.

Nolan had been the only one to treat me with any sort of kindness. Even though I'd been with the department for only a few months, he went out of his way to pass the time with me. He was a bit of a local historian and knew every nook and cranny of his old district, and the dirt that settled in them.

Perhaps what cemented our friendship was knowing

he had served in the War. He wore his medal with pride on his frock coat. Despite his age he had fought in many battles and skirmishes. One of the first things he did was show me where a ball had passed through his side. He was proud of that scar. I didn't show him mine. They were in places you couldn't see. On the inside.

When he saw me walk in, he stopped playing his harp and greeted me. I moved over to where he was sitting. From the window behind him I saw the corner of Fifth and Chestnut. There was a traffic jam already. A wagon had spilled some of its barrels while trying to make a third lane for itself. A few police officers were trying to sort out the mess. Wagons and carriages were at a standstill for about two squares in each direction.

With my head out the window I felt the sun beginning to beat down. It would be another hot one. I said so to Nolan.

"No mistakin' that. I hope the chief puts us on the ferries to-day. I heard there was a lot of buzzin' goin' on along the Shakamaxon line last week. I got a feeling it might be Boston Charlie at work again."

"Boston Charlie?" I asked.

"Yeah. I collared him last year for pickpocketing on the West Jersey ferry. He was inside for eight months. He must've just got out."

"What's so great about the ferries?"

"You don't have to do anything but stand around, that's what! Feel the cool breeze on your brow, pass the time with the ladies, and keep the eyes peeled. Let the scenery go by."

"Sure must smell better than some of the depots."

"You got that right. Seems like we got more tramps stinkin' 'em up than ever."

Nolan was an inveterate enemy of tramps. Arresting them was almost like a personal vendetta for him. When I asked him why he hated tramps so much, he said, "Ain't no reason for 'em to be sittin' around and botherin' the gentle folk. They oughta get a job, or somethin'. That's what we got mills in this town for. They don't wanna work, let 'em join the army and go kill Indians, by damn!''

I had a feeling there was a deeper reason for his disgust with tramps, but I didn't want to press the issue.

Changing the subject, I said, ''Any idea what's on the blotter for to-day?''

The moustache curled downward in a grimace. The little man shrugged and spat in the cuspidor next to his chair.

''Beats me. I saw a swell go in the office just as I sat down.''

''Who was he?''

''I ain't seen him before.''

''Another gold bug who wants us to run errands for him?''

''McCleary, McCleary! Don't let the Bunker thing sour you. Detectives do more than that. Anyway, what're you complainin' about? If you get the dog back for Bunker, you get a hefty hunk of cans for your trouble—am I right?''

''How'd you hear about that?''

''The walls got ears, my boy.''

Just then the door to Cap's office opened and he stepped out, preceded by a gust of segar smoke.

''Awright, boys. C'mon in, now.''

We shuffled through the mahogany doors and into our leader's inner sanctum.

With all eight of us inside, there was barely room to stretch. Cap stood behind a huge desk which was set against the back wall. It was a little smaller than an ironclad, dwarfing Cap with its very official-sized bulk. You could barely see him over the papers and files dumped on his blotter.

Seated beside him was a gentleman. I knew he was a gentleman within seconds of looking at him, just like every other detective in the room did. If we could do one thing, it was take stock of a person by their carriage and dress with one look. That was all we needed to tell us whether a man was a swell or a scamp. If they were walking somewhere at night with a bag, that difference in dress would usually decide whether we stopped them or not.

The man was not exceedingly wealthy, but he was well to do. His coat was a little frayed at the cuffs, noticeable only if you were as close to him as I was. The soles of his shoes were worn down from a great deal of use, yet the shoes themselves were well polished. The top hat he'd placed on Cap's desk was threadbare beneath the brim. A gold watch chain dangled over his vest. On his lapel was the emblem of the Freemasons.

I wondered if he was in mourning. Everything he wore was black. He didn't look at us as we walked in but stared down at the floor, knotting his brow. Once in a while he ran a hand over his brow and eyes, as if he had a headache. His lips were pulled taut and he kept his hands in his lap, kneading them through the whole interview.

He was a thin man with receding hair and a well-trimmed beard. He wore no moustache. Perched on his nose were spectacles with very thick lenses. When he removed them I noticed the impression they'd left on the bridge of his nose.

He seemed small and fragile. Tragedy had etched lines into his face. I felt sorry for him before I knew who he was.

Cap said to us, "Boys, let me introduce you to Mr. Archibald Munroe."

We mumbled good morning.

"Well, I don't know quite how to start. I've never come across anything like this in all my years. Something monstrous has happened."

Our curiosity was piqued. Cap seemed genuinely distraught. We waited silently for his explanation.

But it was Mr. Munroe who spoke next. His voice cracked with emotion as he said, "My boy. They've taken my boy."

"Whatta ya mean, sir?" Nolan said.

"He means," Cap said, "that his child has been stolen. And is being held for a ransom of ten thousand dollars.''

We all gasped. Nothing like this had ever happened in Philadelphia.

''This is brigandage. Pure and simple. This is the kind of thing that happens in savage countries. Like Sicily. But never in our country! Nobody's ever stooped to this level of outrage. Until now.''

Cap looked as somber and upset as the rest of us. Not that we were gushers, mind you. But it was a shock. It was bad enough that the cholera was taking children all through the summer. Now to have a human predator . . . that was too much.

What kind of man, we asked each other, would steal children for profit?

''I don't know of one instance of kidnapping for ransom in the history of the Union. And Philadelphia is not going to let an epidemic start! We are not going to let these despicable creatures ply their trade from city to city! Are we, boys?''

''No, by God!'' we said.

''I am giving this case top priority. All of you are gonna work it until we get that child back. We're gonna see to it that that boy is safe in his mother's arms. I don't give a damn if we have to search every bloody closet in the whole city! We're going to get that boy back! Do you hear me?''

If the kidnappers had been there, we would have had a necktie party for them in no time.

''And we're not letting these brigands escape justice, d'you hear? I want them dragged through the streets and put in Cherry Hill! Better yet, I wanna see them swinging down in Moyamensing! These men are vicious mad dogs, boys. And you know what to do with a mad dog.

''I was there last night when we broke it to the mother. She took it hard, mighty hard. I made a promise to that gentle lady that we would do everything we could to get her baby back. This isn't criminal, men—it's diabolic. We ain't sitting still for it. Don't you worry, Mr. Munroe. If anybody can do it, we can.

"Now, I want you all to listen up to Diefenderfer. I'm puttin' him in charge of the investigation. Mr. Munroe has furnished us with all the details concerning the kidnapping so we have some place to start."

Diefenderfer walked over to Cap's desk and grabbed a slim file. My hackles bristled, remembering his insults of the day before.

Henry Diefenderfer was the oldest of the dicks and a pal of Stokley's. His clout with the mayor was common knowledge and something he enjoyed flaunting. They had been pals ever since they'd been in the same volunteer fire company, the old Franklin Hose.

Even though he was a toady, Diefenderfer was a passable detective. He'd collared some bank sneaks a few months after a gun battle that had left one of the sneaks dead. Aside from his lawful pursuits, he was a known frequenter of black-and-tan fancy houses. Where his taste for colored flesh came from I didn't know. But I had first hand experience of it, having arrested him while I was still a blue belly.

While I was walking the beat one night I heard a scream come from one of the several bawdy houses on the block. Rushing inside I saw two colored girls, half naked, standing over the body of a completely naked white man. They told me he'd fallen halfway down the stairs. He stank like a cell full of drunks. I dragged him back to the station house only to find he was a detective. We let him sleep in the waiting room until he came out of it.

Diefenderfer never forgave me for pinching him. I would've forgotten it if he hadn't climbed on my back as soon as I became a detective. Usually I played it smart and stayed out of his way, unless he got in mine.

Why Cap put that chucklehead in charge I didn't know. Nor did I care. I would do my best to put up with him.

Our ears were perked as Diefenderfer swelled his

chest and started to read. His eyes were placed a little close together under a heavy brow, but they were fly-looking eyes and he glared at us with them before he began. The look said, I'm in charge of this and don't you forget it.

"Here's what we know so far. On June twenty-ninth Mr. Archibald Munroe left his home in German-town . . ."

"What's the address, Henry?" one of the dicks said.

"Two fifty-two Rittenhouse Street. Right near the Wissahickon. Got that?" Diefenderfer spat out the words. He didn't like to be interrupted.

"Okay," he continued, "as he left for work, he no-ticed his two sons Stephen and Edwin playing in a lot across the street on the edge of the woods. He thought nothing of it since the boys frequently were over there. But when he came back home from the city, the boys still weren't back yet. He grew alarmed when they didn't come for supper. When dusk came and went, he sum-moned a neighbor and rode to the local station house.

"The desk sergeant on duty made light of it. Most likely the two boys would come back soon enough. Maybe they were at a friend's house, he thought."

Munroe snorted with disgust and disappointment. He wasn't watching us. All he did was sit there, his head nearly resting on his chest.

"When he returned home, he found that the boys still had not come back. He got ready to go and fill out a Lost Persons form so it could be telegraphed to all the station houses in the area. Then he wanted to see about hiring a carriage to go looking for them.

"It was at this time, just as he was preparing to leave, that Henry Peacock, an employee of the Lehigh Valley Railroad, walked up, having just been dropped off by the streetcar. Stephen was with him. The man explained he'd seen Stephen standing by himself with some crack-ers and candy in his hands, right near the Roxborough depot. When Peacock asked the boy where he lived, he burst into tears. After a while the boy calmed down and gave his address. Peacock skipped supper and took the boy back home by streetcar. After father and son were reunited, the boy related the events of that day.''

"We're sorry to have to go into this again, Mr. Munroe," Cap said. "I know how it must pain you. But I wanted you here in case the detectives have any questions. How are you holding up?"

"Tolerably, sir. Thank you."

"Go on, Diefenderfer."

"Yessir. So, the boy said that morning two men rode up to the lot in a carriage and struck up a conversation. They offered Stephen and Edwin candy and promised to take them to a place where they could buy crackers for Independence Day."

"I told them we could set some crackers off that night. They were so excited. I bought some in town that very day. And some sandbags too. I make sure to spread the sand around so nothing ignites, you know. I bought it all for them." The father's hands were trembling as he spoke.

"You know how shavers are with crackers. Set 'em off day and night. Can't get their hands on enough of 'em," Nolan said.

"Well," Diefenderfer said, "the boys got in the carriage and went with the strangers. This wasn't so strange, because as the boy Stephen tells it, the two men had ridden up to them twice before and asked them questions before driving off."

"What kinds of questions?" someone asked.

"Like, what does your Daddy do for a living, things like that. Obviously they were gunning the place a few days in advance before making their move. The boy didn't remember where they went exactly. It seemed like they made a mess of turns to throw him off the track. After about a half hour of riding around, they came to a store in Roxborough. One of the men told Stephen to go in and get some candy and gave him a nickel. He did so. When he came out from the store the carriage, the two men, and his brother were all gone.

"The boy didn't do anything but stand where he was. Peacock found him there crying several hours later.

"We already interviewed Peacock and he doesn't have any more than this. All he knows is where the kid was when he picked him up. He didn't see any sign of the carriage or the men or the other boy. Nobody in that vicinity did, either. We checked the owner of the store and the bartender at the hotel across the street."

Diefenderfer was finished for now. He turned to Cap, who got up from his chair and walked beside Munroe.

"I talked to the fellas at the Germantown station house. The desk sergeant took down Edwin's description for a Lost Persons form, which I'll circulate later. They figured it was just two drunks that took the boy on a frolic. That was the assumption until yesterday when this letter arrived in the morning mail. Mr. Munroe has been kind enough to bring this letter in to-day so we can all take a look at it."

Mr. Munroe—

Be not uneasy yur son Edwin be all right. We is got him and if you want him back you will have to pay us first. No living power on earth can deliver him from our hand. The cops can't find his hiding place—we got him so any approach to his hidin place will signal his instant annihilation. Don't deceive yurself and think the detectives can get him from us for that is impossible. Put no one in search for him. Yur money alone can fetch him out alive. Ten thousand dollars. You hear from us in few day.

I looked around at the men and their grim expressions mirrored my own. Cap passed the letter around and I got a look at the barely legible scrawl on it. The spelling was bad, but not so bad that it looked like it was faked by an educated person. There were no watermarks on the paper or stains of any kind that provided a clue as to where it had been written. I even held the thing to my nose, smelling nothing but ink.

I passed it on to Nolan and turned to Cap, who was about to speak.

The doors opened behind us. A man walked through the crowd of detectives and approached Munroe, who was staring despondently at the floor.

It was our mayor, ''Sweet William'' Stokley. He was a rotund man with sharp eyes and a clean-shaven face that looked harmless enough—the kind of face you'd trust, and plenty of people did. It was no surprise that Stokley had made his living as a confectioner. He had that pleasant air of the grandfatherly merchant who sends little boys on their way with a free sourball. He was good to the right kinds of people, high and low.

But Stokley was a tough bird. He'd been in a volunteer fire department in his youth. That meant streetfighting was nothing new to him. After establishing a business, he'd climbed his way tooth and nail to the top. After the city had tolerated a Democratic mayor for one term, Stokley was lucky enough to get the Republican nomination.

Now his nostrils were flared with avuncular concern. The tails of his coat fluttered as he strutted over to Munroe. We all hushed up in the presence of the boss.

''Mr. Munroe,'' Stokley said, ''I want to extend my most grievous condolences to you and your family for this outrage and affliction. When I was informed of the situation, I came right back from Atlantic City to oversee this thing to the end with Captain Heins. I think the men will agree with me that this sort of thing must not be allowed to continue in Philadelphia. We have a reputation as one of the safest cities in the civilized world. I'm proud of the job you men do to keep it that way.''

We all smiled dutifully.

''That's why it's so important that we do everything we can, employ every means available, to track these kidnappers down and bring them to justice. I can assure

you, sir, that Philadelphia will not suffer rascals like this
to walk free for long!''

"Thank you, Mayor. I do appreciate the attention
you're giving my son.''

"Please, sir. We will do our best to bring that child
back safely to the bosom of his home. I want you to
remember, Mr. Munroe, this is not just a crime against
your family. It is far worse. This is a crime against the
entire city. We cannot allow it to go unpunished!''

Having made his appearance, the Mayor summarily
departed, probably for a mid-morning libation.

Cap put his hand on Munroe's shoulder and said,
"Mr. Munroe, we're going to have to ask you some
questions since we got the detectives all here.''

The man nodded.

"Now, we're just trying to get at who might have
done this. Chances are, when someone commits a crime
like this they know the people involved, somehow. Uh,
can I ask you if there is any ill will between you and
any member of your family? Your wife, perhaps?''

For the first time, Munroe's head shot up, and he
stared Cap down. It was a feverish stare, full of fear and
indignation.

"What are you suggesting? That my wife kidnapped
the child? That I kidnapped my own son to hurt my
wife?''

"We don't mean anything of the kind, sir,'' Diefenderfer said. "Remember, I told you we were gonna have
to ask some personal questions. Answer the captain.''

"No, no. My wife and I are happy, quite happy.''

Munroe didn't sound too convincing. As if aware of
this, he added, "Were. Until yesterday.''

"Well,'' Cap said, "how about your servants?''

"We keep only one house servant, a negress named
Minnie. She's quite trustworthy and loves the two boys.
No, I can't believe she would do anything to hurt them.''

"Well, maybe it isn't hurting the boy, but it's sure
hurting you.''

"No. As I said, she's very loyal to us.''

"What about jury duty? Have you been on a jury recently? Convicted any men?"

"No."

"Okay. How about business associates? You run a dry goods store, that right?"

"Yes. In West Philadelphia."

"Have any rivals, enemies? In business, I mean? Discharge any employees recently?"

The man was sweating. I don't know if it was the oppressive heat, or being the subject of all these questions and stares from the detectives and Cap Heins. His eyes darted across the space in front of him like he was trying to read his memory, trying to find the answer to the whole problem.

"No, I don't remember anyone or anything that would lead to this!"

"Maybe it didn't seem like much at the time. Are you sure? Because it sounds to me like there's no reason why someone should kidnap your boy."

"I know, I know." Munroe's fingers were interlocked, like he was praying. The knuckles were white.

"Tell us about your business. Is it doing well? Creditors on your back?"

"How did you . . . ?"

Cap wasn't facing the man in the chair now. He was looking ahead in space, watching, just in case something took shape in front of his eyes.

"Yes. Yes, we're having trouble meeting the creditors' demands. Who isn't, after the Panic of two years ago? But I've arranged for the debts to be deferred and both sides are satisfied. That was last month, and from the looks of it, this month we're ready to bounce back. No. It has nothing to do with my business."

"How much would you say you're worth, Mr. Munroe?"

"I don't know. Fifteen thousand dollars, if I sold my house."

"That's a good bit of money, but not that much. I wonder why they picked you?"

"God in heaven, I don't know why!"

Munroe's chest heaved in a spasm of pain. He was about to cry. Cap had the sense to leave off. His hand returned to the man's shoulder.

"It's all right, Mr. Munroe. We're just doing our job, trying to find out who would want to do this thing to you. We're not accusing you. We need all the help we can get. That right, boys?"

We mumbled our agreement and stepped back a little bit. Munroe must've felt crowded with all of us around him. For a second it felt like we were in the back room, giving him a sweating.

"Okay. I think Mr. Munroe's done enough for us this morning. Sir, why don't you wait outside while I talk to the detectives for a minute?"

Then he hesitated, watching Munroe's despondent grimace. Cap said to him, "On second thought, maybe you'd like to hear how we're going to undertake this thing.

"Boys, here's how we're going to play it. I'm pulling bulls from every district in the city to work on this. I've even called in the reserves. We're putting the best coppers in civilian dress with you. We're gonna search every square inch of the whole damn city. We're gonna have men search the depots, barns, unoccupied homes, barges, ferries, you name it. I'm having every covered wagon stopped and gone over with a fine-tooth comb. Every ship on both rivers is gonna get looked over from top to bottom.

"I got a feeling this might be the work of Eye-talians. They pull things like this all the time back there. I want every Eye-talian questioned. And every whore, tramp, and sneak you can spot. This is a monumental effort we're talking about here.

"Now we finally get to your part. We got a bunch of pointers for you to follow up. Diefenderfer has made a list of all the assignments. You're to meet here every morning the same as usual, where we'll both brief you on the progress of the investigation.

"The press has already gotten hold of this story. Expect everyone to be talking about it by this evening. This could help us and hinder us, like always. Some of the papers are offering a reward already for information leading to the arrest of the rascals. How much was it, Mr. Munroe?"

"Three hundred dollars, I believe."

"So. This might help us, too. We'll see. Diefenderfer?"

"Ahem. Half of you are going to Roxborough to interview the witnesses we already got and see if we can dig up anybody else who might've been around to see the kid get dropped off. The rest of you are going with me to Germantown. We're going to interview everybody in the whole damn town. I'm going to the Munroe house to oversee the investigation from there. Why don't I read these off now . . ."

Nolan got sent to Roxborough. So much for his ferry ride.

I watched Munroe while the other dicks got their assignments. He was still sweating. He looked like he was about to fall over. My heart went out to him.

I heard my name.

"McCleary! Quit daydreamin'. You get Walnut and Harvey Streets. Okay, that does it. Let's get to work. Mr. Munroe, why don't you come with us, sir? There're some carriages waiting downstairs."

We all filed toward the door. On the way out, Cap said to me, "So much for Bunker, eh, Mack? What am I gonna tell him?"

I chuckled and said, "Tell him, 'Let the children first be fed.' "

"That Scripture?"

"Yes."

"Hey Mack. Don't forget: 'Even the dogs under the table eat the children's crumbs.' "

This time I laughed outright.

"You must have a lot of faith in me."

"I do."

"I'll take care of it," I said.

THE RIDE TO Germantown took about an hour, because of all the traffic. Along the way we got to read over a more detailed file about the boy. The Lost Person report was there. It didn't tell us much:

Name: Edwin Lester Munroe
Age: 5 years
Height: 3 feet
Whiskers:—
Eyes: Hazel
Dress: Brown linen suit with short skirt, laced
  shoes, straw hat with a broad brim and purple
  ribbon
Hair: Flaxen, long and curly
Last seen: Morning of June 29, 1874, lot near 252
  Rittenhouse St., Germantown

The dicks were all excited. This was something we could sink our teeth into. On the way to the country we discussed what would happen if we found the kidnappers. We came up with some pretty creative tortures.

I was excited to be working on a major case. I didn't want to be happy about a little boy being stolen from his parents. But part of me felt that way just the same.

I sat back in the carriage and let the dust from the

road cover me in a fine mist. The heat brought out the leather smell of the seats. Mine was slightly cracked and the horsehair stuffing was irritating my behind. Some of the other men were telling dirty jokes, but I wasn't interested in humor. There were a lot of things on my mind: Reddy the Blacksmith, Jocko, Bunker, Archibald Munroe, his boy, and the kidnappers—both sets of them.

I wasn't looking forward to walking around in the heat. Looking at the sky, I felt it falling down like a wet dank cloud, submerging everything in a blaring haze. It threatened to swallow me up completely. That made me think of the boy. Where was he? What was on his mind? Was he afraid? Had they hurt him? I tried thinking where I would put the kid if I were the kidnappers. It was too hot to think.

The carriage swung along the Schuylkill, past the Gasworks, the Suspension Bridge, Eastern State Penitentiary, and Girard College. Then we reached the park and the country.

Once we got out of the city proper, things started cooling off. The woods were plentiful and full of shade. Lucky for me, I was next to the window, so I got to peek out.

I didn't get outside the city much. A Sunday trip to the Fairmount Waterworks was like a train ride to grassville. But this was something different.

There were a few homes built alongside the road. But behind and around them was nothing but forest. I pictured Indians creeping through there ages ago. Our windows were down, so I took a sniff of the country air. It was full of earth smells—wet dark soil and leaves. The racket the carriage wheels made was almost a sacrilege.

Somewhere past the trees the Wissahickon wound its way to the Schuylkill. Once, when I had first come to Philadelphia I'd gone there with some friends and ridden a canoe down it. It was one of the happiest days of my life. I'd read all about the wonders of the world, like the Pyramids and Greek temples and such stuff. But this was the place for me. I remember the way the banks looked that day, with all the moss-covered stones and the tree roots intertwining with the earth, and up above on the road there were the swells out for promenades and rides in their four-in-hands. But the best part was the quiet. The only thing to hear was the water moving.

The carriage noise seemed distant now.

We were pulling into Germantown just as I slipped out of my revery. Once again I felt guilty being so calm and happy when a child's life was at stake.

The carriage let me off after some of the other Ds on Walnut Street. I think there must be a Walnut Street in every town in Pennsylvania.

I had the address of the Munroe house and the directions to it. After I was done with my assignment I had to go over there for further instructions.

Germantown was a sleepy place. Along Main, Shoemaker, Church, and Rittenhouse Lanes, there was a variety of homes, from simple brick to pretentious villa. They were all pretty new and freshly painted, with latticework around the porches and gables that looked like the work of a madman with a scroll saw. That was the modern style. I preferred the older stone houses. Behind one I saw some young ladies playing croquet with their young men in a backyard. That sport was getting more popular since the girls didn't need to wear bloomers to play. I watched their cotton skirts gleam in the sunlight for a while. My brain didn't work too well in the heat.

For about two hours I walked up and down the streets, knocking on doors. Stepping from the tenth or eleventh house I tried, I noticed a woman puttering around in a flower garden across the street. I was about to go over and start with her when I saw a gentleman turn the corner and step up to the porch across the way. He had a dark-colored carpetbag in his hands with something shiny sticking out of it. I walked toward him on a whim. When I got to the front door I noticed a brass placard nailed on it beneath the knocker. It said: FORREST MOYER, PHYSICIAN.

Chances were he was the only doctor in the area. It

was a sure bet he would know the Munroe boy. Their house was only a few squares away.

I knocked on the door. From within I heard a voice say, "Come right in."

The door squeaked shut behind me. I walked through the vestibule, where I noticed the carpetbag resting on the floor beside several pairs of shoes. The shiny metallic thing was a stethoscope.

"I'm just washing up, be right with you."

I left the vestibule and walked into the next room, which turned out to be the parlor. Rather, it was a parlor converted into a consulting office. Long curtains kept out the oppressive sunlight. Medical instruments were arranged in orderly array on several tables. Chemical smells lingered in the air. A canvas diagram of the human body was propped on an easel in one corner. Behind it stood a human skeleton.

On the walls of the parlor the doctor had a host of photographs. I noticed they were mostly landscapes of the western lands. A few red Indian faces grimaced at me. Shelves were built into the walls to display artifacts from these tribes. There were dolls and blankets and beads. It was like being in a museum. I must've said something like that out loud. Behind me someone said, "Yes, it is something like a museum."

I turned around to see who was speaking. It was the man I saw walk in. He was washing his hands with a linen cloth that virtually sparkled. His shirt cuffs were rolled up and his collar unfastened. I placed his age at about fifty-five. He was a man of medium height and weight, with a balding head of gray hair. Pince-nez hung on the bridge of his pointed nose. His clean-shaven face beamed with sagacity. His speech was careful and precise, but not too stuffy.

"I took those photographs myself, you know. A hobby of mine. The wife and I like to take trips out west. The Territories . . . California . . . just about every year we get out there, spend a month or so. Can't get enough of that place. Very different, as you can see. One thing I like. It's dry."

"Sounds good to me."

"Yes. Especially on a day like this. Sometimes I ask myself why I come back. Well, at least I have the photographs. The children like to look at them while they're waiting. That's why I hang them up there, mostly."

He stopped looking at his photographs and eyed me for the first time.

"Have we met, sir? Are you here for an examination? How can I help you?"

I shook his hand and said, "My name is Wilton McCleary, Doctor. I'm a detective with the Philadelphia police."

"Oh, my! You must be here about Eddie Munroe. A terrible tragedy."

"You've heard already?"

"Already? Why, the whole town's heard about it! I was one of the first to hear, as a matter of fact. When Archie told Leah what had happened, she fainted! They had to call me to revive her."

"Did you examine the older brother, Stephen?"

"Yes, I did, as a matter of fact. There were some fresh scrapes and bruises on him. He couldn't explain how he got them. Probably from that morning when he and Eddie had been playing in the lot there. It's full of bramble bushes and thistles. Stephen was in shock, I think. He didn't talk to me. Didn't say one word. Just lay on his bed and stared at the ceiling. Terrible, terrible thing. I'm glad he's safe, at least."

"I wonder why they took his brother and not him?"

"One boy is less trouble than two, I suppose."

"I guess you're right. Well, I'm certainly glad I came to you first. You see, Doctor, we're here to-day to ask around and see if people might've seen or heard something out of the ordinary either that day or since then. Something suspicious, I mean."

"Well, let me think for a moment. This thing has happened so fast. It's a shock to me, too. I brought that little boy into the world, you know. I mixed his first medicines and set a broken collarbone when he was four. He used to love coming in here, loved to hear me talk about the 'Injuns,' as he called them.''

Dr. Moyer's eyes grew blank. Half of his mouth curled up in a smile, as if he might wince at any moment. It was the way people looked when they called up a happy memory to stifle something painful.

Something told me he and his wife didn't have children of their own. He was taking this loss as hard as a father would.

Vicious crimes were like rocks thrown in a still pond. The ripples spread out in bigger and bigger circles. There was no way to stop those ripples. The only thing I could do was make sure the hand threw no more rocks. And if I was lucky, I or one of the other coppers would get the boy back. Even then I had to think about the other possibility: that the boy would die.

I pictured him in the room with me, looking at the pictures again. I wondered which had been his favorite. The roaming buffalo herd, or the one with the Chinese coolies laying tracks? How about that squaw with her little baby?

"Just think about it for a moment, Doctor. Think back to that day, June twenty-ninth. Think about who you saw that day."

"Well, I didn't see the boys, that's for sure. In fact, I stayed at home most of the day. That was Tuesday, right? Yes, of course. Let's see . . . I had to remove two warts that afternoon. And the fellow delivering the chemicals was late. I couldn't leave the house because I was afraid he might drive up while I was out and would take the chemicals back with him. So I sat around the parlor, waiting all day.''

"Did he ever show up?''

"As a matter of fact, yes. But well after my luncheon. So I don't think I can help you.''

"Okay. How about before that day? Notice anyone suspicious walking around? Tramps or strangers?''

I watched the doctor stare ahead into space again. After a minute or so his expression changed completely. The pince-nez slipped off his nose. The rest of his face slackened. His mouth opened wide.

"Oh, God," he said. "It just might be."

I fought back an instinct to grab him by the shoulders. Instead, I stood where I was and leveled my eyes directly at his.

"What?" I said breathlessly.

"It just might be, Detective, it just might be them."

"Who?"

"Hold on, let me think when it was . . . yes . . . last week . . . last week exactly. This day. Thursday, June the . . ."

"Twenty-fifth," I said.

"Yes! Thursday, June the twenty-fifth, I saw something odd. Well, not exactly odd at first. It was only the second . . . but I'm getting ahead of things. Why don't I just start with that day? Good Lord, I can't believe this slipped my mind!"

"That's okay. Just take it one step at a time. What did you see on the twenty-fifth of June?"

"I frequently take the shortcut through McKinny's Quarry to get to the Wissahickon Turnpike. The mill there calls me now and then to dress cuts and the like. On that Thursday, as I was walking through the forest to get to the quarry, I noticed a carriage was parked in a clearing, with a horse tethered to it. A couple of men were sitting down beside it, but I didn't see them too well. I thought it was all a little strange because they were so far off the path. You know how something out of the ordinary like that catches your eye. And like I said, they were set so far back from everything that they seemed . . . like they were hiding. Well, maybe that's not what I thought at the time. No, of course it wasn't. I was merely interested in what they were doing back there with the carriage, but I didn't have time to worry about it. I was late that day."

"You mind telling me why you went back that far yourself in the woods?"

"If I didn't, I'd have had to walk all the way down to Rittenhouse and then follow that till it leads into the turnpike. Then I'd have to follow the turnpike a ways while it winds to the mill. This other way just saves me a lot of time, that's all. Besides, I like the woods. The quiet and all that. You know what I mean?"

I admitted I did.

"So that was Thursday last. Then, I guess it was the next day, Friday the twenty-sixth, and I was making a house call in town. It was about nine or ten in the morning. And I saw the same carriage with two men riding it. As they drove past, I got a good look at them. This was on Harvey Street, just a square from here. I couldn't stop to see where they went. But that Saturday I was on my way back from church. We have a Saturday evening worship service, starts at six. So I was making my way past the Munroe house, as I always do on the way back from church. And . . . have you seen their house?"

I said no.

"Well, it's set up on a hill beside the woods that lead to McKinny's Quarry. There's a spacious lawn in front and back and a stone fence around the perimeter. Looks like a miniature Hadrian's Wall. Anyway, at the top of the hill there, past the house, I saw the carriage again with only one fellow in the driver's seat. Then I looked up at the house and saw something move. I stayed where I was to watch."

He paused a moment for dramatic effect.

"It was the other man, climbing over the stone wall and heading for the carriage. I immediately got the impression that he'd been on the grounds there."

"Why didn't you tell someone about this sooner?"

The doctor covered his mouth with his hand like he was about to cough. The hand trembled slightly. He knew what a mistake he'd made.

"I honestly thought it was the men from the gas company at first. Archie told me they were putting some new pipes in. Complained about the cost. I know all about that. I had to have my sister's house redone. There was a little explosion in her kitchen.''

I started to get impatient. ''You thought it was the gas men? Why wouldn't they go out the front door instead of climbing over the fence?''

''You're right, of course. In fact, as I made my way home, I kept thinking on what I'd seen. And the more I thought on it, the clearer it was to me that they were burglars. It's not the kind of thing that happens in our neighborhood. Maybe that's why it hadn't come to my mind at first. But I started to leave the house to go look for a policeman. And then Mrs. Miller came rushing down the street, babbling hysterically. Her little girl had fallen from a tree on East Walnut Street. I had to go right away.

''And I simply forgot the whole matter. Until right now. I swear that's the truth, Detective. I just hope this helps.''

''Me too.'' I pulled out a small tablet of paper and a pencil. I asked him to describe the two men. Did he get a good look at them?

''Yes, I did. The second time, on Harvey Street, I did. Especially the one in the carriage. Very queer looking chap, too.''

''Queer? In what way?''

''The thing I noticed first were these goggles he was wearing. They were tinted a greenish color. I'd never seen ones quite like them, not on a burly fellow like that.''

''Did he have a beard or moustache?''

''Both. The moustache was thick, with gray hairs mixed in with the brown. The side and chin beards were brown as well, and bushy. He had a straw hat on, pretty dirty looking. Broad band around it.''

Between each sentence there was a pause, as if he were describing new details of a picture that was at that moment being drawn. His memory dredged up the details slowly, painfully.

"What about his clothing?"

"Couldn't see much from where I was. Only thing I noticed was a gray alpaca duster."

"Any other details about his face?"

"Yes! That's right. His nose was deformed! When he saw me watching him, he glowered at me and turned away. So I saw his profile. His nose was very flat. Peculiar looking. And halfway between the bridge and tip of his nose there was an indentation which made the bottom of the nose turn up, like this."

He tried it on his own good nose. It looked like a child imitating a pig.

"How old would you say he was?"

"I don't know. I'm not much good at guessing people's ages. Forty, maybe. How old are you, by the way?"

"Thirty."

"Hmm. With your moustache you look older. I would have said thirty-five. You see what I mean? That's quite young for a detective, isn't it?"

I felt my face blushing. He was right. I was the youngest dick there was. The others held it against me, as I saw the first day with Bunker. Suddenly I was aware of how much I wanted to prove myself to them, to everybody. To show them that I wasn't too young, that I could pull my weight and more. I had been young in the War, too. Only nineteen when I was captured. I lied about my age when I enlisted. They weren't too discriminating about that in those days.

I'd lost my chance to prove myself in battle back then. Now I was in a different kind of battle, with a different kind of enemy. I was determined to win.

I ignored the doctor's comment and got back to his story.

"What about the second man? Didn't you notice anything about him?"

"The only time I saw him was that last time, when he was climbing the fence. I wasn't that close to the Munroe house. The second man was heavier. Younger looking. Also had a full beard, brown hair. He was wearing a linen duster. Gray, like the other man's. And the same kind of straw hat with a broad brim. That's about all I can tell you."

My wrist ached from all the writing I'd done. I had five sheets completely filled up. I turned to the next one and said, "Describe the carriage."

"Yes. That I can do, because it was very distinctive."

"In what way?"

"Do you know anything about carriages, Detective?"

"A little. I collared . . . I mean, I arrested a horse and harness thief last year who worked for a carriage fence . . . a receiver of stolen goods. So I had to bone up on models and such."

"All right. The carriage had a cab front and a yacht-like body. But the top was collapsible."

"Sounds like a type they make in Bucks County."

Dr. Moyer smiled. "You do know your carriages. Yes. You don't see that kind of carriage made outside of Bucks County."

"Very good. What about the color?"

"Pretty drab. Gray wheels and chassis with a green cab."

"And the horse? The same one both times?"

"Yes. It was a nice-looking bay about . . . fifteen and a half hands high."

I laughed and said, "I got to hand it to you, Doctor. You'd make a great detective."

"Not at all. I'm simply observant. This is my little piece of the world and I'm naturally interested in everything that goes on. It's hard not to notice strange vehicles and men. This is such a quiet place."

"Yes, it is." I closed the notebook.

"Do you think this will help?"

"I have a feeling. I think you do, too."

"Yes. They're the ones, aren't they?"

I nodded and said, "They sound like family men to me. Certainly not gas company employees."

"Family men?"

"Sorry. That's what we call thieves, people in the criminal life. They must have been gunning the house, watching it from the woods for at least a week. Waiting and watching. They might have been planning to steal the kid from inside. That would explain what they were doing climbing the fence. Either that or they're tramps, gypsies who saw a chance to get rich quick."

"But why Munroe? He's not a wealthy fellow. Well off, yes. But there are far richer men."

I shrugged and said, "Criminals aren't known for their brainpower. But you're right. There's some reason why they picked Munroe."

And something told me the answer was two streets down, at 252 Rittenhouse.

"Thanks a lot, Doc. I think the Munroes are going to owe you a lot when this is over."

"Just as long as that boy comes back safely. That'll be my reward."

"If this turns up something substantial, I'll be in touch with you. You might have to come downtown and make a formal statement. Thanks for your time."

I left Moyer in his parlor. He turned to the western photographs as I left. His eyes were closed.

5

THE PROPERTY AT 252 Rittenhouse was just as Dr. Moyer described it. A sloping lawn led to a new house of vine-covered verandahs, bay windows, and a mansard roof. A wall of stone surrounded the property like it was a castle.

It wasn't such a large house, but it was no shack, either. A fresh coat of paint covered the wooden boards and the grass was cut. All in all, it looked like a prosperous but modest man's home.

A vegetable garden was planted along the side of the house that faced the woods. It looked like an involved enterprise. From where I was on the road I saw tomato vines, rows of carrots, and beans. An apple tree grew to one side. There were flowers, too. Marigolds, some roses and dahlias, and a host of huge sunflowers. They looked quite pretty.

One of the carriages from the Central Police Station was parked on the street. The horse was dozing in the heat while bluetail flies took care of its dumpings. A sheep dog was lying in the sun near the porch steps. When I walked up, it started barking at me.

The noise brought one of the boys to the porch.

"Oh, it's you, McCleary."

"Sure enough. Diefenderfer in?"

"The parlor. He's been sweating the nigger woman

for an hour and getting nothing. Keeps it up, though. Guess he enjoys it.''

''I couldn't imagine anything more fun. Where is he?''

''Down the hall here,'' the dick said.

The house was quiet inside. And dark. All it needed was a black wreath on the front door and a corpse in the parlor. I tried shaking that image out of my head. It didn't work.

I asked the dick, whose name was Bowie, how many more of us were there.

''Just me and Diefenderfer. The rest are out making house calls. I'm surprised you're back already. Did you get both streets covered?''

''No. But I did get to talk to someone.''

''That's it? One person?''

''One person who happened to be the right person. He saw the kidnappers.''

Bowie grabbed me by the shoulders and asked, ''Are you serious?''

''Damn right I am. That's why I came right over.''

A voice came from the parlor.

''Who's jawin' out there?''

''Just me and McCleary,'' Bowie said.

''What's he doin' here?'' Diefenderfer growled.

''Got some news for you,'' I said, and walked in.

The parlor was well furnished and tasteful, but not extravagant. The lace curtains, trailing to the floor, were draped to keep the flies from coming in through the open windows. A small piano stood in one corner with its legs tastefully covered. In the fireplace was an attractive display of wildflowers that took the place of logs in the summer. On the mantel were photographs of the family and several arrangements of stuffed birds protected by glass covers.

A large pendulum ticked back and forth in the corner. It was part of a huge clock that looked as old as Philadelphia itself.

Stylish wallpaper covered the walls above dark cherry

wainscoting. There were several paintings and prints hung up, as well as a few stitched mottoes. The one I noticed right away was *The Fear of the Lord is the Beginning of Wisdom.*

Diefenderfer had the colored house servant sitting on the piano bench while he stood right in front of her. Both of them looked at me when I came in as if I'd just fallen out of a tree.

"Well? What have you got?"

"I was talking to a doctor on Harvey Street. Just a square down."

"I know where it is. And?"

"I think he saw the men who grabbed the boy. He gave me a complete description of them and their vehicle."

"How do you know it was the kidnappers he saw? Did he actually see them take the kid?"

"Actually, no, he didn't. But I have a feeling that these two did it. Now all I have to do is talk to the older brother, Stephen, and see if his identification of the men matches the doctor's."

"That right? Okay. Now listen. First thing. I'm the one who deals with the Munroe family. Heins put me in charge, and by damn, I'm going to stay in charge. I don't wanna turn this thing into a circus. We gotta do things nice and orderly. That means you give me what you got and I run it past them. Besides, I don't want you upsettin' the kid. Or the mother."

"What's wrong with them?"

"She's taking opiates for her nerves. The kid . . . he doesn't say a word. I tried questioning him and it's no good. The shock and all that, I guess."

"I wasn't going to bother her. Or the kid. I just wanted to get some corroboration here."

"You leave me the description and I'll get it."

I said nothing. All I did was stare at him staring at me.

"See," he went on, "I don't want to give you somethin' that delicate, Junior. You might fuck it up, and then where would we be? The kid might have a fit or some-thin'. Just gimme the description and I'll ask about it.''

"Well, why not let me go and ask, since you're busy down here?''

I was being pushy. I wanted to meet these Munroe people. Plus I was annoyed that Diefenderfer was trying so hard to keep me out of the investigation. I didn't take it personally because he was probably acting the same way with all the other dicks.

"McCleary, listen carefully. You got a lot more work to do. Leave me the fucking report and I'll take care of it.''

Suddenly I got sick of his rudeness. I wasn't going to let him take advantage of me. Fair was fair. I had a right to follow up on my own pointers. So what if he was in charge? He was just another dick, same as me.

I wanted to pop him in his fat lip right there, but I decided to do the more intelligent thing. I said, "I must've dropped it on the way.''

"Well, tell me what the doctor said!''

"I can't.''

"Why the hell not?''

"Because I forgot.''

I walked out on him and back to the porch.

Bowie followed me out. I grabbed the verandah with both hands. My knuckles were white with rage.

"What's the matter with you, boy? Who do you think's in charge of this whole thing?''

"I know who's in charge.''

"Then if you got something on the suspects, you gotta turn it in to Diefenderfer. That's the way it works. We follow orders around here. Even when we don't like who's giving them.''

In his patronizing way, he was trying to make me feel better.

"I don't have a problem with taking orders. It's just that I get the feeling Diefenderfer's in this to make lieu-tenant. He makes us do all the work, then gets the credit and the promotion. I don't think it's fair.''

"Who said anything about fair? You were in the War, weren't you? You know how it works!"

"Yeah. I guess I do. Maybe that's why I'm miffed about it now. I had enough of that back then."

"It doesn't stop. No matter where you go."

"I know. Thanks."

"That's okay. Listen, I'd feel the same way if I was young like you and gave a shit. But I just got out of the hospital. Last case I was working on, this beerslinger who ran a policy shop out of his saloon barked me when I tried to collar him. I was laid up for weeks. Still hurts my leg where the ball went in. So I don't feel the need to stick my neck out. I'm content to watch from the balcony, if you catch my drift."

"Sure."

"I seen what Diefenderfer's up to. He wouldn't let us get close to the family. Wants them all to himself. That way, he's the only one they trust and talk to."

"I think he likes all that power."

"He's always been that way. He's got his ambitions, like everybody else. Mine stops with what I got right now. You got ambition, too, I'm sure. So right now he wants to have his hands on the whole business. Keeps talking to the father and his wife. The wife, she's not a bad piece of muslin, either. She's got quite a face on her. I musta seen her in town. Was she an actress for a while?"

I shrugged.

"Coulda been. Ah, well. I ain't seen her much. She's up in her room, bawlin' over the kid. Understandable. Hell of a strain for a woman like that."

Listening to him had calmed me down. I was curious about the rest of the Munroes. I wanted to tell them myself what I'd learned. I wanted to be the one to bring that hope to them. Maybe it had something to do with the guilt I felt—guilt about seeing the case as an adventure, a problem, and not the endless anguish it must be to them.

As I stared off the porch, thinking on these things, the smell of smoke reached my nostrils.

I turned to the dick and said, "You smell that?"

"My sense of smell ain't so good. What is it?"

"Smoke. Nearby, too. Who'd be burning something when it's this hot?"

"Dunno. I seen some gas company men working around the house. Maybe that's it."

"No, I don't think so." I took another sniff and walked off the porch.

All at once I saw the smoke and heard two screams.

The smoke was coming from a shed in the backyard. It was more like a small barn. Smoke was billowing from under the doors. Those same doors were shaking. Screams came from behind them. I started running toward the doors.

Another scream came from the house. I gazed upward and saw a woman leaning out of a window. She was saying, "Oh, my God! Stephen! Help! Fire! Fire!"

It took me a few seconds to make it to the barn. From the single window I could see a fire had started inside. It was still manageable, but it wouldn't be for long.

There was a boy lying on the ground. One hand was wrapped around his ankle. The other was banging on the doors. I took hold of the knob and pulled. The doors were unlocked, but they still wouldn't open. The jambs were warped. The boy had probably pulled them shut tighter than usual and they'd gotten stuck.

Not that I was thinking on any of this. The only thing I cared about was getting the child away from the fire. His screams of terror pierced my heart. Deep down, even then, I think, I realized how much I had always wanted to save a child's life.

I threw myself against the doors with all my strength. They gave, sending a wave of pain up and down my left side.

The boy was right at my feet. His knee breeches were on fire. The whole shed was ablaze by now, unbearably hot. My flesh got singed as I dragged the boy out. He was screaming hysterically.

When we were far enough away from the shed, I beat the fire out on his leg. I grabbed him by the shoulders and said, "Are you okay?"

The boy's lower lip trembled as he mumbled, "Yeah, I think so."

"Stay here. I'm going back."

The fire was spreading to the rear of the shed. A few buckets of water were lying next to some garden tools. I heaved them at the wall. The water hissed against them, snuffing out the climbing flames. Part of the floor and some burlap sacks were still on fire. I used the rest of the water to put them out.

When I was done, the shed was a charred mess.

The boy was still lying on the ground when I came out.

"What're you doing here?"

"I can't move! My ankle got twisted when I tried to get out!"

From the house I saw a black-clad woman dash toward us, her arms flung outward. I picked the boy up and carried him across the sward to his mother.

She nearly tore him from my arms, clutching him to her.

"Oh, God! I thought . . . Stephen! Thank God you're all right! You *are* all right, aren't you?"

"He's fine, ma'am," I said, wiping sweat from my brow. "I wish I could say the same about your shed."

Her eyes took me in for the first time. They were large, gray colored, and intense.

Despite the mourning dress draped from her chin to her ankles, I could see she was a handsome woman. Even in that hysterical moment her beauty was evident. But it was a fragile, soft beauty, like a flower toward the end of its blooming. Her features were hard etched, with piercing eyes surmounted by gossamer-thin eyebrows. Her severe-looking nose arched over small lips, parted now with fear and relief. There was a bucolic innocence in the way she wore her dress and the way she carelessly tied her hair back with a tortoiseshell clip. But there was something else in her eyes, a tired worldliness, as if she were used to trouble like this.

I must have stood there for three or four seconds without saying anything, watching her. It seemed like much longer. Finally, she said, "What is your name, sir?"

"Detective Wilton McCleary, ma'am."

"Sir, we are in your debt. I don't know how to say . . ."

"Don't worry about it, Mrs. Munroe. I'm just glad the boy's okay."

I tried to act as modest as possible, but inside I was swelling like a balloon. All my life I'd waited to do something like this. My body tingled with satisfaction. The way the mother clung to her son and kissed him moved me deeply.

I'd saved people from gunfights before, but this was different. This time I had saved someone and hurt no one in the process. It was a good, clean feeling, and I thanked the Lord I had been where I'd been and acted when I'd had to.

Diefenderfer was just a few paces behind Mrs. Munroe. I've never seen such a look as the one he had on his ugly mug. A dash of rage and a smidgen of disappointment. He was probably thinking he should have been the one to save the kid and not me. I got the impression he wanted the boy to go back in the shed so he could set it on fire and have his shot.

Mrs. Munroe and I walked past him while he fumed. Then he stuck a segar in his pursed lips and headed for a carriage, probably to sic Cap on me. But he was too late. He didn't know it, but the investigation had just slipped through his fingers and into mine.

We met Mr. Munroe who was standing at the back door, his mouth wide open.

"What *happened*?" he cried.

"Your boy must've been playing with matches or something in the shed. You keep kerosene in there?"

"Yes," Munroe said, his face draining of color.

"Probably some of it spilled and got sparked by the matches. Children play with fire all the time. Especially around this time of year."

"Playing with crackers, more than likely. He must've found out where I hid them."

"Could be. The doors got stuck when the fire started and he panicked. Something's wrong with his ankle, too. Sprained it, I think. But don't worry. He's all right."

The man shook his head with relief. I could hear his thoughts: losing one is terrible enough. But to lose both . . .

"Wish I could say your shed was in A1 shape, but it got smoked. Some of your tools are wrecked, and the walls and floor might need replacing."

He nodded and said to me, "I remember you from City Hall, but I've forgotten your name."

I told it to him.

"Mr. McCleary, I can't thank you enough. Why don't you come inside and let us look after you for a spell? You weren't burned, were you?"

"Me? No! I got my hands on your water buckets before . . ."

"Glad to hear it. Well, the shed can be rebuilt. As long as no one's hurt."

His tone was unconvincing. It was one more heartbreak for him. From the looks of his yard, gardening was a favorite pastime.

"The tools. Well, the garden will have to wait. Maybe I can borrow some tools from the neighbors." Replacing all those tools would cost money. Money that he needed to save his boy's life.

He turned to me again and said, "Won't you come inside? Minnie'll make you some lemonade and you can sit and take a load off! It's bad enough you have to walk up and down the streets on a scorcher like to-day, but then all this . . ."

"I'm obliged to you. Lead the way."

We went through the back door and into the kitchen,

where there was a small table and two chairs. I sat down on one of them, unfastening my collar. I grabbed a newspaper and fanned my neck. It felt great.

"Minnie, fetch some lemonade for the policeman!"

I heard her say from somewhere in the house, "Right away, Mr. Munroe."

The kitchen was well kept. A cross-stitched motto hung over the doorway to the rest of the house. It said, *Give us this day our daily bread.* Some antique molds and strange-looking tools I didn't recognize were hung from the walls or placed in orderly piles in the pantry, the door of which stood open.

"Those look like confection molds," I said, by way of breaking the silence. One of them was in the shape of a fish, the other a boot.

"That's right." He turned to me and smiled, pleased. "My father was a confectioner. Those are some of the molds he brought with him when he came to the United States."

"From where? Scotland?"

"Well, originally my family came from there, way back. But first they lived in Canada. Up in New Brunswick."

"And they had a confectionary up there?"

"That's right. When he moved to Philadelphia, he brought some of them with him just for old time's sake."

"So he didn't set his business up here as well?"

"No, he came to . . . well, he was old and wanted to spend time with his family."

"Ah, I see! You'd already set yourself up here and he came to stay with you."

"Yes. He died just two years ago, God rest his soul."

Munroe got quiet for a while and stared at the fish mold.

"That one," he said pointing to it, "he used to make licorice. The red kind. Gosh, how I used to love those things. I remember in his shop he had these barrels where he stored the candy. Old things that looked like they'd been thrown overboard during the Boston Tea Party. And you'd go from one to the other, lifting the lid and seeing licorice one place, taffy another, chocolate another, and then you'd lift the last lid and inside would be a dead cat!''

He chuckled. So did I.

''I think it was my father's aunt's cat that she'd stuffed years before. When she passed away, he was cleaning out her place and found this cat. For some reason he didn't throw it away but kept it in one of the barrels as a joke. Nothing he liked more than watching a little girl lift that lid up, thinking she'd see some sweets, and have that bug-eyed thing glaring at her!''

The smile and the stare on his face were both for another time, one that had nothing to do with to-day. This was probably not the first time he'd retreated back there, to hide from the horror of the present.

''Thank God Father didn't live to see this happen.''

I wanted to take his mind off brooding. There was a Bible on the table with a Lutheran book of worship beside it. I said to him, ''You're a Lutheran?''

My question jolted him out of his revery.

''What? Oh, that. Yes, I'm a Lutheran. These days I've been reading and praying more than usual.''

I used this topic to lead in to what was really on my mind.

''I was just talking to a person to-day who belongs to your congregation.''

''That so?''

''Yes. Dr. Forrest Moyer.''

''Of course! How is the good doctor?''

''Not too well, I'm afraid. He's as worried about your son as everyone else.''

''I can remember all those times I took the boys to his office. Those pictures of his! Quite spectacular, I think. Someday I should like to go out west. See the red Indians and the canyons, and plains, and of course the buffalo. Eddie loved going there just to see those pictures. I told the doctor he should publish a volume of his photographs.''

It was as if he didn't want to talk about the kidnapping or anything related to it. The memories were acting like a barrier. I had to climb over it.

''The doctor told me something very interesting. I was planning on telling you about it first thing when I called on you, but I got detained.''

''Detained?''

''By Detective Diefenderfer.''

''It's very curious. At first I was relieved when he came and took over things. It meant I didn't have to think anymore. But over the past few days I've begun to feel . . .''

I waited for him to find the right description.

''I don't know . . . it's as if I should be the one taking care of all this. Don't get me wrong, I appreciate what all of you policemen are doing very much. Both of us do. But it makes me feel weak. Powerless.''

''Guilty?''

He was in the mood to confess things to me now. All the bottled-up feelings came out. And I was lucky enough to be around. It helped that I had just saved his son's life.

The answer to my question was a whisper: ''Yes.''

Then he said, ''They wouldn't have gone with those men if I hadn't said they would get no crackers this year. But I didn't mean it! That day I bought them some. It was a surprise, understand?'' He was pacing back and forth, biting his nails.

''Sure. Take a seat.'' I wanted to get him calmed down. ''You love your children very much. Anyone can see that.''

''Of course I love them! Both of them! But I'm not doing anything to get Eddie back! Why can't *I* help?''

''You have helped. You told us everything you knew. What more can you expect of yourself?''

''I'm tired of your Detective Diefenderfer being the one to talk to the *Ledger* and all the rest. I'm tired of him being the one to talk to my wife, calm her down. He's taken over my house and kept me in the dark about everything! The way he talks to me, you'd think I was an imbecile! I can do something, too, you know! I may be a fool, I may be on my way to the poorhouse, but I want to get my son back! Even if I have to lose everything else!''

There was no way he could even buy his son back. He couldn't fight the battle that needed to be fought. Others were doing it for him. He didn't have what it took. At least, that's what he was thinking.

And I knew exactly how he felt. That's why my heart went out to him again. As he wept with his face in his hands, I held him to me, like a comrade in arms.

The colored woman came in with our drinks. She saw Munroe and stayed where she was, shocked. I pushed the air in front of me with my hand. She got the message and left.

''Mr. Munroe, I think I can help you,'' I said.

''How?'' It came out with a sob.

''Dr. Moyer may have seen the men who kidnapped your boy.''

For a few moments he stared at me dumbfounded. Then he said, ''Tell me everything.''

It took about twenty minutes. He interrupted me after every detail. Finally I asked him, ''Does this sound like the men Stephen told you about?''

''It most certainly does. By God, McCleary! I think you've got them!''

I laughed a bit and said, ''Hardly. We still have to catch them. We have no names, no places last seen, no witnesses other than the doctor. And I need to talk to the boy, just to make sure. Is there any chance I can talk to him now?''

He shook his head and said, ''Now probably isn't the best time. It's his piano lesson. His mother's very religious about it. Every day at three o' clock. Especially since this started she's been there with him for an hour each day. I hardly ever get a chance to see him anymore.

If I do, he barely says a word to me anyway.''

"Keeps her mind off things, I guess.''

"That's right. They both need to do that.''

"Well, maybe I'll go out and knock on some doors in the meantime. Are you sure you don't remember any men of this description? Maybe at your store?''

"No. I'm sure I would have remembered a man with a deformity like that.''

"I'm almost sure your son can remember a little bit more than he's told already. Right when something happens, it hits you like a brick and you're stunned. You can't always remember all the little things. They come back over a period of days. I've seen it happen. And it's those little things that I'm interested in. Out of the little things come the big things.''

"I'm no detective, so I couldn't say. Listen, why don't you come back and talk to Stephen when you're finished? I'm sure he won't mind answering your questions. And, Detective McCleary? Could I ask a favor of you?''

"Certainly. I'm at your disposal.''

"Don't tell Detective Diefenderfer about this. Keep this between you and me.''

I was no devotee of Diefenderfer by any means. A part of me was glad to work behind his back with a chance at breaking the case, making him look like the ass he was. Yet I still felt compelled to ask Munroe why he didn't want me to go to my superiors.

"You seem to understand me, McCleary. You know what I'm going through and you've talked to me like I wasn't some idiot who couldn't take care of himself or his family. You don't know how much I've needed someone to talk to these past few days. What I'm trying to say is . . . I trust you.''

I could feel myself blushing. I wasn't used to this kind of confidence coming from a man. But the crisis was bringing it out.

"I trust you to understand my motives. I want to get Eddie back. Understand? I need to know that I am doing something to help. I have something to prove to myself and . . . everybody else.''

I said, ''I understand.'' He had no idea how much I did. ''I'll tell you what. If you want to help, talk to your son and anybody else in the house. Give them the description of the men and the carriage that I just gave you. See if they have any recollection of them. You can work from here, you know.

''I have to tell Diefenderfer sooner or later. It's better that way. The more the detectives know about the kidnappers, the easier it'll be to catch them.''

''Let me help you find them!'' His hand clutched my arm.

''I can do that better on my own,'' I said. ''You have no idea the kinds of places I'm going to have to look. And the people I'll have to talk to. You're better off here, taking care of your wife. I won't tell Diefenderfer yet. Okay? I'll work this end myself and see what happens.''

He was chewing his nails again. Something was bothering him.

''You're sure this is all right? That is, I don't want this to hamper the efforts to find him. Maybe it would be better just to tell everyone.''

''No,'' I said. ''We know they're still in the city. The ransom letter had a Chestnut Street postmark. Now, if Diefenderfer gives the press boys their description, we'll be on to them, sure. But they'll be onto us. If it turns out they are the kidnappers, it's better that they don't know we're looking for them. As long as no one goes after them, they'll stay put.''

''Are you sure?''

''I think so. We have a better chance of catching them this way than if we went to Diefenderfer. If it's these men at all. Once we know for sure and we find them, that's when we call in the rest of the detectives.''

''You're right, I think. I'm sorry. I just doubted for a minute. Doubted that I could go through with it. I'm afraid, McCleary. I just want to find him.''

"Well, we can work on this for a day or so. You still have to get the next letter, the one that'll describe how they want to get their money. Until then we'll see what happens and keep this between the two of us, like you said."

I stood up to leave. Munroe got up with me and grasped both my shoulders. He didn't say thank you with words. But it was in his eyes. Somehow I was grateful, too.

I SPENT THE rest of that afternoon wearing out my soles on Germantown streets. I tried the description of the two men and the carriage on every single person I questioned but it got me nowhere. By the time I was finished rubbering around it was about half past five. I had had enough of the Edwin Munroe kidnapping case. When the carriage from downtown clattered by looking for me, I hopped into it and rode back to the city. The boy could wait until tomorrow.

I wasn't exactly sure how I felt about my agreement with Archibald Munroe. I understood his motives fine. His masculine pride was in question. That was part of it. His wife had something to do with that. From the first time I saw her, I figured there might be problems in that department.

Munroe wasn't a bad-looking man, but he was older than she was by at least fifteen years. And she was a beautiful woman.

I thought on Mrs. Munroe and called her face to mind as we rode back to Philadelphia. I understood why he might feel threatened by so many other men in the house. But maybe it was in his head. If she had borne two of his children, it might just be that she loved him. At any rate, he had something to prove to himself and to his wife. And he also wanted to atone for a crime that

79

someone else had committed but that he felt responsible for.

That was the easy part of the equation. Then there were my reasons for going along with him. I hoped I wasn't just trying to spite Diefenderfer and show him up for the lunkhead he really was.

None of this mattered, I realized. As soon as Diefenderfer met up with Cap, he would tell him all about what I'd said at the house. Cap would call me in and ream me out for holding something back. That would be the end of it. Unless I could convince him with the same argument I'd just used with Archibald.

I had a mind to beat Diefenderfer to it that evening. Cap was going to show up at Bunker's later, and I was headed there, too. The next letter from this group of kidnappers would surely arrive and Bunker would be getting ready to settle with them, one way or another. The rat classic was in two days and he would need Jocko. The kidnappers knew that. He would be willing to pay, I thought. But there were still two days. A lot of things could happen in two days.

The city carriage let me off a few squares from Bunker's diggings. I walked down the quiet street, past a lot where some boys were beheading thistles with sword-like sticks. Bunker was standing on his front porch with a ukelele in hand. His fingers strummed a minstrel tune, one that I had never heard before. The large, waxed moustache he wore jutted out like an awning over his lips, pursed in concentration.

"Can you sing, too?" I asked him.

"Only when I'm three sheets to the wind," he said, and smiled. "I was in the minstrel show we put on at the firehouse last May. You shoulda seen me. I was blacker than Reddy.

"Glad to see you again, my boy. Heard about your business with Reddy this morning."

"So the cat's out of the bag?"

"Yessir. I was ready to give him a capital kick in the ass. I don't know why I keep that old nigger on sometimes. Oh well, at least he makes good horseshoes.''

"It might help if you kept the spirits in a safe place.''

"Wouldn't do no good. He'd bully Ben into giving 'em to him.''

"Is Devers around, by the way? I wanna talk with him.''

"Sure. Last I saw of him he was out back, watching a peddler grind our knives.''

"Is Devers the one who talks to the peddlers when they come by?''

"Yeah. He don't bother the missus. Lets her stay in the parlor, where it's cool.''

Bunker put the ukelele down and leaned against the door. He bent his head and regarded me for a moment without saying anything. This was part of his theatrics. He had an announcement to make.

"I got the letter.''

My patience was all used up. I said, "Give it to me.''

Bunker said, "Wait a minute. Lemme read it to ya first.''

I ceded him that dubious honor. The letter went like this:

Dear Bunker,

We see from your response in the Ledger *that you is willing to deal. Just two more days until the big day so Jocko needs to rest up. If you want your dog back alive bring ten thousand dollar to the Fairmount Waterworks at eleven o'clock tomorrow night. There is a gazebo there (you know the one) that overlooks the forebay. Come there with the money in a carpet bag. And come alone. Tell no one else, especially the detectives. If you bring them along it will signal the instant annihilation of your dog. We will be watching you.*

Something about the letter bothered me. It was one of those vague feelings of disquiet. Like when you leave a place and know you've left something behind, but you have no idea what it is.

I was about to say something to Bunker. It was on the tip of my tongue. Then it sank back into the morass. I couldn't retrieve it.

I sighed with exhaustion. "Do you plan to go along with them?"

"What choice have I got? If I want Jocko back I got to! Christ, why'd they haveta do this? They wanted money from me they coulda broke into my house and stolen my guns! At least it woulda been over quick!"

"Don't give up hope. I have a plan."

"Yeah, so do I. I'm bringin' my Winchester with me tomorrow night. The first one of 'em I see I'm gonna put a hole through."

"That's not talking sense. Where would that get you?"

"Same place I'm goin. Nowheres. You think they're really gonna give me the dog back?"

I tried to put myself in the minds of the kidnappers. That was hard to do. At last I concluded, "Probably. It's not like the dog's going to tell us who kidnapped him. They'll be safe. The only reason they'd kill the dog would be out of sheer spite. And that in itself would be a clue, 'cause we'd know it had to be someone with a grudge against you."

"Swell. That would be about all the Democrats in my ward, plus more ratters Jocko's kicked the tar out of than I could count."

"Well, that's somewhere to start. But let's not worry about that yet. Here's what we'll do. Tomorrow night *I'll* go to the waterworks. If there's any shooting to be done, I'll be the one to do it, understand?"

"They said they'll be watchin' me."

"I'll go disguised as you, in your carriage, walking out of your house. It'll be dark. They're not going to be too concerned about whether or not it's you. Just if the money's there or not."

"I don't know, McCleary. I feel like this is personal. They want a piece out of me."

"Maybe they do at that. But it's all the more reason for me to go. And if they really *are* watching, I'm going to have to go alone."

"Ain't there some way the rest of you detectives can . . ."

"Naw. Especially not now. Cap's got them chasing leads on another case. By the way, I thought he was supposed to show up here to-night."

"He sent word he'd be delayed. That other case, he told me, is forcin' him to put in extra time until it's done."

"I know all about it."

I was relieved. This meant I had a few more hours to follow up on my private investigation of the Munroe case.

"Did he tell you what happened?"

I didn't want to say anything I wasn't supposed to.

"The Germantown boy? Yeah, he told me about it last night at the bowling alley."

"Well, if Cap's workin' extra hours, you can bet the detectives are, too. They're not gonna want to work ten-hour days looking for the boy and then pull night duty doing the same for your dog. Cap's overworking them as it is."

"So what are you doing here?"

I stroked the ends of my moustache for a time. Then I said to him, "Because I like to finish the things I start."

I didn't want to get into the deeper reason. The one that had to do with a battle I needed to fight with myself.

Bunker beamed and said, "A capital trait, boy."

"Yeah. Anyway, you have me at least until tomorrow night. If I can round up some bluebellies from the Central Office, I'll bring them along with me. But I won't promise anything except that I'll do my best to get your dog back."

"That's all I can ask for then." He clapped his hand on my shoulder to signify his satisfaction.

I wondered why I was so dead set on doing things myself. I had something to prove. But what good is that if it gets you or someone else dead? Who was I to think I could solve every problem without anybody's help?

I needed someone I could trust.

The only detective who fit that shoe was Nolan. I would ask him to come along with me when we convened at City Hall the next morning.

I left Bunker and went around the house to find Devers. There were some things I needed to go over with him. Since neither Reddy nor the Edgerton boys had panned out, I figured I could go over the details of both their stories with the boy to see if he could add anything to them.

Devers was cleaning fish when I walked inside the kitchen. Blood dotted his forearms and the front of his apron. Despite the fierce stink, he seemed to be happy. He was whistling a popular tune. I think it was, "I Guess I'll Have to Telegraph My Baby." The knife was keeping time on the chopping block.

I whistled a chorus along with him. He dropped the knife and turned around. He was a handsome kid, and well spoken, too. He'd actually graduated from the high school.

"Hello, Mr. McCleary," he said, firmly grasping my hand. "It's good to see you again, sir."

"Likewise. How're things?"

"Passin' fine. I have no complaints."

"What're you makin' for to-night?"

"Filet of flounder. The missus likes it. Mr. Bunker caught them himself last Tuesday, in the bay."

"I've always wanted to go on one of them sea fishing trips."

"Me too. He was describing it to me. Sounds like a lot of fun. But I get seasick. Even when I go on a steamer."

I thought of my last swim in the drink and shuddered.

Then I asked him how his folks were.

"They're okay. Pa got a job with the *Christian Recorder*. He's mighty happy with that."

"The *Recorder* . . . that's the negro newspaper?"

"That's right. They got him working on the devotional stuff."

"Well, that's fine. I'll have to pick a copy up one of these days."

Devers laughed and said with a trace of bitterness, "That'd be a sight to see. A policeman reading an issue of the *Recorder*." Then he stopped smirking and said, "I'm sorry, Mr. McCleary. You're not like other cops we know. Ma and Pa and me, we know you're our friend. We don't forget what you done for us on that election day in seventy-one."

The Fifteenth Amendment had just been ratified back then. There was a lot of trouble that year. Even the assassination of a prominent negro, Octavius Catto. I'd saved Devers's father from a similar fate.

"It's just . . . hard to trust any of them after what's happened over the years."

"Still happening, too, I'm afraid. But you gotta remember, Benny, coppers are like the rest of the world. There are good ones and bad ones. I hate to say it, but maybe there are more bad ones than good ones. At least, the kind who would rather do nothing than do something when it might cost their neck. But there are a few, more than a few, who fight on the right side."

"And what is the right side?"

My heart could answer that, but not with words. I changed the subject and said, "Listen, I came over to have a talk with you and Reddy before I knock off for the day."

"About Jocko?"

"That's right."

"But I already told you what I know."

"That's what you think. But it's been my experience that memory can change from day to day. You might be walking down the street and look at a pigeon on a telegraph wire and suddenly remember something you hadn't thought of in years. That ever happen to you?''

Devers nodded and said, ''I see what you mean.''

''So. I guess you heard about my run-in with Reddy this morning.''

''You bet. He made one hell of a fuss, after you left. Told the boss about the dog and getting drunk.''

''And what did Bunker do about it?''

''Same thing he's always done. Calls Reddy every four-letter word in the book and then some and breaks every bottle in the barn. You'd think he was on a one-man temperance crusade. He even lectured Reddy about drink. This comes from a man who owns about half a dozen saloons and dancing halls!''

'' 'Do as I say, not as I do,' I guess.''

''That's right. Anyway, things settled down and Reddy's back banging on his anvil. The boss won't do anything about it. In fact, they were back in the kennel this afternoon, working with some of the dogs.''

''Bunker has some he can use instead of Jocko?''

''I don't know too much about the dogs. I know he has a few he's plannin' to use on Thursday night. But they don't have anywhere near the chance of winning that Jocko had. Has.''

''Well, we got to get that dog back, then.''

''The boss is mighty upset about it. He doesn't eat much these past few days.''

''Maybe you can help us out. Did you hear what really happened to Reddy that day?''

Devers shook his head. The two of them apparently didn't talk that much. Reddy was suspicious of a ''high-tone nigger'' like Ben, who had a little education and polish.

I told him what had transpired. With each revelation he shook his head. When I finished recounting the story, I said to him, ''It seems like Reddy and the Edgerton boys are out of the race. I don't think Reddy would stoop so low as to deliberately ruin Bunker's chance of winning the big classic, do you?''

"No. Reddy's loyal to the boss. That's for sure."

"Then that leaves us with the peddlers. They're the only outsiders around the house that day. The first time we talked, you didn't tell me anything about them."

He stared at me with an almost stupid expression, as if my words were meaningless.

"You told me you spent the whole day in the kitchen."

"Well, that's right. I did exactly that."

He was stammering. I walked right up to him. With a quick movement I grabbed him by his apron and pulled his face to within an inch of my own.

"I think you're lying to me."

Devers started chewing his lower lip.

"How'd your folks feel if I told them their son was a liar?"

That got him. I knew it would. Ben was very attached to his folks.

"I-I-I wasn't here for a half hour that m-mornin'."

"Where were you?"

"With a . . . girl."

"What girl?"

"She works two houses down. Her name is Lucille. She and I met on the streetcar a few weeks ago. I just spend a little time talking with her. She's mighty nice. It's when everybody's out of the house and I don't have to be doing nothin'. Anything, I mean. No harm done, you know what I mean?"

"And you just spend time . . . talking with her?"

"Just talking. She's not that kind of gal."

"I hope she isn't. So you weren't around when Jocko was grabbed. You might have seen the kidnappers if you hadn't been dallying with your sweetheart."

Other men who didn't know Ben as well as I did might have asked him for the address of the place where Lucille worked. I didn't need to follow up on that. I believed his story. Bunker treated him well and he made better money than most negroes his age. He had no motive for kidnapping the dog that I could see.

I shook my head and started walking out of the kitchen. Ben rushed up and grabbed my arm.

"You're not gonna tell on me?"

I smiled just a bit and said, "I'm sure your ma would like to know."

"Aw, c'mon! It's nothing! Really!"

"Just talking, eh?"

"I swear on my pa's stack of Bibles!"

"Stay out of trouble, Ben." I patted him on the shoulder and left him there.

For the boy's own good I would tell Bunker to keep an eye on him during the afternoons. I didn't want to get him fired, but I wanted him to stay out of trouble, the female kind.

Things were not working out. I really thought Ben might have remembered something about the peddlers. Now it looked as if I was back to where I'd started. With nothing.

I went through the kitchen and into the parlor room where Mrs. Bunker was dusting off her ceramic dogs. I introduced myself again and chatted with her for a few moments about the heat and the humidity.

Then she said, "Have you found Jocko yet?"

I had to admit I had not.

"That's too bad. I don't worry Joe about his business too much. He's a very private man, you know. You'd think not, because he's a politician. But I know him better than anybody. Men tell women the darnedest things."

Bunker had told me his wife hated rats and kept her distance from the kennels. She kept out of his other affairs. For most of the day, from what he told me, she was around the house, tidying up and writing religious tracts for her temperance society.

She was a quiet woman, the kind that stays in the background. The few times I'd called on them I'd barely seen her. It was a good way for a politician's wife to be. All kinds of deals had to be made, and it was best for her not to be around to hear them.

The first time I questioned them he'd spoken for her, telling me no one had seen anything or anyone unusual. Perhaps he was afraid to have me talk to her, afraid of what I might learn about things other than Jocko's kidnapping. I'd discounted her completely because Bunker had.

But that was before I'd heard from Reddy about the peddlers.

Now for the first time I had a chance to talk to her without her husband being around.

I asked her, "Ma'am, do you remember any peddlers coming around that day? The day Jocko was stolen?"

The woman twisted an opal ring around her finger like it was a gear in her brain. Right away she said, "We get all kinds of peddlers here. Usually Ben takes care of them."

"Reddy told me that day he saw some peddlers who were selling poison."

The opal ring kept going around and around her finger. I waited for a few seconds. Then she said it.

"Yes. Rat poison."

"You saw them?"

She sat down on a sofa and fanned herself. Her lace-trimmed and heavily tasseled crinoline skirt looked like a balloon in the process of deflating. There was a glass of water on the table beside her. She took a sip and waited to answer me, obviously enjoying the effect her words had on me.

After a few dainty sips she said, "I saw them. I was upstairs and told Ben to answer the door. When they kept on knocking, I figured Ben was out running an errand."

If she only knew, I thought.

"Finally I got up from my desk and went to the door myself. And there was the strangest man I'd ever seen."

"How was he strange?"

"Well, he looked like most peddlers, I suppose. Very frowsy, and he smelled a bit like the stables." She giggled and said, "You should have seen him. He looked like some character out of a romance."

"Tall, dark, and handsome?"

She giggled again, like a vapid schoolgirl. Mrs. Bunker was enjoying this attention too much. Her husband must not have given her a lot of that. I felt sorry for her.

"No, no. He looked like an appar . . . ?"

"An apparition?"

"Yes, that's the word! An appar . . . ition. I couldn't see his eyes, first off. He was wearing green spectacles."

I had my notebook out and was writing this down.

"And a queer-looking straw hat."

"How about his face?"

"Big, bushy beard, like a mountain man. Gray and brown. And the poor thing's nose."

My hand stopped writing. I gripped the note pad till it bit into my palm.

I asked her, "What about his nose?"

Her flaccid face wrinkled up with disgust, barely disguised as pity.

"It was all flat, like this." She pressed her nose against her face.

"Like it was," I tried to remember the word someone used before. "Deformed?"

"Well, I guess so."

"Mrs. Bunker, let me ask you, now. Was this man wearing a gray alpaca duster?"

"Why, yes. He was. I like alpaca. It has such a nice feel to it. But not in July. Ugh."

"And was there another man with him?"

"Yes, there were two of them, but the other one was in the carriage."

My hands were shaking. She was looking at them. Sweat poured down my face. The collar felt like it was strangling me.

"Was he also bearded and wearing a gray linen duster?"

She nodded and asked, "Do you know these men?"

I ignored her question. "What about the carriage and the horse?"

"I don't take much notice of horses. They look the same to me."

"You don't remember the color at all?"

"I think it was brown and white."

"Or maybe a reddish-brown and white? A bay?"

"It could have been."

"And the color of the carriage?"

"Gray and green. I was thinking about his spectacles, the green ones. They were very queer."

I could barely keep myself together. What I was hearing was too incredible. I walked over to Mrs. Bunker and asked if I could have some water. She poured me a glass. I gulped it down before I realized it was more gin than water. After a hearty cough, I asked her, "What was your conversation about?"

"The man wanted to sell me poison for rats. He called it Rat-Oh and said he manufactured it himself. It was a bad time for rats, he said, with the summer miasmas and garbage left outside. For the safety of children and the protection of food and property, the best thing to do was poison them out of the house. I couldn't agree with him more, even though we never had children. We have a pantry that they're always getting into. Ugh! I hate to even think of them.

"So I bought a few bags of the stuff and told him to go back behind the house and let Reddy take care of it."

"Do you still have some of this Rat-Oh left?"

"I don't have it. Reddy might. He's the one in charge of getting rid of pests."

"And that's all that was said between you?"

"Yes, I think so. Do you think those are the men who stole Jocko?"

"I'd bet my left leg on it. Did he tell you his name or talk about where he lived?"

Mrs. Bunker thought for a moment, then shook her head. "No, he just talked about Rat-Oh like it was the greatest invention since the locomotive. Told me many major concerns had purchased Rat-Oh to get rid of pests. Especially meat-packers and slaughterhouses. He told me a story about watching rats devouring a carcass in ten minutes flat! That's what sold me on it, I think. Sent shivers up my spine.''

''And that's all you can tell me about them? Did the other man ever approach you, or did he ever talk to the other man?''

''No. He stayed in the carriage.''

''And once you bought the bags? How much were they, by the way?''

''He wanted a dollar for a bag. I talked him down to seventy-five cents,'' she said proudly. ''After that he thanked me and said good day. That's it.''

''Did you notice anything about his speech? Foreign-sounding? Southern?''

''He sounded normal to me. Like everybody else around here talks.''

My head felt like it was ready to burst. I couldn't take any more in. I got up to leave the Bunker house and head back for my diggings.

''Mrs. Bunker, you have no idea what you just told me.''

She clapped her chubby hands gleefully.

''Wait until I tell Joe. He'll be so happy! I might even talk to him about that new wallpaper I've been looking at for the bathroom. It's expensive, but after this I think I deserve it.''

''You sure do. Listen, I'll be back to take a formal statement from you, okay? And try to remember if there's anything else you may have forgotten. Every little thing helps.''

''Who would have thought?'' she exclaimed.

''You can say that again.''

I left her in the parlor with her ceramic dogs. The walk to the streetcar stop went by like a hazy dream. I thought back to what had been on the tip of my tongue when Bunker had shown me the letter. And I couldn't believe I'd overlooked something so obvious.

They'd used the phrase "signal the instant annihilation" in both letters.

My mind's eye could see only one thing, like a huge shop sign emblazoned in the sky. The sign said, THE SAME MEN STOLE THE DOG AND THE BOY.

And I was the only one who knew about it.

I rode past my stop. The jostling of the car lulled me into a mesmeric trance. I let the car take me through its entire route again. I needed time to think.

I WOULD GET nowhere fast hitting up every informant
of mine in and out of prison with the descriptions of the
two suspects. Chances were the kidnappers might be
alerted sooner or later. I wanted to keep them in the dark
at least until to-morrow night. Once we got to the waterworks, they were going to find out that I had their
number.

If I could just get them to-morrow night, I thought, I
could tie both ends up so nice they'd be talking about
me at the Central Office for years.

But as it stood, I still had no names or whereabouts.
I figured the best way to get those was to start with the
easiest thing to trace: the carriage from Bucks County.

Dr. Moyer knew his carriages well. A model like that
would be noticeable enough to the various fences and
thieves I knew who dealt with that kind of merchandise.
They wouldn't have any idea I was looking for anything
but who'd stolen the carriage. But they might feel a little
cagey about selling one of their brothers out for a collar
that could take them all the way to the gallows.

I had no idea what the punishment for kidnapping
would be. Since it had never been done before, that
would be something for the judge and jury to decide.
But if I knew the mood of the city and the press they'd

push for the stiffest of all. This was not the kind of crime to encourage with light sentences.

If they were smart, they would break down fast in the back room and cough up where the kid was stashed. That might buy them a round-trip ticket to the chokey instead of a one-way ticket to a necktie party.

And there was the boy, too. I wondered if he and Jocko were sharing accommodations. Where in hell were they?

After pacing back and forth until I got light-headed, I decided to go for a walk.

I wound up on Eighth and Vine after the streetcar left me off. Locker's Oyster and Dining Rooms was right on the corner. The gaslight was blazing from inside and good smells reached me, carried on the moist summer air. A wooden sign was propped on the curb. It said TRY OUR 30¢ ROAST DINNERS. Two other signs advertised 20¢ STEWS. Gray's ales were five cents a glass, though I don't often imbibe when I'm on the job. In fact, I rarely go for liquor at all. Still, it sounded tempting. I had some change in my pocket and I figured it would be a long night. So I strolled through the gaudy entranceway with its marbleized Corinthian columns and ornamented gas lamps and into the restaurant.

I left a half hour later and headed south toward Arch Street. This was the edge of the business district and there was a lot of bustle even this late at night. Cellar doors were propped wide open while shopkeepers unloaded barrels from a plethora of wagons. I noticed a uniformed copper talking to two whores camped beneath a streetlight. I saw some money exchange hands. He gave one of them a tweak on the rear and headed in my direction. At first he gave me the typical scowl reserved for strangers on the beat. I gave him a scowl back.

The bull was about to give me some grief when I pulled the detective star out of my pocket and palmed it at him. He got respectful pretty quick and mumbled, "Evening, sir. Ya need my help?"

"No thanks, Officer. I was just on the prowl looking

for crooked cops to put the pinch on. You know the kind I mean? The ones who bug from whores and sneaks? Look the other way while a second-story gang robs a warehouse here and there?"

The officer made for his billy club. Not like he was going to use it just yet. But he was getting ready.

"You seen any of them around?"

I pulled my revolver out, pulled the hammer back slightly, and spun the cylinder. I said nothing. The metallic clicking sound it made said all kinds of things.

"Incidentally, Officer, I spent my last dime on dinner. You wouldn't happen to have some change on you to see me home, would you?"

The gun was still out. I pretended to clean it. The barrel was pointed at a slight angle from his belly.

Sweat trickled from under his cap and down his clean-shaven cheeks.

He got the picture. When I held out my hand, he slapped the whores' money into it.

"Thanks a bunch, pal," I said. "Be seeing you."

I waited for him to walk away. When he peered back and saw me staring right at him, he quickly turned and started running down Arch like a rabbit.

The whores at the streetlight had witnessed the whole transaction.

"Dog eat dog, eh?" one of them said to me.

The other said, "Interested in sharing some of what you got there? We can have all kinds of fun."

"Give me your hand," I said.

One of them slipped a soiled palm my way. I put some of the bills on it and said, "Merry Christmas. Now, find another street lamp."

They didn't have a smart comment to answer me with. All they did was stare at the money I'd given them. They didn't bother thanking me as I walked away. Politeness was not a part of their disposition.

They must've counted it. One of them hollered, "What about the rest?"

"I really do need cab fare."

I watched them strut off. Their cheap perfume lingered.

I pulled my watch out of my front vest pocket and tried to read it under the light. It was getting late. I had to do a little more work before the night was out.

A few squares down was a flash drum I needed to visit. With a little luck I could get the story on the carriage.

A flash drum was a saloon reserved especially for the criminal class. It was not just a watering hole but also a place of business. And an information center. There were dives like this all over the city. They weren't advertised in *Appleton's Handbook of American Travel*, nor did they have lurid signs out front, like Locker's. But if you were a part of the family, you knew where your home was.

It wasn't a good idea to advertise the fact that I was the law. Being in plain clothes helped. But when you went into a flash drum, they had other ways of telling right off if you were with the family. The most effective was to speak flash to you and see if you had the slightest bloody idea what they were talking about.

Flash was a language criminals used to keep their deals secret. They used it in the prisons and in the station houses as well as on the streets. A few articles had been published here and there which purported to be dictionaries of criminal cant, but they were always out of date by the time they saw print. Flash was like any other language, subject to constant change. The best way to learn it or keep up with it was to speak it. That meant spending time at flash drums and cribs where you had no one but criminals to talk to.

I was lucky enough to have had the equivalent of a college education in the flash language while I was in Andersonville. One of my tent mates was a fellow I saved from getting his throat slit for his boots. He never made it out of there alive, but while he held on he taught me all kinds of things. Before the War he had been a safecracker, an aristocrat among criminals. Most of what

I knew about Philadelphia's underworld came from him. His friends eventually learned about what I'd done for him. We did favors for each other now and then.

This particular flash drum was a home away from home for one of those men, named Gilbert Davis. His underworld moniker was Gasper. Gilbert had consumption.

I had a good idea he would be there that night, if he wasn't out on a job.

Davis was well acquainted with most of the horse and carriage fences in the Quaker City. If any of my informants could lead me to the men who had stolen that carriage (and I was almost certain that it had been stolen), he was the one.

The drum looked like any other cellar dive. The wooden doors were flung open to let in as much air as possible. Even so, it was as stuffy as a backhouse at noontime.

Just about everyone was watching me as I stepped inside. Their vision was partially impaired by a wall of smoke as thick and rancid as the harbor water near the docks.

It was a fairly respectable hellhole. No guns were openly displayed. The men seated at the tables were well attired and groomed. Women and men mingled with each other, like in a negro saloon. I had arrested two of the ladies last year for shoplifting. I had to shift my hat over my head to keep them from noticing me.

I managed to overhear some conversations:

"...We was padding the hoof to the popshop to fence some swag Billie buzzed off this shakester. The ikey mo says, 'One shine for the reader and five for the yack.' I says to him, Go be blowed..."

"...So I mowed this bleak molly right there in the panny with her old man upstairs..."

They went on detailing their crimes and bragging while I approached the bar.

The beerslinger eyed me suspiciously. "Hob or nob?" he asked. That meant what would I have to drink?

"Sky blue," I said. The beerslinger knew what I was talking about. He gave me a shot of gin.

After I downed it I told him, "That's the blue ruin."

Telling him it was bad gin only elicited a shrug. But he was evidently satisfied with my spattering of flash. I was allowed to pass toward the tables.

A hurdy-gurdy player was cranking out some old tunes in the back of the room. One of his legs was missing. Most likely he had lost it in the War. I went over to him and tossed the rest of the whores' money into his hat.

Then I scanned the room to see if Gil was around. Before I even started, I felt a tug at my sleeve.

"Hey, fella, you make a better door than a window."

I turned around to see who the smart aleck was. A pint-sized man was slumped against the wall, beneath a framed and yellowed portrait of an actress with more than her ankles showing.

His eyes were the color of choleric skin. A thin moustache curled around his lips like a limp rag. The top of his head was bald and shiny with sweat. Salt-and-pepper curls ran around his ears. He hacked into a handkerchief and stuffed it back into his pocket. Then he took another swig from the pail of lager beer in front of him.

"You heard me, McCleary. I wanna see the man play."

I moved out of his way and sat down beside Gasper. All the eyes that had been on my back went to look at something else.

Gasper's chest heaved with a minor convulsion that wound its way up to his face. Then he broke into a smile and said, "Nice to see ya, Wilton."

"Likewise. How's business?"

"Stinks. They put the pinch on my whole gang a few months ago. I've been flying low ever since."

"Cracking cribs is getting to be a risky business."

"Don't I know it. I've been dipping my hand into something else lately. You're not going to believe this."

"Try me."

"Well, I had a little jack saved up from the last casa we bagged. Actually quite a load, if I do say so myself." The chuckle he made turned into another cough.

"This damn humidity doesn't do wonders for my condition."

"I know what you mean."

"Makes me want to go to the desert or something. Or the Catskills."

"Those spas are expensive, from what I hear."

"Yeah. But all kinds of bleak molls, too."

Looking at Gasper, I didn't think the women would clamber after him. I left his fantasy alone.

"Mmm. If I could get me into one of those places . . ."

"Keep dreaming. You have just enough to rent that place of yours in Kensington."

"How do you know about that?"

"I keep up on my friends, Gasper. Remember, I'm the one who got that charge thrown out last month."

"Yeah, I heard about that, and I thank you. That was bullshit, though. They had no right to pinch me first and *then* search my sack."

"Sure they did, and you know it. Any copper can collar a known criminal on suspicion. We don't have to have a reason."

"Well, that's bullshit. I got rights, too."

Having a legal discussion with Gasper Davis was a little too strange for me. I decided to get him back on track, somewhat.

"What's this about you going into a new business?"

"Well, like I was telling you . . . by the way, you want a drain?"

"Not while I'm on the job."

"Oh, you're not paying me a social call?"

" 'Fraid not."

He got up and swayed to the bar. When he came back his pail was full.

"This is my celebration to-night," he said after his first gulp.

"What're you celebrating?"

"Like I told you, my new business venture. I've said goodbye to second-story jobs. I've got a nice crib in Kensington now, as you know. But what you may not know about is my stables."

"Stables?"

"That's right, McCleary. Meet the newest and finest of Philadelphia's colt men."

A colt man kept horses, but not just for anybody. His job was to supply transportation for thieves—when they needed to dust out of town in a flash. He also alibied the horses and by extension, the sneaks who used them on a job. It was a nice criminal enterprise devoid of risk. Certainly less dangerous than pulling second-story robberies. I complimented Gasper on his choice of a new career.

"How many horses do you have?"

"Six so far, and I've been saving for a seventh. Champion bits of blood. Got 'em from a friend of mine."

"Who stole them, of course."

"Of course. But not from Philadelphia, so don't get your hackles raised. They were all gipped from Jersey." Gasper smiled at the alliteration.

"That soothes my conscience."

"Damn right. I take good care of them. I got my cousin helpin' me out with all the chores. You'd be amazed the kind of deals I cut with my customers."

"Oh, yeah? You actually ask for a piece of the take?"

"Sometimes, instead of a flat rate. It depends on whether I know them really well. Some of my pals from Cherry Hill patronize me every few weeks and we do really well together."

Cherry Hill was better known as Eastern State Penitentiary. It was just about the only social club these scamps ever belonged to.

"Hey, Gasper—you have any bays in your stables?"

"No, I don't. Why?"

"I'm interested in a particular carriage drawn by a

bay. And the two men who were driving it.''

"Well, maybe I can help you at that. What have you got to trade?"

It was bad enough having to frequent flash drums and brothels to collect dirt. I didn't have to pay my pigeons like I was a customer.

What I did instead was trade information with them. It could be that I had violated every principle I had by doing this. But you couldn't function as a dick without having a score of sneaks and buzzers on your side. And to get them there, you had to be willing to make deals.

My way of getting around this moral dilemma was a form of prophecy.

"The Athletics are playing the Phillies on the thirteenth."

"No kidding. So what?"

"It's the Seventh Championship game. A big one."

"I know that, Mack. I got it marked on my calendar."

"Well, knowing you're a Phillies fan, I didn't want you to come away disappointed."

"How do you mean?"

"I have it on good authority that the Athletics are going to win the game."

Gasper whistled and started hacking again.

"Don't take it *that* hard."

"Oh, shut up. The Phillies would've won. The Athletics can't field worth a damn."

"You got that right."

"What about the game on the Fourth?"

"The Sixth Championship?"

"Yeah."

"I didn't hear about that one. Maybe it'll be a fair game."

"Anyway, I won't make it to that one."

"Oh yeah?"

"That's the day I'm goin' to see the new Zoological Garden at the Park. You hear about that?"

"Yeah, opened yesterday."

"I never seen a buffalo before. They got a buffalo pen."

"Monkey house, too. You'd fit right in."

"Funny." Gasper coughed up something and spat it in the cuspidor.

"You better watch where you spit. Expectoration is hazardous to the public health. I could run you right in."

"Kiss my ass, you dumb mick. How long you gonna sit around and waste my time? I have a meeting to get to in a few minutes."

Gasper didn't fool me. He had nowhere to go and he didn't get much of a chance to talk to anyone lately. All of his friends were in jail.

He rubbed his bald head and ran his hands through the curly tufts of hair above his ears.

"You got a smoke?"

"You know I don't smoke, Gasper," I told him.

"Why not?" he asked me, as if smoking were as natural as breathing.

I ignored the question and said, "All right, let's get down to business. *My* business. I'm looking for a carriage, green body with gray wheels and chassis. Cab front and yacht-like body. Has a collapsible top. It's pulled by a bay about fifteen hands high. It probably came out of Bucks County somewhere. Sound familiar?"

Gasper shook his head.

"Let me describe the drivers."

I went into as detailed a description as I could give him of the two men, including what they had been selling, the poison Rat-Oh.

"I could use some of that. Got rats all over the stables. Those sons of bitches get into everything. When you see 'em, you tell 'em I'll buy half a wagon full."

"Do you know them, or what?"

"With a mug like the one you're describing, it sounds like he belongs in Colonel Wood's Museum. How'd his nose get like that?"

I knotted my fist and held it in front of his face, saying, "Maybe this helped."

"All right, all right. Don't get bent out of shape. I'm only fooling with ya. I haven't seen them. Or the carriage."

"So you're telling me I've been wasting my time?"

"Now, would I let you do that? Especially after all the money you're going to make for me on that game? Believe me, I wouldn't forget two scamps like that. But maybe I can help you. You ever hear of Pete Shields?"

Most of us knew the names of every criminal worth jailing in the city. But I couldn't place the name with a face or anything else. I shook my head.

"He's a harness thief, mostly. Was inside Moyamensing for a few months on account of being caught making off with a dandy bridle. Right in front of the shop, too."

Gasper started laughing and coughing again. It was hard to tell where one left off and other began.

"What's so funny about that?" I asked him.

"I heard from a mutual friend that no more than a week before, he'd sold a few crates of brand new harnesses he'd taken off a wagon. Must've made hundreds of dollars. And here he gets pinched while making a nickel-and-dime grab. Now, I call that funny."

"So he went inside for a while, eh?"

"Yeah, but he's been out for a few weeks now. He promised his mother he'd go straight and get a real ten-hour-a-day job. I think he was working at some slaughterhouse for a while."

"Which didn't last too long, I take it."

"You know how it is. Working to the whistle just don't cut it."

I smirked and said, "So how's this Shields character going to help me out?"

"Aha! See, Shields knows every horse-and-carriage fence between the rivers. Before he went in for harnesses he was a horse thief. Good one, too."

"What happened?"

"He got shot in the leg. Scared the shit out of him. Make sure you got something to hold on to him with. When he smells copper, he bolts."

I wouldn't forget to bring along the bracelets.

"What does he look like?"

"A little shorter than you. Always wears a hat. One of them new derby things. He goes for those short jackets, too. He might still be wearing a beard. Big nose, like a beak. Pox scars on his cheeks. And he's got these big brown eyes like a wild man of Borneo. You can't miss this character."

"Where can I find him?" I asked.

"He's moved since the last time I saw him, for sure. The best place is probably the Herkness Bazaar. He likes to attend the auctions."

"Have you seen him lately?"

"Not for a few weeks. The last I heard of him . . ." He looked me straight in the eyes. "Say, that's right! Oh, boy, you're gonna like this!"

"Well, spit it out."

"I remember him saying something about going out to grassville for some fresh air after he quit at the slaughterhouse."

"Which grassville? There's a lot of countryside around. Chester County? The Pocono Mountains?"

"No." He smiled and waited, to build up suspense. "I think it was Bucks County."

I stroked my moustache and said, "My thanks to you, Gasper."

"Glad to be of service, Mack."

I gave him a smile and stood up. I had walked a few paces from the table when, just for curiosity's sake, I turned back and asked him, "By the way, do you remember the name of the abattoir Shields worked at?"

Gasper took a draught of lager beer, emptying the pail. After a subdued belch, he said, "I forget the name. I know it was somewheres near the waterfront."

"Much obliged. Take care of that cough."

He gave me a slight wave and put the soiled hand-kerchief to his mouth.

I went home to get some sleep. I wanted to be ready for Shields in the morning.

EARLY THE NEXT morning I took the streetcar to the Central Office and met up with Nolan. He was assigned to supervise a search of all barges on the Delaware waterfront in the hopes that Eddie Munroe was hidden on one of them. I told him about the affair at the waterworks planned for that evening. He made a joke about fireworks a day early and agreed to go along with me in exchange for a bottle of Scotch. While I had his attention, I asked him about Pete Shields. Nolan was the one detective who investigated horse crimes. His memory was a better rogues' gallery than the one they had on display downstairs. I got a good description of Shields from him. It tallied with Gasper's.

"What's Petey done this time?" Nolan asked me.

"Nothing yet. I just want to ask him some questions."

"When you meet up with him, give him a big hug for me."

"You the one who pinched him last time?"

"That's right, lad. I was keeping an eye on him for weeks. The one time he pulls a job at the harness shop I was home in bed with a fever, sweating like a pig. When I found out what he done, I said to myself, I'm gonna run that scamp in no matter what. It didn't take long to catch him dead to rights."

"He a dangerous fella?"

"Not as long as you don't get close enough to smell his breath. That's enough to choke on."

"Don't forget. Ten-thirty at Bunker's. And don't come with your back teeth afloat. This is a very delicate situation."

"A doggy's life hangs in the balance."

"Maybe a hell of a lot more than that."

It was getting muggy already. I complained about the weather to Nolan for a bit and then said, "All right, I'm off. Tell Cap I'm working on a lead."

"Oh, I heard about that."

"You did?"

"Sure. Diefenderfer blew his top about it yesterday evening. Wanted Heins to write a letter to the mayor about you. Get you demoted to patrol duty. Heins is looking for you. He wants it straightened out."

"I don't have time for that now. Stall him if he asks about me."

Nolan laughed from under his huge moustache and said, "You're a plucky lad. Let's get away from the door then so they won't catch you."

We moved behind a pretzel vendor's cart. I bought a pretzel and devoured it while Nolan interrogated me about yesterday.

"I can't tell you everything," I said. "Let's put it this way. I think I might have the boy and the dog back sooner than anyone thinks. And we might be a pair of regular heroes. Look, I gotta go."

"Aw c'mon. Let me in on it. Whatta ya mean, we're going to be heroes?"

"To-night. Bring your self and I'll bring the Scotch. When it's all over we'll have a drink and I'll tell you all about it."

I dashed across the street and caught an omnibus headed for the theatre district.

I got off right in front of the Walnut Street Theatre. Some colored boys were sweeping the sidewalk. I walked up Ninth Street to Sansom. There were loose cobblestones scattered here and there with loads of horse manure dried up and coating the streets like a fine patina. The city hadn't been too conscientious about cleaning it up.

For three weeks there had been no rain. Most of the time that was how the streets got washed. Now, with all the heat, the filth dessicated and blew about like clouds of pollen. I'd been downtown for just an hour and I was already brushing the manure dust from my clothes. It got in your lungs, too.

In fact it had probably gotten all over that pretzel I'd just eaten. I decided to write a letter to the editor of the *Ledger* and complain.

The Herkness Bazaar was on Ninth and Sansom. There was no way to miss it. A horde of carriages was parked in front, from sporty laundalettes to victorias with their tops down, the swells inside squinting and fanning their whiskers in the sun.

I stood around for a while admiring the carriages. Then I took a stroll up and down Ninth Street, keeping an eye out for a man fitting Gasper's description. For about an hour I didn't have much to do except stare at the bazaar.

The building was completely round and looked like a brick watertower. It had been built a few years after I was born to house the cyclorama of Jerusalem. I remember seeing it on a visit to Philadelphia when I was a little shaver.

Eventually the cyclorama had been dismantled and the building left standing. Alfred Herkness took it over. So there would be no mistake of ownership, he painted his name in huge letters over the brick. Three gables poked out of the top and the entrance was fashioned into a typical storefront with three facets. Right above the doorway was another sign for the myopic which said: ALFRED M. HERKNESS HORSE & CARRIAGE BAZAAR. On either side of the storefront structure, painted on the round brick surface, was all the information you needed to know. There were auction sales every Wednesday and

Saturday. Not just horses and carriages, but harnesses, too.

That must have been what drew Pete Shields.

Some harnesses hung from the two open doors at the entrance. As I walked by for the seventh or eighth time that hour, I noticed a man scrutinizing those harnesses. He wore his derby hat tipped over his brow, covering most of his bearded face in shadow. From the profile view I took note of his nose. Just like Gasper had said. Broken and sharply pointed. His shabby suit was covered with dust that made it look more gray than the black it really was. The elbows were a little worn.

I approached him from behind a crowd of gentlemen going into the bazaar. They were talking about the Brady salvage claim, the front page news that morning.

Then I heard one of them say to his companion, "Did you hear about the boy in Germantown?"

"The kidnapping? Yes, a terrible, terrible thing. The papers are certainly full of it to-day."

"Can you believe they're going to search the entire city? I've never heard anything like that in my life!"

"They might actually earn their keep, for once."

I didn't take offense. I was wondering how I should play the game with Shields. There were two options. Beat the tar out of him until he talked, or chum up. I opted for the latter. The heat was making me drowsy. I was in no mood for rough-housing.

I tapped him on the shoulder and said, "Hey—Pete Shields?"

The man turned around, slouching, and said, "Whatta ya want?"

His eyes were glossy and bloodshot. The smell of his breath got me tipsy. You didn't have to be a detective to know he was intoxicated.

"Looking at the harnesses, huh?" I said.

"What's it to you?" He was really friendly.

"My pal Gasper Davis told me I could find you here. Told me you know a lot about harnesses."

He closed one of his eyes and tilted his head back. I thought he was going to fall over.

"You a pal of Gasper's, eh?"

"Sure. He told me where to find you. I got a business proposition."

Shields motioned me away from the door. One of Herkness's assistants was scowling at him.

"Looks like your reputation precedes you."

"I got a right to look like anybody else. Don't mean I'd take nothin'. I done some good business with Herkness in my old days."

"Some less than honest business?"

"What're you, a cop or somethin'?"

"Something. Why don't we go over here?"

I led him down the street to the Fifth Baptist Church, as round as the bazaar. I noticed that Shields walked with a limp.

There was a wooden fence leading to the Herkness stables. We paused at the entrance to the alley there.

"So? You got something you want to sell?"

"Not really. I need some information."

"What kinda information?" he said suspiciously. He yanked a square bottle out of his coat pocket, uncapped it, and took a swig.

"Drinkin' mighty early, aren't you?"

"What's it to you? My leg still hurts from the ball that bastard cop put into it."

"It must be your imagination. You got shot months ago."

"So? You think they took good care of me at the Moyamensing infirmary? Fat chance. It's still a bitch for me to walk. Can you believe that? I never done nobody any harm in my life and this is what I get. I tell ya. I got a right to have a little liquor."

"Specially after going dry for a few months."

"Gasper tell you about my stretch?"

"Yeah."

"Well, then you can imagine what it was like. Ain't no picnic, by damn. And I got a mother to support."

"Yeah, that's rough." It was going to be easy to coax things out of him. He was drunk enough that he wanted to talk. If I was a little careful, I might get everything I wanted.

All I had to do was keep him standing. Shields had slumped down to the pavement, propping his back against the fence. He was drunker than I thought.

I don't like dealing with drunks. They are unpredictable. They might cry on your shoulder, dance a quadrille, or stab you in the belly, depending on their disposition. Even though Shields seemed docile, I kept my guard up.

I decided to lead into the carriage nice and easy.

"You still working at the slaughterhouse?"

"Hell, no! I got my fill of that stinkin' hole. Ten fucking hours walking in blood up to your ankles. And the stink! Whew! Try goin' home and washin' that off. Impossible!"

"Still, it must've made your mother happy, knowing you had a job and all."

"Yeah, bless her. I guess it wasn't all that bad. I met up with some pals there. They were a bunch! We had some good times. When they quit, they offered me a job peddlin' with them."

If I'd been a dog, I'd have licked my chops and drooled a big, thick gob. I looked away from him and said, like I wasn't interested at all, "That so?"

"Yeah, coulda peddled this Rat-Oh stuff Glick invented."

"*Glick*, did you say?"

"Why, you know him?"

"Yeah . . . I heard of him." At least now I had. "I think he's one of the fellas I'm looking for. Him and the other guy . . . what's his name?"

But it didn't work. Shields' eyes looked sharp now. He blinked at me and stood up, his hands in his pockets.

"Just who did you say you were?"

"I didn't. The name's McCleary."

I oughtn't to have said that. My reputation preceded me, too.

Shields pulled his right hand out of the pocket where the bottle was. It must've been a roomy pocket. There was a revolver in his hand now.

"You stink like a copper to me."

"You shouldn't put revolvers in your pantaloons like that. Liable to cause an accident."

"Shut up! I'm gonna put a pill in that bastard lunger for this! I ain't done nothin'! You ain't pinchin' me on suspicion this time, you bastard! I ain't goin' back in! You hear me?"

I had heard stories about some of the things that went on in prison. Things that happened to a man. Mighty ugly things. Shields might've had a reason to be as desperate as he was.

"You sent one of my buddies to Cherry Hill last year. You and that Nolan. The one that put the ball in my leg."

He started laughing, mean-like. "He didn't come out. They had him for supper! See? I been waiting to even the score for him."

I cursed Nolan for telling me Shields wasn't dangerous. Prison had changed Pete Shields in a big way.

"Don't get excited, Pete. I'm not interested in you at all. I just wanna talk with Glick and his pal. If you tell me where they are, I might forget about you getting the carriage and the bay for them. I might forget I saw you to-day."

It was a bluff. I had no proof he'd stolen the carriage used to steal Eddie Munroe and Jocko.

I didn't have time to test my theory. A hay wagon was coming toward us from the stables. When the driver saw Shields holding a gun on me he froze, too afraid to urge his horse forward or backward.

Shields kept the gun pointed at my face as he edged along the fence toward the wagon. Without looking at the man grasping the reins he shouted, "Get out of there!"

The driver complied, clambering out of the seat, nearly falling head first. Then he stood there, shaking and immobile.

"Now, get!" Shields told him.

He did as he was told, running back toward the stables.

The gun gestured for me to come toward the wagon. It was like a magnet. I had to go where it told me.

"You're makin' a big mistake, Pete. Gasper was tryin' to do you a favor. I'm not looking to collar you. I just want to know where I can find Glick and his pal."

"Peach to a pig like you? I ain't tellin' you shit! Over here."

My hands were raised as I walked toward him. I could feel sweat trickling from my armpits down my ribs. That was all the fear I allowed myself. Guns in my face were nothing new.

I tried stalling him, hoping the people at the stables would come investigating.

"Where are we going?" I asked him.

"You ain't goin' nowhere. You're gonna sit here while I steal this wagon."

"Who's to say I won't run after you as soon as you're out of the alley?"

"I'm gonna put a pill through your leg, same as you done to mine."

Shields was as mad as a June bug. He probably blamed every policeman on the streets for what had happened to him in jail, and for getting shot. That son of a bitch Nolan would owe me a bottle of Scotch after this. No, a case.

"Sit down," he told me. "So I can aim good."

"Try not to shoot my foot off. I don't fancy getting a peg leg."

He was gripping the wagon's brake with one hand while the other held the gun. The horse seemed to steady him. There was so much liquor in his gut he was about ready to fall over.

I was about three feet from him, my back against the

fence. My hands were still in the air. But not for long.

"Don't make me tell you again, damn you!"

I was not ready to sit down and get shot in the leg. Besides, he hadn't pulled back the hammer yet.

My hands darted out toward his gun arm just as he pulled back the hammer. My left clasped directly below his wrist, aiming the gun away from me. My right wound above the elbow. I pushed both inward. The bone beneath them went in two different directions.

Shields screamed, as the pain sent a shock wave through to the trigger. He pulled it.

The explosion tore through my ears, stunning me. Behind me, I heard a part of the fence splinter.

At the same time, the horse hitched to the wagon went berserk from the gunfire. With a jolt, it jerked the wagon forward and tore down the alley. Shields was thrown forward and lay on the ground, groaning in agony.

Men ran toward me from the stables, rifles in their hands. They were a little late.

"What happened? Who are you?" they shouted at me.

"Detective with the Philadelphia police!" I shouted back, as I ran after the wagon. "That man's arm is broken! Don't let him out of your sight!"

The horse was heading down Ninth Street, cutting a swath through traffic.

As I ran after it, I hollered at the pedestrians, "Runaway! Get out of the street! Move! Move!"

I had to catch that wagon. Otherwise there might be another accident like last week's, when a young boy was killed by a runaway beer wagon. The horse had buckled, sending beer kegs spilling out of the back and rolling down the street. One of them had crushed the child, who was waiting for his mother to step out of a store.

Nothing like that was going to happen again if I could help it.

The horse reached the intersection of Ninth and Walnut. I kept shouting for people to get out of the way.

A streetcar was proceeding past the theater and into

the way of the speeding horse and wagon. I was only a few paces from the wagon bed. With a burst of speed I shortened the distance.

I flung myself at the back of the wagon bed, trying to get a hold on something. My hand clawed at the edge of the left side, above the wheel. Splinters ripped through my palm and fingers. It was all the hold I could get.

We flew across the tracks, right in front of the streetcar. I could smell the horses that pulled it, they were so close. The startled team buckled and threw their car off the rails. People screamed as they spilled out onto the street. The driver fell off his seat and onto the rumps of his team. That was the most I could get a glimpse of before we were past the intersection, speeding down Ninth Street.

I had both my hands on the side of the bed, but I couldn't climb in. My legs dragged behind me, ready to get squashed like grapes in a wine press under the huge metal-capped wheels of the wagon.

For a block or so I let myself be dragged along the street. Once I thought of putting my foot on the bolster of the hind gear. But it was too far off for me to stretch. If I fell, I'd crack my head on the cobblestones or get trampled.

I was dimly aware of pedestrians screaming at me to jump off while I could, but there was no chance I was going to let this thing get away from me. I had to stop that horse.

Suddenly the wagon jolted. The front wheels had passed over a huge pothole and sent the back wheels flying. My legs got tangled in between the spokes of the wheel. In a second they would be dragged around and snapped in two.

I put one foot on top of the hub, the other dangling in space. Then I hoisted myself up and over the side of the bed.

I slammed down on the hard wood. The taste of blood was in my mouth. Another pothole jolted the wagon and banged me around. I wiped the trickle of blood off my lips and got up in a crouch.

The horse was still going full speed down the street. The center lane of traffic was wide open. A copper crossing the street jumped out of our way just in time. As we sailed by, he started rapping his nightstick against the corner lamppost.

I could see ahead to the intersection of Ninth and Locust. Even with the clatter of wheels and hooves I could hear the band that was marching through there. From the looks of them, it was a Ladies' Temperance Union parade. And we were set to cut right through them.

Quickly I crawled over to the driver's seat searching for the reins. Scrambling over the "lazy back" which poked into my breadbasket, I saw it was no use. The reins had fallen forward and were lying on the whiffletree. No chance of getting them in time.

The brake. That might work. I reached over to try it, but the damn thing was stuck. Shields had been holding onto it when I sprained his arm and must've bent it out of whack.

The springs on the seat kept me bouncing as we steadily approached the parade. They were making so much noise they couldn't hear us drawing near.

Since I'd had so many opportunities to break my neck and had failed each time, I decided to give myself one more chance.

I clambered over the seat and put my heels on the front edge of the bed. My eyes were focused on the back of the horse, my hands groping for it like it was some unfulfilled dream.

I gave a push with my boot heels and sprang into the air.

Part of me landed on the horse's back. The rest slipped to the side and got caught in the trace. We were about half a block away from the parade.

I stretched my arm to the breaking point and touched the bridle with the tips of my fingers. Wriggling a little bit forward, I had enough of a grip to pull. I screamed at the brute to slow down and kept tugging desperately.

We were close enough for me to recognize the tune the band was playing. It was "When Johnny Comes Marching Home."

I closed my eyes and got ready to be thrown forward when we ran right into the tuba section.

But we never interrupted their music. The horse slowed down to a slow shuffle, my hands gripping the bridle like it was the last thread of my life. Finally the animal came to a complete stop, jutting into Locust Street. The marchers had to move around the horse. They were giving me dirty looks. A policeman approached the wagon.

I fell off the horse and onto the cobbles. My head was spinning and I was short of breath.

The copper pulled me off the ground and said, "What the hell are you doing?"

I pushed him out of my face and took my star out.

There wasn't much air in my lungs to say what needed to be said.

"Runaway . . . from the Herkness stables . . . gun went off . . ."

I walked over to a water vender parked on the corner and poured myself a glass. I drained it in a single gulp, rinsing the blood from my mouth. I handed back the glass and a nickel that miraculously hadn't fallen out of my pocket.

"I'll take the wagon back myself. You can return to your duty."

I patted the horse's snout and got back on the seat. Turning the wagon around, I headed back up the street. As we went past some of the pedestrians who had just witnessed my clumsy antics cheered.

"Way to go!"

"Huzzah!"

I broke into a smile and waved at them.

The smile faded when I pulled up to the Herkness Bazaar. There was an ambulance there.

I jumped out of the wagon and dashed to the back of the ambulance.

"Who got hurt?" I said to the nurse with a compress in his hand. But I knew the answer before I finished the question. Shields' oblong head poked out from under the blankets of a stretcher. The uncovered face told me he wasn't dead.

"He sick, or what?"

"Severely sprained arm. And a concussion, I think. Witness said he hit the pavement. Who are you?"

"Police. Where are you taking this man?"

"Pennsylvania Hospital, I reckon."

"He's unconscious?"

The nurse nodded. "He'll be in dreamland for quite a while. Lucky for him. He'll be in a lot of pain when he comes out of it."

"If you move him from Pennsylvania Hospital or anything else happens, I want to be notified. My name's Wilton McCleary. I'm a detective at the Central Station House."

"Will do, Detective."

"There any other policemen around here?"

"Yes. One questioning the driver of the runaway wagon."

I thanked him and went back to the harness bull. When I showed him my star, he got respectful and quiet. I said to him, "Go with the ambulance and make sure our patient stays put. His name is Pete Shields. He's a harness thief who pointed a gun at me. And I want him taken care of, see? Don't worry. I'll take responsibility for pulling you off the beat."

He was all too happy to get out of the heat and into the hospital, where he could fall asleep in the waiting room.

I cursed my luck. It might be a long time before Shields could give me any more answers. But I had gotten one priceless thing out of him: a name.

The name of someone Shields got a carriage from

Bucks County for. The name of someone he worked with at a slaughterhouse.

The name of the man who had kidnapped Eddie Munroe.

Glick.

I was looking forward to meeting him.

9

A THERMOMETER HANGING outside a shop told me it was eighty-three degrees. My clothes seemed to weigh three times as much as they should have. The city's masonry trapped the heat and threw it at my face like a blast furnace.

By the time I got to the Central Office I was ready to pack it in for the day. It was only about ten o' clock in the morning, the time when all the detectives were supposed to assemble with Cap and get their assignments.

I was not in any hurry to go up to Cap's office. No doubt I would catch hell for telling off Diefenderfer at the Munroe house. I could usually count Cap on my side, but he had to be fair. The other dicks wouldn't take too kindly to any more special privileges bestowed on me.

When I walked inside, I made my way to the desk sergeant and told him I wanted to see the rogue's gallery. This was a large leatherbound volume full of photographs of every scamp we had gotten our claws on and maneuvered in front of a camera. It was hard getting the rascals to sit still long enough to capture their ugly mugs on film.

This was a pretty new development in police work. I used to take it out for a few hours now and then and memorize as many faces as I could. More than a few criminals were pinched red-handed or picked up on suspicion because the arresting officer remembered their faces from the book.

Beneath the tiny photographs were written in perfectly legible bureaucratic script the worthy occupations of the individuals depicted. Lots of women pickpockets and male bank sneaks. Hearty doses of confidence men and hotel sneaks. A few horse thieves.

As I flipped through the pages I noticed the picture of one Peter Shields. It was a good likeness, his eyes slightly blurred by the flash. His derby was in place on his long, thin head and his mouth gaped with chagrin or surprise. The poor bastard had no idea what was in store for him in the chokey.

Since it wasn't alphabetized, I had to go through the whole darn thing, looking for that name Glick. It was possible he used an alias, which would make my whole search a waste of time, but that was the chance I took.

After several minutes of checking, I wound up with no Glicks. He either hadn't been collared recently or he went by another name.

I handed the book back to the sergeant and headed upstairs.

Before I cleared the staircase, Cap's voice thundered, "McCleary! Get your ass in here! Now!"

Cap was in a livid mood. He stood at the door to his office, his hands on the jambs like a miniature Samson. Diefenderfer stood behind him, smirking at me.

I strolled up with as innocent an expression as I could muster and said, "Good morning, sir. What's the problem?"

"What's this blasted stunt I hear you pulled in Germantown yesterday? You withholding evidence from Diefenderfer here? The man I myself appointed to head this business? Is that what I'm hearing?"

Diefenderfer nodded and said, "The smug bastard came dashing in yesterday with information he was just dying to tell me. As soon as I told him I was the one to question the family, being the one in charge, like you said, sir, he got all belligerent and stormed out of there."

Cap turned to me and waited.

Everything Diefenderfer said was true.

I said as much.

"Do you know what insubordination is, McCleary?"

"Yes, sir."

"How'd you like to get your ass kicked out of the detective force and back on the beat?"

I put my head down and frowned. I felt like I was back in school and about to get the switch across my knuckles.

"You know I got only so much patience with you. You gotta cool that hot head of yours off mighty quick." He reached out and grabbed the back of my neck.

"Now you gonna speak your piece?"

"Yessir."

"All right, then." He moved to let me in the office where the rest of the detectives were sitting around eavesdropping.

"What about an apology?" Diefenderfer said. "I think I got one coming."

"Go eat coke," I told him, and took a seat.

Cap followed me and said to the detectives, "Before we get briefed on the status of the investigation, I want Wilton here to impart some information he gained yesterday."

They all looked at me. Some of them laughed under their breath. It was one of the more humiliating experiences of my life. I don't think he actually thought of booting me back to patrol duty. He believed I was a good detective, but now I needed to be taught a lesson. We both knew that. I didn't want to be alone on the streets. The detectives there might have the choice to help me one day or leave me to fall on my face. I wanted them on my side.

I told them what Dr. Moyer told me. I left out everything else. Glick, the ransom letters with that "signal instant annihilation" phrase in them, the slaughterhouse where they worked with Shields, everything.

That was mine. And now more than ever I wasn't going to tell them one bloody word. The only way I could stop from feeling like an ass was to solve this thing myself. Nolan could come along for the ride that night. But it was going to be my show.

They say pride goeth before a fall.

I was going to fall hard. But I didn't know it then.

After Diefenderfer went over the general assignments, which involved painstaking searches of every suspicious or probable place of concealment in the city and its environs, Cap took me aside.

"I don't want you to take this too hard, McCleary. But I'm taking you off the Munroe case for a few days. I'm tired of you and Diefenderfer going after each other. It messes up a smooth operation. I want you back on the Bunker case, full time. Understand?"

I barely suppressed a smile. Now I'd be left alone to do what I had to do. No answering to Diefenderfer.

But Cap added, "And that means stay away from the Munroe family. That's Diefenderfer's turf. Get it? He told me you practically burned our only real witness alive yesterday trying to save a shed from getting torched."

"That's what he told you, huh?"

"I heard the other version from Bowie. He said you were a big help to him while he was putting out the flames. Pulling the kid out was a good move, even if you did sprain his ankle."

I sighed and murmured, "Sons of bitches."

"Maybe I put you on something big too soon. You go take care of Bunker. Get that dog back and make him a lot of money when they play the classic on Thursday."

I turned away without a sound and he put his hand on my shoulder.

"Hey. Don't mind me. I'm not holding anything against you, okay? I just want things to cool off for a spell. Eddie Munroe made the papers this morning. They'll be on my back until this case is solved. The Mayor's calling it 'one of the most atrocious crimes perpetrated in our nation.' This will make or break all of us, McCleary. We can't slip up. If the press gets wind of conflict in the detective department, that'll look bad for us. Understand? That'll make me look bad. You want that?''

''No. Don't worry. I'll get you results on this one.''

''I know you will, boy. Now, get.''

I was glad he hadn't heard about Pete Shields and the runaway horse incident. He might not have been so conciliatory with me.

Nolan grabbed me on the way out.

''What'd he tell you?''

''I'm off the Munroe case.''

''You don't look that disappointed.''

''That's because even though I'm not on the case I'm still on it. Make sense?''

''No.''

''Don't worry about it. You're not going to let me down to-night at the waterworks?''

''Count on me being there. With a barker in tow.''

''Me, too. And, uh, incidentally—after it's all over, remind me to kick your ass from here to Broad Street.''

Nolan looked bewildered. ''What're you talking about?''

''Pete Shields. He almost put a ball through my leg to-day when I tried to get him peaching.''

For some reason that made him near bust a gut. He was still laughing when I bade him a fond farewell with a single-finger salute.

As I walked past our clerk, he called my name.

''Sorry. These arrived for you.''

There were two parcels. One was a telegram and the other a letter. I thanked the clerk and went over to a window where the light was better.

The telegram was from Leah Munroe. It said,

WISH TO CONVEY THANKS FOR YESTERDAY IN PER-
SON. SHALL CALL ON YOU AT STATE HOUSE IN
MORNING WITH MY HUSBAND.

MRS. ARCHIBALD MUNROE

The letter came from, of all people, Reddy the Blacksmith.

*I got to meet you. I got some information about
some men your looking for. Meet me at Fitzgerald's Tavern on Front St., South of Dock at noon,
and I can tell you what you want to know.*

Signed, Reddy

Reddy was an illiterate. The name at the bottom was
barely legible. The handwriting looked like Ben Devers',
which probably explained the letter's vagueness.

Maybe I wouldn't have to worry about getting shot at
the waterworks after all. I patted my revolver in the holster under my coat. Pete had caught me unawares and I
hadn't had time to draw it. That wasn't going to happen
to me again this day. I hoped.

Leah Munroe could wait. It would be about noon by
the time I got myself over to the waterfront. If Reddy
was playing it square, I might have Glick and his crony
before the sun went down. But I didn't trust the blacksmith. He'd lied to me the day before and might be lying
now. For all I knew, he might be in league with the
kidnappers. This rendezvous might very well be an am-
bush.

As I walked out onto Chestnut Street I saw Archibald
Munroe getting off an omnibus. He saw me almost immediately and waved. I made a quick motion for him to
follow me through the archway to the park on the other
end. I didn't want anyone to witness our meeting.

The State House bell tolled eleven as we strolled under the lines of trees in Independence Square. Houses

and office buildings on either side gave the park a cramped feel, like it was an oasis of green in a desert of red brick. I said to Munroe, "I thought your wife was coming with you."

"She was, but at the last minute she received something in the mail and said she couldn't accompany me."

"Was it anything important? Maybe another ransom letter?"

Munroe stopped and knotted his brow, like he had never considered that.

"I don't think so," he said. "She would have told me, surely."

Not necessarily, I thought. But I didn't want to make him more upset than he already was.

"Have you seen the papers this morning?" he asked me.

I told him I hadn't.

"My son's name was all over them. The journalists found out about it yesterday."

"Who told them?"

"Diefenderfer, of course. He explained putting the descriptions of the men in the papers might get us results faster than we imagined."

"He has a point," I said begrudgingly. "But it also might make them more nervous. If they were in Philadelphia they might think about getting out, and fast. Damn."

"What is it?"

"I wanted to tell you, Mr. Munroe. I think I know the name of one of the men who stole your son. Glick. Does that mean anything to you?"

He shook his head, obviously disappointed.

"I'm on his trail. I know a number of things about him already. In fact, I'm hoping that by to-night at the very latest I can have him for you on a silver platter."

"And what about Eddie?"

"We have all kinds of ways of making men talk."

"Well, who is this Glick? How did you find out about him?"

"I'd prefer not to say at this point. Maybe it's superstitious, but I don't want to jinx it. I don't have him yet."

Even though I trusted Munroe, I didn't want any of this getting back to Diefenderfer or Cap. Munroe might happen to say something in passing to them and then Cap would have my *ass* on a silver platter.

"But can't you tell me anything at all?"

"I can say this. I'm mighty close, Mr. Munroe, mighty close. I don't know where your son is being kept. All I really know is that name. Glick. But I know a few places where *he* may be, or where someone might know him. And if I can find *him*, I know I can find your son."

"Don't forget your promise, McCleary. I want to be a part of this."

I was tempted to speak about the waterworks and Jocko. But I decided against it. Too dangerous. If things worked out that night, he would be the first to know. I might even let him take a pound of flesh out of Glick before we got to the station house.

"You will be, don't worry."

"Are you really close? You're not just trying to inspire some hope in me?"

"I wouldn't lie to you. I've got a name and I might just get another name and more than that. That's where I'm off to now."

"Then Godspeed, my friend."

We shook hands. I hopped the fence and headed toward the waterfront.

10

THE OLD COLONIAL buildings on Chestnut Street looked
stately and out of place in our ornate century. I was
tempted to dally looking at them. Sometimes I get
caught up in the beauty of a scene. A particular tree
branch swaying in the wind or the sun shining on a brick
wall sets me into a mesmeric trance. For just a moment,
I felt something close to peace.

It was an odd time to feel serene going to meet Reddy
the Blacksmith. What he was doing at Front Street was
anyone's guess. And I was dying to find out what he
had to tell me. But at the same time I hesitated, almost
took my time getting there. It was as if another part of
me didn't want to hear what he had to say. I felt that
sense of expectation when you know something big is
going to happen. Like waiting for the first shot of a battle
to be fired.

The Delaware was close enough that you could smell
it. Stevedores carried their heavy loads through the
streets to waiting drays. Strangers to the city wandered
about, sharing the expression of many waterfront deni-
zens—the look of the lost.

I walked past the ship joiners and telegraph offices,
the run-down hotels for sailors and newly arrived im-
migrants, the cooperages and oyster bars. They bore the
old Franklin fire insurance hand-in-hand insignia on

their upper stories like dubious badges of respectability.

The buildings on the Delaware waterfront are some of the oldest in Philadelphia. Their dilapidation makes them look even more ancient. I'd spent more than my share of time rounding up tramps who'd fled to the waterfront like it was the last bit of dry land in a huge ocean.

Debris littered the streets, burst from crates and sacks, or tossed from wagon beds. The sun illuminated the street like a coroner's lamp. Rickety wooden awnings afforded the only shade. I was afraid to take shelter under a few of them. They looked like they could cave in at any moment.

Workers sauntered through the streets on various errands. Their women were out buying groceries, the hem of their ready-made skirts touching the dusty cobbles and sidewalks. They gossiped with each other in thick city accents, far removed from the polished bantering of Rittenhouse Square matrons.

Groups of children clustered on the corners looking for victims. They were bands of pickpockets. Looking into their joyless eyes, I knew what hunger really was.

I finally made it to Fitzgerald's Tavern, my heart as light as a kite. The Irishman was doing a brisk noon trade. Stevedores and sailors and apprentice chandlers were scooping up his oysters and chowder with abandon. I asked for a bowl of the chowder and was about halfway done when Reddy walked in. He called to the beer-slinger.

"Hey, Mike."

The Irishman waved a dishrag and resumed polishing a mug.

The others didn't pay him much attention. Colored and white men drank in the same places here, but usually not at the same tables. Everyone was too occupied with their soup to notice Reddy join me.

"Nice of you to come, Mistuh McCleary."

"I had no choice, after that letter you sent me."

"No, I guess not. You mind if I get some dinner fo' we gets to talkin'?"

"Go ahead."

I watched Reddy head up to the bar and converse with the man he called Mike. They appeared pretty friendly. I couldn't exactly hear what they were saying. Reddy handed Mike a slip of paper and took some money from him. Mike barked a name. A child appeared and then, after listening to the man, disappeared into the next room. A moment later he returned holding a package in one hand. It was covered with a thin cloth. Reddy took it in his own hands and gave the boy some more money. He returned with the package and a bowl of soup, smiling.

"What's in the package, Reddy?" I asked.

"Ain't no package," he said, laying it on the floor. "It's a cage."

Lifting the cloth up a bit, I peered through the bars. Six large rats squeaked at me, the gaslight reflected in their tiny eyes. I drew my hand back with surprise.

"That your dinner?" I asked him.

He thought that was funny. "They's fo' our dogs. We gots to train them with live bait."

"I see. Sparring partners for Jocko and his pals."

"That's right. 'Cept these babies don't leave the pit alive."

"You do your buying from a lot of different people, then?"

"Sho'. I get as many as I can take. And Joey's stables is mighty large. I like these here 'cause they big. The closer you be to the river, the bigger they get. We want the fattest, juiciest, meanest critters for training."

"To separate the men from the boys?"

"Somethin' like that. We gots ta make the dogs fearless and ready to kill. That's the only way they gonna win in the pit."

"How long does that take? Training to kill?"

"Months, up to a year. But it's worth it, believe me. See these here?"

He pulled slender slips of paper out of his overall pocket.

"Maybe I shouldn't be tellin' you this, but Benny say you all right. Joey's got me keeping the book fo' all the bettin' done on rat matches, with special attention to them matches with our dogs. And I tell ya, we make a pile. A mighty big pile. Ol' Reddy livin' mighty high for a nigger cause of all the money we made."

"Bunker shares the take with you?"

"That's the way it's always been. I took care of his daddy and him too when he was a chile."

"He respects you, Reddy."

"Well," he nodded, embarassed. "I always done my best to take care o' him."

I was stalling, feeling bad about what I'd done to him the day before last. I wanted to atone, let him see I had nothing against him.

"You taking bets for Thursday night?"

"The classic? You bet. Takes *fifty* dollars to buy a ticket on the steamer, but anybody can bet on what happens."

And Joe Bunker would collect his piece of that, I was sure. Bunker had more than a few books to his name.

"Joey's told me 'bout the steamer where they's gonna have it. Mighty sumptious, he said. We gonna cruise the rivuh the whole night. They's gonna be women there and gambling and such. Gonna be one hell of an affair, I tell ya."

Fifty dollars was one hell of an admission charge. Bunker wasn't kidding when he told me only the most powerful men would be there.

"You gonna be there, Reddy?"

"You bet. Been waitin' all year fo' this one. Now alls we need is Jocko."

The wrinkles in his forehead got deeper. He stared into his soup. Inadvertently he had led us into the conversation he too seemed anxious to avoid.

I stared at him from across the table and said, "Tell me about Glick."

After a deep sigh, Reddy began.

"It's all my fault. Reddy go shootin' off his mouf when he drunk. See, I gots these friends o' mine. We met 'cause we all show up to the rattin' matches. We all gots dogs or take care o' them somehow. So naturally we gets to talkin'. Well, I gots some o' these friends fo' ten years and mo'. One of them has work in a slaughterhouse. Met up with these white fellas workin' there and they gots to talkin' 'bout dogs and such. Now, he don't invite them to our meetin' or nothin', they bein' white and all. But they be talkin' and hear him say my name and they just dyin' to meet me, 'cause they say I gots a reputation. I'm the best trainer they heard of.''

He stopped talking and looked over my shoulder, trying to recapture the feeling of pride that had given him.

"So I said, Well, stop by one day and I'll show you my dogs."

"And they did?"

"Just one of 'em. He came over with my friend after they knocked off at work."

"When?"

"This was 'bout a month and a half ago. Anyway, he was a foreign fella. I think he was a Spaniard or Eyetalian. So we gets to talkin' 'bout the dogs and set out there in my workshop. My friend, he pulls out a bottle and we start drinkin'. After awhile my friend's gotta go 'cause his woman's gettin' off work, but the other one stays and we keep drinkin'.''

"What was his name, this man?"

"Franco."

The other name I'd been waiting for. I clenched my fist with excitement and kept listening.

"We keep drinkin' and after a while I'm fixin' to fly, I so drunk. Now, I been drunk befo', but this was no kind of drunk I ever heard of. I think the son of a bitch put somethin' in my drink. Cause I was up and over, man."

"Could have been laudanum, or hydrate of chloral."

"I don't remember much, but I musta told him 'bout

the classic and showed him the kennels. I coulda told him all kinds of things and not remembered a bit. In fact, I forgot the whole thing till the day you came the first time.''

"You don't remember anything else he did? When he left you?''

"Hell no, man. Felt like I just had a pail full of ether.''

"Why didn't you tell me this when I saw you the first time?''

"'Cause I was afraid. Afraid Joey'd blame me. I . . . dint want to let him down.''

His lower lip trembled, as it had the last time I saw him. But the emotion was coming out full force. He was getting it all off his chest, not just a sliver of it.

"You fool,'' I said to him. "I might've been able to find this Franco. Might've saved another man a lot of trouble.''

Reddy wiped a tear from his cheek and said, "I know who you talkin' 'bout. The boy in Germantown. What's his name? Munroe?''

"Aw. So you heard of him?''

"How could I miss it? Benny read the whole front page to me this mornin' and that was takin' up half o' it. And when I heard them descriptions that boy gave o' the men what stole him and his brother, I knowed what I had to do.''

"So what really happened the day Jocko was stolen?''

"They come, like I told you. I remember this Franco fella. This time he brought his friend. I say, I thought you was workin' in the meat house. They told me the place closed down but that didn't matter 'cause they had a product they was peddlin'. That Rat-Oh stuff. Franco, he pull out another bottle and we gets to drinkin'.''

"And you pass out again.''

"Yeah,'' he said, grimacing like a shaver waiting to be paddled.

"Did you meet up with them any time since they stole Jocko?''

"I tried to. I tried gettin' my friend to tell me where they lived. But he left his woman. She dint know where he gone to."

"Maybe with Glick and Franco."

"I don't know."

White criminals didn't often associate with colored ones. Even in their world that line was usually drawn. But kidnapping was far from usual.

"What was his name, Reddy?"

"Albert. Albert Johnson."

I had Reddy give me his last known address and the name of his woman. Then I told him to go on.

"I remember Albert tellin' me they used to get together, the three o' them, after work at this tavern."

"Where?"

"Eighth and Market, or there'bouts. I remember 'cause I went there to leave a message fo' them. See, Albert told me they knew the man who runs it. Name's Boylen. He uses the place for ratting matches. Also got some faro tables. And a girl in the back room. She don't give you much for your money, though.

"I been there a few times with the boss. In fact, Jocko's been there, too. Won the pot that night. Ten rats in as many seconds. That was a sight to see."

I wrote down the name and address and said, "I'll bet. So Boylen knows Glick and Franco? Is he the type to talk to the police?"

"Dint talk to me. He know I's Joey's man and he hates Joey plenty. Lost a lot of money to him over the years. But when I told him I got a message for Franco and his pal, he listen up."

"What'd you tell him?"

"That I want to talk to them. Maybe we can make a deal."

"Reddy. I'm disappointed."

"Well as long as we got Jocko back, what difference it make if I makes a little money on the side? If I told the boss who they be he'd snap his fingers and they'd

be . . .'' He drew his finger across his throat and made
a cutting sound.

"So I said I'd make sure they got their money, but I
wanted some of it fo' keepin' my mouf shut. As long
as we got Jocko back, of course.''

"And you were going to meet with them to-day to
square things away before the waterworks to-night?''

Reddy nodded at me like I was an apt pupil. ''That's
it.''

"Why write to me?''

"Well, I gots a conscience, like any man. Benny be
readin' the paper to me this mornin' and I read that
description. And I know too well who those men be
what took that chile. I know it's the same ones I's goin'
to meet to-day. And I said to myself, Reddy, you ain't
gonna let them steal no child. Unh-huh. I draw the line
well before that. Hot damn right.''

Reddy's ethics went through changes quicker than I
could blink. My head was spinning.

"I'm gonna prove to Joey once and fo' all that he
done right by keepin' me on. I'm gonna prove myself
to him. We gonna get Jocko back, and we gonna get
that boy back, too. Me and you. Right now!''

This scheme was as half baked as his blackmail game.
And Reddy was far from trustworthy. Still, the thought
of breaking the case this fast was intoxicating.

"How exactly did they get in touch with you?''

"Got a letter this mornin'. Said to meet 'em at the
slaughterhouse where they was workin'. Right around
here. Two squares down. There's no one there no more,
so we can have us some privacy.''

"You sure set it up right, didn't you?''

"Nobody's ever gonna doubt ol' Reddy's the man
after this!''

"When's the meeting?''

"One o' clock. Y'all dig into yo' chowder. We don't
got much time.''

"Y'know, Reddy, they're not going to want to go
quietly.''

"That's why I brung you along. You the po-lice."

"That's not going to mean much to them."

"Yeah, but this will."

Reddy pulled a revolver out of his pocket.

"Where'd you get that?" I asked him, before I pushed it back into his pocket.

"I borrowed it from Joey's collection. He won't know I took it."

"You know how to use it?"

Reddy smiled and said, "Joey showed me how when he was a little boy."

I fingered the barker in my holster.

"There's going to be shooting, I think."

"I'm ready fo' it. In fact, I's lookin' *fo'ward* to it. Specially if that double-crossin' nigguh Johnson's with 'em."

"Cool it, Reddy. Let me handle the gun play. If we're lucky, it won't get to that. Now I gotta run back to the station house."

"What fo'?"

"To get me some more coppers to take care of this mess."

"We don't have *time,* man. We gots ta be there in five minutes!"

"So we'll be a little late," I said, halfheartedly.

"They ain't gonna be there, man! We gots ta go now or we missed our chance!"

Why I trusted him was beyond me.

Whatever his reasons were, he was leading me to the men who had kidnapped Eddie Munroe. Both of them. Or maybe all three of them. There was still Albert Johnson, a wild card that I knew nothing about except what Reddy had told me.

Reddy wouldn't be much help in a fight. He was too old and feeble. I would face them alone.

There wasn't enough time to worry about reinforcements or anything else.

I grabbed Reddy's arm and said, "Let's go."

As we left Fitzgerald's Tavern I felt elated. No, that's not the word for it.

I felt fey.

It was only a few squares to the slaughterhouse. That it was deserted didn't surprise me. Businesses all over the city sprang up quick as shoots in April and withered just as fast. All of America was like that.

My hand was thrust in my jacket pocket where I had some dollar coins. I shuffled them between my fingers nervously. Reddy was in a good mood. Where he got it from was no surprise. He held the bottle in his hand like it was a family heirloom.

Whistles were blowing on the river. They sounded mournful.

Reddy and I kept quiet. There wasn't much to say. I had to stifle a desire to run to the slaughterhouse.

"This is it," Reddy whispered to me with awe.

It looked like any other warehouse, the front shaped like a stable or barn. Some letters from the name of a previous owner were still emblazoned on the upper stories, spaced between the windows. A marble factory, then a slaughterhouse, now an abandoned place of assignation for us to conduct the ugliest kind of business.

We tried the front door, but it was locked and bolted. The neighborhood children had been at work with the windows. Most of them were shattered, the glass shards scattered on the ground like some new kind of pavement.

"Looks like there's the only place we can go."

Reddy pointed to a narrow alleyway between the slaughterhouse and a residence. I looked behind me at the street. A building had collapsed or been torn down, leaving more open space than I was used to in the city. Few people were on the street. This was an industrial area. Next to the slaughterhouse was a house that didn't look occupied above the ground floor. Its front door was ajar. A parked wagon waited outside. It said SOUTH-WARK TACKLING CO. on it. The horse looked bored while it waited for its driver to come out of the house.

"Did they say anything about where we were supposed to meet them?"

"Nossuh. Just show up at this here place at one o'clock."

I pulled out my watch. One o'clock on the dot.

"Let's explore the alley. I want you to go first, Reddy. I'll cover our back, in case they try to trap us in there."

I was also thinking the Southwark wagon might be a ruse. But I wasn't going to open its doors and get shot in the face if they were hiding in there.

Reddy was taking his gun out when I told him, "Keep that in your pocket, Reddy. Let's hear what they have to say first."

Our boot heels clacked against the cobbles, the echo ringing against the pitted brick walls. As we approached the turn to go behind the slaughterhouse, I looked over my shoulder. No one coming yet. The wagon and its driver might have nothing to do with us, after all.

I whispered in his ear, "I'm going to stay right here."

"What fo'?" Reddy asked, scared.

"I don't want them to know I'm with you. Yet. Let them think you came alone. Don't worry, I'll hear everything. If there's someone there, start whistling. If they make you go inside the building or off down the alley, keep whistling. I'll have to come out into the open then."

"You like the wild card."

"That's right. Let's save any surprises for them until they've had their say."

"All right. Here I go."

Reddy made the turn while I stood just beyond it, my back against the wall. The brick was cool against my neck.

Whistling started up. They were there, all right.

My eyes went back to the street. Still no one coming.

Reddy was saying something.

"Where's your pals, nigguh?"

Another voice that sounded like a negro's said, "They comin'. They gotta make plans for to-night."

"I guess."

"So get to the point, Reddy. How much do you want from us?"

"I want my fair share. What I'm entitled to."

"You ain't entitled to nothin'."

"Not the way I see it. I gots a tongue, and it's gonna wag to Mistuh Bunkuh. And then you gonna be fish food, Albert. Or you can give me a quarter of what yo' takin' from to-night and I'll keep on forgettin' I know yo' ugly ass."

C'mon, Reddy, ask him where Jocko is. Ask him something.

But the old man just wanted to bait Johnson. Reddy wasn't interested in the dog anymore. He wanted a piece of the friend who betrayed him. The baiting was going to lead to shooting unless Reddy kept his mouth shut.

There was a pause, and then Johnson said, "That don't sound too good to me."

"You ain't got no choice! You wanna live or die? I don't know 'bout yo' white friends, but nobody's gonna spare yo' black ass! Serve you right fo' setting me up. Some colored man. Some friend you is. I trusted you. Let you drink from my bottle."

That was a real concession for Reddy.

"We all gots to make us a livin', friend." The last word was accented with venom. "What right you got judgin' me, huh? You nothin' but an old slave! That's all you is and that's all you ever was! You givin' us airs all the time cause you Bunker's man, the one with the roll of money and the prize dogs. And you love to play the high-tone nigger, don'tcha? But I don't need my *massa* to keep me breathin'!"

Reddy screamed with rage. I turned the corner, with my hand under my coat, ready to draw.

The old man was fiddling with the gun in his pockets, trying to yank it out. I said, "Get your hands off the gun, Reddy."

He didn't listen to me. Blood was the only thing on his mind. I rushed to him, clamping my hand on his arm. My revolver was still in its holster for the moment.

"Gimme the damn gun."

Albert Johnson hadn't moved. I figured he was un-armed. The sweat streaming down his dark forehead confirmed my supposition.

I got the pistol from Reddy and kept it trained on them.

Then I said, "Now we're going to have a talk. Nice and civilized. No name-calling. Understand?"

"Who the hell are you?" Johnson said. His voice was raspy now, with the gun on him. He took a gulp and kept staring at it.

"I'm a friend of Jocko's. Where is he?"

"You from Bunker?"

"I'm asking, Albert. You're answering. Where is Jocko?"

His eyes moved to the back doors of the slaughter-house. A pair of locks were on the ground directly in front of them. Around the latches where the locks had been there were heavy scratches.

"Let's go inside. Albert, go and open the door there. Reddy, follow him."

Johnson walked steadily over to the doors and yanked one aside. Then he stood in front of the door that re-mained shut. He didn't seem nervous anymore. His face was a placid mask, like that of a butler waiting to take your hat and coat.

I looked inside but saw very little. The sparse light in the alley was too weak to illuminate the interior. But there was a strong stench that made me nearly lose my chowder.

"You first," I told Johnson.

"This is it, McCleary," Reddy whispered to me. "We gonna get Jocko back. I got a feelin' he's inside this place."

I went ahead of him into the dimness. Johnson was still in view. The reek of rotten flesh and blood nearly choked me.

As soon as I stepped inside, someone hit me in the

head with a slung shot. It rapped against my skull like a steam-powered jackhammer. I fell to the ground, stunned. Reddy's gun was torn out of my hand. My gun stayed where it was in the holster, hidden under my coat.

Something dark passed over me. I heard Reddy's voice. It sounded far off, though he was probably no more than a few feet away. He was pleading for his life.

Johnson dragged him through the doors and slammed them shut. A voice, another voice, said, "Now finish the job, Albert."

I lay on the ground and bled, my eyes shut. My lips pressed against the cold stone floor. The last trace of cattle blood hadn't been washed off too well.

I didn't want them to know I was still conscious. My hands were too far from my waist. If I made a move for the barker they'd notice it right away. I couldn't do anything but play dead.

"Use his own gun. Don't worry about him. He'll be out for a while, the way I hit him."

I had to resist smirking at the unknown voice's overestimation of his pugilistic talents.

"Don't shoot me, man! I'll keep my mouf shut! You got nothin' to fear from me!"

"Now you don't talk so big, do you, old man?" Johnson said.

"Go ahead, Albert."

There was a pause. Johnson was hesitating.

"You know the deal. You want to be our partner in this thing you gotta do your job. I thought you might be able to handle it out there just now. Otherwise I woulda come and lended a hand."

A little coward. I wanted to open up my eyes and get a look at him. Was it Glick or Franco? I wondered. The voice didn't have a Spanish accent, but that didn't mean anything.

"Just get it over with. We got things to do."

Reddy screamed before I heard the hammer fall. There were whooping and gurgling sounds. Then something heavy hit the ground with a thud.

But there had been no shot.

"I didn't even pull the trigger!" Johnson cried.

"That may be," the unknown voice said. And then, after a pause, "But this nigger's deader than last year's corpse."

"Sweet Jesus," Johnson said.

"His pump must've called it a day when you pointed that gun at him."

I strained to keep the emotion off my face. Maybe they hadn't shot him. But they had killed him just the same.

"What're we gonna do with him?"

"Dump him in a barrel over there."

"Where we put the carcasses? Just look at 'em, man! There's rats climbin' all over that mess still!"

"So what? Rat needs to eat, same as anybody."

That made him laugh.

"You one cool son of a bitch, Glick."

Glick kept laughing. There was no joy in the laughter. It was an ugly sound, like a death rattle.

"Get moving. The dab's comin' any minute."

Dab meant a woman, in the flash cant. More to the point, it was a part of a woman.

I heard Johnson drag Reddy's body past me, into the stink.

Glick walked up to me. Without warning he landed a heel in my kidneys. I had to bite into my cheek to not make a sound or expression. I tasted blood again. The blow hadn't hurt that much. But it was no love tap, either.

"He's still out of service. Hurry up, Albert."

Something rapped against the doors to the alley.

"Drop him!" Glick called to Johnson. "Damn it! Where the hell did Franco get to? *He's* the one who should be here! This is *his* problem! How long does it take to bag a damn boat?"

A voice said tremulously, "I've come."

I recognized the voice. Leah Munroe.

This was too much for me. A moment before I was

ready to spring up and bark Glick point blank. But not now. My kidneys throbbed with pain while I listened.

"Did you bring the money?" Glick asked.

"Yes, it's all here. Now you can go crawl somewhere else. Just make it far away from us."

"That'll all depend, won't it? C'mere and count the money, Albert!"

After a minute Johnson said, "All there."

"Who is that lying there?" Leah Munroe asked.

"Search me. He came with the place." Glick laughed again. I prayed she wouldn't tell them who I was. I wanted them to keep thinking I was one of Bunker's thugs.

Somebody answered my prayers. Leah said, "Then I'm going." She sounded anxious.

"Wait a minute, sweetheart. You're not going to run out on us so fast. No. That wouldn't be ladylike, would it? And you are a real lady, that right?" Again he laughed.

"Let go of me, let go!"

"I think Albert and I'll hold on to you until Franco joins up with us. He'll want to see you, won't he? Oh yes, I think he will. I think he'll want to have more than a few words with you!"

Glick's ugly laugh rang off the walls. It got into my head and bounced around inside my skull. The only way to get it out was to stand up.

I got to my feet, my hand ripping the barker out of its holster.

My eyes were adjusted to the dim light. I could see Glick now.

The doctor's description was a good one. The deformed nose, the beard, the alpaca duster. His mouth hung open in surprise. A withered arm clutched Leah Munroe's neck. She was bent back, her hair undone and falling over her shoulders. A small bonnet lay on the floor. Glick planted his boot on it. A button had popped off her jersey. Glick looked like he was going for another.

Albert Johnson was not where I thought he would be. He must've moved after counting the money. Now he stood by a large barrel of offal not more than ten feet from me. Reddy's corpse was at his feet.

Leah Munroe gasped with recognition.

"We have one corpse already," I said. "Who wants to be number two?"

No one spoke a word. We were petrified like four objects in a still life.

Another person came through the doors to the alley. For a second my attention was drawn to him.

In the same moment, Glick turned and said, "Franco! Get outta here!"

Then Albert lobbed a huge barrel at me and kicked over another one. I stumbled backward out of the way of the first one. It crashed against the floor, spilling rotten meat. Rats scurried out of the debris in all directions.

A thick gush of blood poured out of the second barrel. It washed over my shoes and the cuffs of my trousers. But I wasn't too worried about the damage to my apparel. Albert had taken advantage of my surprise to close the distance between us. He was springing at me with a meat hook in his hand. It was about to go into my ear when I shot him. The revolver made a noise like thunder. It filled the air with a greasy, thick cloud of smoke.

There had been no time to aim. The first ball bored into his chest. Albert cried out and went to his knees, dropping the hook. He fell to the puddle of blood around him and pumped some of his own into it. Then he died.

In the meantime I turned to where Glick and Franco had been, but there was only Leah Munroe. She was on the ground. It looked like she'd been struck in the head. The side of her face already had a small but livid bruise on one cheek. I was surprised I hadn't noticed it before. Now a second red mark coated her jaw.

I ran out to the alley. When I got to the street, the wagon was gone.

I staggered back to the slaughterhouse. First I carried Leah Munroe outside. Then I went in and dragged

Reddy out of the pool of blood and offal he was lying in. His body was heavy for such an old man. I got all the way to the doors before my muscles gave out. I collapsed to the floor. A wave of darkness washed over me and I went under.

11

SLOWLY MY EYES opened. The lashes struggled, caked
together with bits of dried blood. I was in my room at
home. The gas lamps were burning. Through the window I could see the sun going down. The clouds over
the tree there were burnished with purple and deep blue.

The twilight imposed a stillness on the room. My eyes
shifted from the window to the wallpaper I'd put up a
week ago to the crucifix hanging on it to the counterpane
where my hands were resting. I realized I was naked
then except for my drawers.

There was another set of hands beside mine. They
were smaller and more slender. Feminine hands. They
were attached to a body covered by a black mourning
dress. For an instant I thought I was dead and attending
my own wake with a single symbolic mourner at my
deathbed.

Leah Munroe spoke and shattered the illusion,
"You're awake. No, don't get up. You have a nasty
bump on your head."

She wiped the side of my head with a damp cloth and
rinsed it out in my washbasin. In the stuffy heat of the
evening the cool water felt wonderful.

I couldn't read anything from her expression. It was
impassive, businesslike. As she rinsed the cloth I stared
at her face, hoping she wouldn't notice. It had been a

147

long time since I'd felt what I was feeling.

There was an incredible fragility to her prettiness, as if a master hand had made a charcoal sketch of beauty without adding the deeper tones of a brush or quill.

Strands of brownish-blond hair curved around cheeks as pink as if she'd just scrubbed them. Her small lips were the same color. Just above the collar of her dress I caught the hint of a pale neck. I wanted to see the collar disappear for a moment. Then I squelched the desire. She was a married woman.

She turned to me with a slight smile and said, "You're very brave. I owe you my life."

I was embarassed, not just from her praise, but also from realizing she had been the one to undress my bloody clothes and put me in bed.

"How did we get back here?"

"You were conscious half the time, though you probably don't remember it. I propped you up and walked you to the Market Street Terminus. It was only a few squares away, but it seemed to take hours. We climbed on the car and rode down here. I had to ask a young man to help me carry you upstairs to your bedroom."

"But how did you know where I live?"

"That was easy. I asked your Captain Heins this morning when I came to the city. I wanted to have some flowers sent to you."

"Flowers?"

"For saving Stephen. And now you've saved me, too."

"You'll have to send more flowers."

She smiled and said, "I've come in person this time."

Part of me resisted saying, "Does Mr. Munroe know where you are?"

"No. He's probably worried sick. But I wanted to make sure you're all right."

I touched the side of my head and felt tiny threads poking out of my skin.

"You needed two stitches. I took care of it."

"You're mighty professional. Did you ever work in a hospital?"

"Oh yes," she said, her eyes looking past me, "during the War."

"Is that where you met Archibald?"

Her eyes turned to me again with surprise. "You certainly are a good detective."

"Not really. Just a good guesser."

"You guessed correctly. I met him at the Citizens' Volunteer Hospital. Not too far away from here, actually, at Broad and Prime Streets. You know the one I mean?"

"I'm sorry. I wasn't in the city during the War."

I could see she wanted to ask me more, but the bitterness in my voice stopped her short.

I said, "What made you become a nurse?"

"I wanted to be of use somehow. I couldn't fight. So I went to the hospital. I'd gone once before, but they were reluctant to take me because I was a woman. As the War dragged on they stopped caring so much about that. I was," she paused as if searching for the right word, "working at the time. They expected the women to volunteer. I started going a little bit, and then the more I was there, the more I liked it. Eventually I quit working altogether and made the hospital my home. There was plenty of food around. Not spectacular, mind you. But enough for me to live on. And there were cots when I felt like sleeping. Which wasn't often."

The smile on her face seemed joyful and tragic at the same time. She said, "That was the best time of my life."

The weight of anguish was taking its toll. The fragile beauty of not just her self, but her life, was beginning to fade. She seemed to feel that dissolution. With her words she was trying to snatch at that beauty before she lost it completely.

"I met Archibald in sixty-four. He came in with a large group of men from Sherman's March. At first it looked like he was going to lose part of his leg. What amazed me about him was his lack of anger. He accepted whatever happened to him with such . . . peacefulness. I'd never known someone like him. He used to sit there on his cot and write in a leatherbound journal. The first few times when I asked him what he was writing he showed me. They were poems. Some of them were about the War, about how horrible it was. The others were about the places and people he'd seen. They were wonderful poems. I asked him to make copies for me. I took them to my cot and read them over and over again while he slept.

"Then one day he wouldn't show me what he was writing. I wanted so much to see that I waited until he was asleep and then peeked through his book. The poem he'd written that day was about me. I cried when I read it."

Her eyes were watering even now. Archibald Munroe must've had a way with words.

"When he was well enough to leave the hospital, he asked me to go with him. As his wife."

"That's the first happy war story I've heard in a long time."

"Do you have any war stories, Mr. McCleary?"

"Call me Wilton. You wouldn't want to hear them. They're not so happy. I was a prisoner of war."

"A prisoner of war." She repeated each word as if it was new to her. "Then you know how I feel now."

"What do you mean?"

"Nothing. This hideous business. My baby."

I took hold of her shoulder and sat up. "Don't you worry, Mrs. Munroe."

"You can call me Leah. I think you've earned the right."

I smiled and said, "We're going to get Eddie back. You saw how close we were to-day to getting the men who kidnapped him."

For the first time since I'd awakened from my stupor it occurred to me to ask her, "What were you doing at the slaughterhouse, anyway?"

"I got a letter this morning that said I should meet them at that address and bring the money. Then they would tell me how to get Eddie back."

I had a feeling their goal was to get some money quick and dust out of the city before anyone could spot them.

"And you came alone? Were you mad?"

"They told me to. They warned me if I didn't they'd . . ."

"Let me guess. It would 'signal his instant annihilation'."

She nodded. "Like the other letter."

"What about the money? Where'd you get it from?"

"I had some of my own saved up."

"Did they take it with them?"

"Yes. I think the man with the . . ." She touched her nose, wrinkling it at the same time with disgust.

"His name's Glick. So they took the ransom. But no Eddie, right?"

She bowed her head.

"Did they say anything about releasing him after you paid the money?"

"Yes. But they weren't too specific."

"Where's the letter? Can I see it?"

"You can't. I destroyed it."

"Why would you do a thing like that?"

"I didn't want Archibald to see it. I didn't want him knowing I was acting alone. It would hurt him so. He wants to do something himself. But I'm worried about him. His health hasn't been too good since I met him. I have to take care of him as much as the two children."

"He loves you very much. And the boys. He wants to help, somehow."

"I know."

"Speaking of the boys, how is Stephen? Any harm done in the shed?"

"He got scorched some on the back of one hand. But I soaked it in cold water and kept the swelling down on his ankle. He's all right, thanks to you."

"I've been wanting to talk to him. About what happened when Glick and Franco grabbed them."

The names had no effect on her.

"He's already talked to the police, hasn't he? Is there any need to torture him further?"

The angry tone made me lower my voice placatingly. "I don't want to torture him. I just want to see if he remembers anything more about that day. Maybe they talked about where they were taking Eddie."

"He would've told me by now, I think."

"Perhaps you're right. Has he talked to Diefenderfer at all?"

"Oh no. He stays in his room mostly. Sometimes . . ."

She drew in her lips as if to stop the words from coming out.

"What is it?" I asked.

"I don't know. Perhaps I'm worrying too much about trifles. It's just that . . . sometimes I'm afraid for Stephen as much for Eddie."

"What makes you say that?"

"The whole incident in the shed. It wasn't the first incident he's had. There were two more."

"What kind of incidents?"

"The first happened in our parlor room. Archibald and I were outside, setting up a picnic table. Eddie was with us. Stephen was in the house by himself. He always likes to play by himself. Reading in his room. He's a very solitary boy. The only friend he has is his brother."

"What happened?"

"Yes, well, I heard this crash from inside the house while we were laying the table. I rushed inside because I thought he might have hurt himself. In fact, he did cut himself a little bit. But he had broken a statue I'd had for many years. It was a keepsake from my mother. The only one I had of her."

"A statue of what?"

"Oh, a pair of ceramic birds," she said, like she was embarassed.

"And he broke them."

"He said it was an accident, but I thought twice about it. They were set on the mantel. He couldn't bump into them, or anything. I got the feeling he did it deliberately."

"Maybe he was just curious. I'm sure he felt bad about it."

"No. He wasn't remorseful at all, that was the strangest thing. I made him stay inside while the three of us ate our picnic. Maybe it was the wrong thing to do."

"Sounds like you did what any good parent would have done."

"I don't know. The second incident was just a week later. It was Eddie's birthday and Archibald bought a miniature base-ball bat. He used to take the boys to the Athletics games in town every now and then. They loved it.

"So Archibald hid the bat in the shed. He usually keeps it locked. The night before Eddie's birthday he went to get the bat, but it wasn't there. He questioned both of the boys about it. But they said they hadn't seen it. He told me later he suspected Stephen had stolen it."

"Why would he do that?"

"He loves his brother. But sometimes he can be very jealous."

"Was anything else stolen from the shed? Or missing?"

"Not that we could see. It was all very strange."

I thought of Glick and Franco messing around there. Hadn't Dr. Moyer seen them lurking around the grounds? But why would they take a base-ball bat?

"What were the dates of these events?"

"Eddie's birthday is June eighteenth. So we found out the bat was missing the seventeenth. And my birds were broken a week before. I don't know, sometimes I'm afraid I'm losing my other son, too."

Her voice trembled.

"Stephen acts so queer since the men abducted them. He hardly says a word, doesn't want me or his father to touch him. I'm afraid, Wilton. Afraid they might've done something to him.''

She couldn't hold it back any longer. Dry sobs wracked her body.

It was hard to watch that. I took her in my arms and held her while she cried. All kinds of thoughts went through my brain. I wanted to kiss her, very much. Once she looked at me like she was waiting for me to do just that.

I wanted to. I really did. But I could not bring myself to. She was as vulnerable as a child.

My eyes were drawn to the crucifix on my wall. They refocused on it, barely visible in the shadows thrown off by the gas lamp.

I held her until she stopped crying. The next time she looked at me it was with surprise and a new emotion I hadn't seen there before. It looked like affection.

She apologized. I told her there was no need.

"You need to talk. That way you can ignore all that's on your mind by worrying about little things. That's what this business with Stephen sounds like to me. Little things.''

"You're right, I suppose." But she didn't sound so sure.

I decided to change the subject.

"Perhaps you can help me.''

"Anything I can do. Just ask.''

"It's a question I've been meaning to ask you. It just slipped my mind till now. Did you happen to notice a dog in the slaughterhouse, or a kennel of some kind?'' I didn't have the time to look.

With a sniffle and a wipe to her cheeks she pulled herself together, putting on the veneer of the business-like nurse.

"Not that I could see. Why?''

Briefly I outlined for her how the kidnapping of her son was linked to that of Alderman Bunker's fox terrier.

"These men are in for big money. If they collect both ransoms they'll have about twenty thousand dollars.

That's enough to pay the rent for a while. How much did you pay them, if you don't mind me asking?''

She hesistated before saying, "Maybe five hundred dollars. All my savings. It was all I had left.''

Her voice was bitter.

I was puzzled. "It doesn't make sense to me why they'd take money from both of you. And five hundred dollars doesn't cut it. They were asking for ten thousand.''

"All I know is what they told me. Bring what I had as a down payment.''

"And in return they set up the exchange? I'm itchin' to get at these scamps to-night.''

"To-night? What do you mean?''

"They've also delivered a letter to Alderman Bunker. To-night at the Fairmount Waterworks there's going to be an exchange. The money for the dog. Except what they don't know is that I'm going to be there in Bunker's place. And faded into the woodwork will be a friend of mine, a detective like me. We're going to catch them with their drawers down. With only two of them left, it should be easier.''

I told her the contents of the Jocko ransom letter. The carpetbag, the gazebo. All the rest. She was a good listener. I couldn't remember the last time I'd talked to a woman. I felt close to her. Not just out of gratitude. Or pity. She seemed to need someone. I wanted to be needed.

"Don't go to-night," she said abruptly.

"Why not? I've got my friend to back me up. After what happened to-day, I may get some more coppers to join us.''

"No, please. What happens if they're killed? Before they can tell you where Eddie's being held?''

"Don't worry. I won't shoot unless I have to. And I'll tell my friend the same. We're going to be careful. I want them alive, too. Quick deaths aren't as good as slow decay in prison. Trust me, I know.''

I looked out the window to the darkening sky.

"In fact, I gotta get up and get ready to head over to Bunker's place. Nolan'll be expecting me. It's set to go at eleven o'clock. What time is it, by the way?"

She reached over me to the nightstand where my watch lay. Her bodice touched my chest for an instant. Warmth surged through me. She was so close. I wanted to just touch her face, where the bruise was. Kiss it, maybe.

I stopped the thoughts by asking her, "How'd you get that bruise on your face? I don't remember seeing it the day I called on you."

"Oh, that? I must've fallen to-day."

But that bruise was too old. Something had happened since I'd last seen her in Germantown, something she didn't want to talk about. I hoped Archibald wasn't taking out his sense of helplessness on her.

"It's nine o'clock," she told me, "but I really wish you'd stay. You shouldn't be getting up with those stitches in your head. You need rest."

But I got up, wrapping the sheets around my waist.

"Would you mind fetching my trousers? The ones on the chair there?"

She brought them to me and then turned around while I put them on. We were both silent, very aware of each other.

My eyes were focused on the shirt front I was buttoning. Then I heard her bustle skirt trail across my wooden floor with a soft swish. Her shaking hand touched mine. She said, "How can I convince you to stay here?"

My throat was dry. I couldn't look at her face. Instead I fastened my gaze on the hand that curled around my own. I had no idea what to think or do.

So what if Bunker didn't get the dog back? What did I care?

Let them take the money. We'd get them sooner or later.

What if there was gunplay, and they were shot, like she said. How would we find the boy?

What if I got shot? Hadn't I had enough excitement for one day?

There was not enough time to request a detachment of harness bulls to back us up.

It was all wrong. She needed someone. She needed me.

She needed her husband.

You need to do your job, I thought. You need to catch Glick and Franco and bring Eddie back to her. You need to snap yourself out of this and get moving.

Suddenly I felt ashamed, then angry. Going to the waterworks was the only way for me to snap out of it.

I got up and put my collar on.

"I'm afraid, Wilton. I don't want you getting hurt. The whole thing sounds too dangerous. Won't you please stay here and lie down? Can't your friend take care of it?"

"No. I want to see this thing through. It's my responsibility."

"Well, if I can't talk any sense into you, then I'm going to catch a car back home before they stop running for the night."

"Shall I walk you to the stop?"

"No, thank you. I'll be all right. Please stop by the house tomorrow."

I wasn't too concerned with what Cap had told me that morning. So I said, "I will. And thank you. For saving *me*."

She laughed and said, "You owe me a penny for each stitch." She kissed my cheek and said, "You're a very strange man. A good man."

Then she left me alone.

I sat on my bed, cleaning the chambers and barrel of my revolver. As I wiped the rag across the metal I thought of her. Of what I had done and hadn't done. I tried to make sense of what had just passed between us. I was completely bewildered. But more than ever, I wanted to find her son and bring peace to her family.

Loading the revolver was a complicated process. Cradling the barker in my hand, I picked the old percussion caps off the nipples. I brought it back to half-cock and spun the barrel. Then I put the new caps on. Next I poured powder into the six chambers. After the powder I stuffed each of the chambers with a ball and wad. The revolver had a built-in ramrod to pack the balls in tight. The last step was a special precaution I took. I smeared grease on the rim of each chamber. That way when I fired, a spark wouldn't set off the other five balls. That could be pretty messy.

I wanted to see how fast I could load the thing. Working as quickly as possible, I still managed to take up a minute and a half with the whole process. I hoped six shots would be all I'd need. Better yet I hoped not to use it at all.

When I finished I tied my necktie in front of the mirror on my washstand. Then I clambered down the stairs to catch the last streetcar.

12

THE RIDE TO Bunker's was quiet. Most of the people in the streetcar were pooped after a ten-hour day in the oilworks near my home. They craned their necks out the open windows and cooled their sweating brows. The jingle of the team's harness and the clatter of their hooves against the cobbles drowned the few snores and coughs of the men in the car. We slid along the tracks relatively smoothly, jostling only now and then. I nearly dozed off.

There were one or two colored men in the car with us. Only seven years ago they would have been beaten to within an inch of their lives if they'd tried to get on any of the streetcars or omnibuses. I felt old, remembering that time before they could ride with white men. Things had changed since the War, all over the country. Though perhaps not enough.

It was a long ride up to the Northern Liberties. The colored men got off well before then. I don't think there was one colored resident in Bunker's whole ward. Except Reddy.

When I got off the car, I wound around the block to the alleys behind Bunker's crib. I didn't want anyone seeing me enter. I knocked on the back door and Mrs. Bunker let me in.

"This is so exciting!" she blurted out.

I walked through the kitchen into the smoking room. Bunker was there, leaning on the mantel. He was loading a Winchester rifle.

Nolan sat in a chair smoking one of Bunker's segars.

I greeted them both and said, "What are you doing with that rifle, Mr. Bunker?"

"Reddy's dead."

"I know. I was with him at the slaughterhouse."

Bunker strode over to me, the rifle still in his hands. He brandished it at me like I was the cause of all his troubles. "What happened?"

I recounted the events of that afternoon. I left out the part about Reddy trying to blackmail the kidnappers. Let bygones be bygones.

"Did you tell him, Nolan?" I asked.

"No, Mack. I just got here."

"Heins told me. A woman sent word to him that you'd been hurt and Reddy was dead. I went there as soon as I heard. Reddy's out back now," he said wistfully.

"So Cap knows all about what's happening to-night?"

"Yeah," Bunker said. "But don't let that worry you. I told him I'd take care o' things, he needn't trouble any more detectives. You got one already, so that narrows things down a bit. Good work, lad."

I didn't feel proud about killing a man. It would have been better to keep Albert Johnson alive. And we still didn't know where Eddie Munroe was.

"I don't want you coming, Bunker. This is a very delicate situation."

"The hell it is. These bastards killed my Reddy and stole my dog. I'm not lettin' 'em get away with it. I'll take care of things to-night."

I paced around the leather upholstered furniture and tried to calm myself. I didn't want blood lust ruining our one chance of capturing Glick and Franco. We had to keep our cool. If we lost it, we would make mistakes. Fatal mistakes.

I told him so, but he wasn't listening. "What difference does it make if they're dead as long as we get the dog back, Mack?" Nolan asked.

So I had to spill the beans. "This isn't just about Jocko, Nolan."

"Whatta ya mean?" they both asked me.

"There will be two men there to-night. I hope. If they haven't turned tail and gotten out of the city by now. But I don't think they will. They want that fat juicy ten thousand dollar steak you're going to throw them to-night.

"Their names are Glick and Franco. They're the same men who kidnapped Eddie Munroe in Germantown."

"What? How do you know that?" Nolan was out of his seat.

There was no use hiding it anymore. I would've gone to City Hall that afternoon if I'd been able. I told them the whole story, everything I knew about Glick and the Spaniard.

Stunned, they waited with their mouths open for me to say more. When I didn't add anything else, Nolan said, "We gotta get more men."

"There's no time! In a half hour we're gonna have to be there!" I told him.

"Bunker can telegraph the station house."

"Nope. I'm coming with the two of you. I wouldn't miss this for the world now. Think how this is gonna look when we nab these scamps, boys. You'll have any nomination you want in the next election, I tell you. This is priceless!"

He was getting Nolan wound up, too. I could see delusions of grandeur swirling across their eyes.

"Don't forget the boy. And your dog, Bunker. With a little luck we'll have both within an hour or two."

I supposed Bunker would be all right. He was clutching his rifle to his expansive chest like he was battle ready. I didn't know where his eagerness came from. But I needed any kind of help I could get.

We planned it like this. I was to go in Bunker's place

with the carpetbag, in his carriage. Nolan and Bunker would follow me and take positions around the mill-house, entering through the woods leading to the reservoir.

Gunfire would be the signal to close in. I made it very explicit that Glick and Franco were to be captured alive.

Then we shook hands, wished each other luck, and went our separate ways. Mrs. Bunker gave me a top hat and jacket from the rack. I would look enough like Bunker to satisfy the kidnappers, but only if they regarded me from a distance.

I took the front door to the street, where a sporty break was hitched to the post. The animal snorted impatiently as I grabbed the reins. Then we were off.

Traffic was not especially heavy in the city at this late hour. I followed Callowhill Street till I was out of the city, drove past the Wire Bridge along the east bank, and stopped a short distance from the waterworks, at the beginning of the graveled walk.

On the mount to my right was the reservoir, Philadelphia's water supply. It was one hundred feet above tidewater in the river and gave a good view of the works below it. Nolan and Bunker would approach from there. Of course, Glick and Franco might, too. But something told me they were already in position. The hairs on the back of my neck were standing on end. Just like they were when we marched all those years ago. I felt like the whole sky was going to fall on me at any moment. Maybe it was having those twenty-six million gallons of water up there on the mount. I imagined the reservoirs erupting like a watery volcano, drowning all of us.

The whole waterworks took up about thirty acres, but I had a feeling most of the action would be confined to the buildings curving from the dam to just short of the Wire Bridge. Some lights were aglow in the upper stories of the millhouse and the newer adjacent buildings. They perched over the Schuylkill like miniature Parthenons. In the moonlight the whole scene reminded me of a phantasmagoric city of the ancients, lonely and full of ghosts.

As I approached the buildings I noticed a couple of young people leaning against the railing that stretched from the bridge to the works themselves. It wasn't Glick and Franco, unless one of them had taken to wearing bustle skirts. They giggled and held each other. There was just enough light from the night sky and the city beyond the mount to see them. Staying in the shadows, I spoke to them in a harsh whisper.

"What are you doing here?"

They took their hands off each other and stared at me, petrified.

At first I thought it might be a whore with her catch for the night or at least the next half hour. But they were well dressed and both young.

The boy summoned up some bravado. "Don't we have a right to go for a walk?"

"Listen, sonny," I said, showing him my star. "There's going to be shooting around here mighty soon. Go paw at your gal someplace else."

My tone was harsh. Seeing the two of them there made me angry. I didn't know why.

The young couple fled the way I had come.

The evening was so pretty I wished I could just take a stroll around the works and enjoy the peacefulness of the night. I could see the stars better out here. There was the Big Dipper. I couldn't remember the last time I had bothered to look for it.

Leah Munroe came to mind and I thought on what she'd told me. I remembered the way it had felt when she'd touched me that one time.

I felt incredibly weary when I remembered everything else about the past few days.

I watched the black river slide over the dam and past the temple-like pier. The noise of its fall swallowed up every other sound for a moment.

I remembered falling into it myself. In the hot humid night, I shivered.

The metal railing I gripped was cool under my hand. I wanted to touch something real. To be sure of my own existence. I looked toward the reservoir where the standpipe poked into the sky like a minaret. Nolan and Bunker should be passing it by now.

Beneath the last set of trees before the open space of the waterworks I paused. The crickets stopped singing when I got near them. Mice ran here and there through the grass. They were invisible but I could hear them, the only sound other than the water.

I had this crazy idea that if I listened closely I would be able to hear the invisible Eddie calling for help. I pictured him hidden like the mice, under foliage and tall grass, his tiny voice so quiet you could barely hear it over the rush of noise that daylight brought.

My weariness was leaving me. Blood surged through my veins, my heart pumping furiously. Thinking about Eddie did away with my impromptu revery, which I now realized was a symptom of fear.

Does he feel the way I'm feeling now? I wondered. Frightened? Afraid of dying? Afraid of never seeing home again?

It was the way I always felt before confrontations in the War, in prison, on the beat, right now.

Fear has a way of making men weak.

But I wouldn't let that happen to me. My fear turned me, as it had always done, to prayer. When I was done the fear was far away. And the loneliness, too.

I was ready to meet Glick and Franco.

The carpetbag I carried was heavy with all of Bunker's money. It was a hell of a ransom to pay for a dog. I was looking forward to meeting a terrier that was worth ten thousand dollars.

Nolan and Bunker were nowhere to be seen. I didn't waste any more time worrying about whether they were there or not. I took the graveled path behind the buildings.

Moon and starlight fell through spaces between the slender columns of the millhouse portico. The formal

Greek architecture was eerie, impassive. Behind any corner or column I was expecting a shadow to metamorphosize into one of the kidnappers. There were so many shadows, so many places for a man to hide. They had picked a good place for the exchange. Once they had the money they could scatter in a host of directions. Up the mount, toward Boathouse Row, over the Wire Bridge, down to the river, practically anywhere.

And we had only three men to box them in. Silently I cursed the lack of time and my own stubborn pride. If only we had a bunch of coppers from the local station house . . .

But it was no use now.

It was as quiet there as among the other Grecian buildings not far off, the tombs in Laurel Hill Cemetery.

The river kept going over the falls. The noise would have been pleasant any other time, but not now. It seemed to get into my brain like Glick's laugh, bouncing around in there.

I wanted to turn off the water so I could listen for them. Coming behind me.

I turned quickly to see.

No one there. Just the millhouse.

On my right side was a bit of the Schuylkill, trapped between the footpath and a bridge that used to face the forebay. It led to a tiny peninsula that perched on the tip of the dam. At its extreme point was the stone gazebo. Trees grew thick over the path leading to it.

I walked up the stairs leading to the promenade on the forebay, feeling like an actor on the opening night of a production. The skies were like curtains. I could feel a huge hand lifting them, a light shining on me and me alone.

For a moment I stopped to look at the elaborate fountain perched on the forebay rocks. Slender jets of spray trickled down the shadowy precipice. In the moonlight I could see the old sculpture of Leda and a bittern—William Rush's symbol of the Schuylkill River, the scantily-clad Leda regarding me with a mockingly placid expression.

A steamer was docked at its landing stage on the other side of the forebay. I walked over to a bench and pretended to count the money. I thought of putting my barker in my coat pocket. But it was too big. I left it in the holster and picked up the carpetbag.

I was ready now.

As I entered the path to the gazebo the trees engulfed me in darkness.

I was in a tunnel of foliage. It curled around me like a clenched fist. The night at the other end gleamed in this deeper darkness.

I held on to the wooden stock of my revolver for dear life.

I trod across the path, the light at the end getting closer. The sound of the river seemed to issue from that point, drawing me toward it with hypnotic power.

A twig snapped. At first I thought I must have stepped on it. But before I realized that no such twig was on the path, I felt something cold and metallic nuzzle into my ear.

"Keep goin'. Slow."

The voice was one I hadn't heard before.

I walked silently, one hand on the money, the other on the revolver.

His gun moved behind my ear to press at the base of my skull. My back arched involuntarily.

Finally we reached the gazebo. The voice behind me said, "Drop the bag and put your hands where I can see them."

There was no mistaking the foreign accent. I made to turn around.

"Don't move."

Franco walked in front of me. He stood there silhouetted against the black river.

"You're not Bunker."

"He sent me in his place. Count the money. It's all there."

He opened the bag and took a quick look at its contents. His gun was still trained on me. My hands stayed where they were.

"You come alone?" he asked me.

"Like you said in the letter."

He came close enough for me to get a good look at him. His chiseled good looks were about to go to seed. Long black hair hung over his shoulders like an Indian's. His dark beard was carefully trimmed. The rest of his face was devoid of emotion, a desert pitted with pockmarks.

He flashed a set of nice teeth in a joyless smile.

"You a copper? Huh?"

His thick hands went through my pockets. Out came the star like Judas. And my barker from its holster, like a fair weather friend. Franco tossed it aside.

"A detective? How about that."

"I'm a friend of Joe Bunker's. I brought you your money. Now, where's the dog?"

"The dog? Oh, he's here. Closer than you think." That made him laugh. "Get down on the ground with your arms and legs spread out. Do it now."

I did what he told me. There wasn't much else I could do with his gun pointed at me. Franco picked up the carpetbag and walked back toward the end of the gazebo. The gun never moved from its target, my face. I had little to do but stare at it.

Franco backed away from me, still training the pistol on my face. A narrow walkway extended from the gazebo, bordering the dammed river. He went about halfway along the path and peered over the edge, down to the river below the dam. At first I thought he was going to take a dive. It wasn't much of a drop, maybe twenty feet.

I stayed where I was, curious. Franco seemed to be looking for something. The dim moonlight wasn't helping him. Finally he straightened with recognition. I heard him say, "You got it?"

A voice from below him said, "Yeah, go ahead."

Franco hoisted the bag over his head and tossed it downward, toward the water. I didn't hear a splash, of course. Glick was waiting down there in a stolen boat. Now I remembered him mentioning it at the slaughterhouse. Now, when it was too late to help us.

As Franco leaned over the railing to make sure the bag reached Glick, a sound came from the river.

A dog, barking.

Franco walked over to me and said, "Now, here's how we're gonna play this. Down there is a boat. The dog is in a cage which my pal is holding on to. I'm going to walk down those stairs"—he indicated a set of stone steps leading to a lower tier of the promontory, just above the river—"and climb on the boat. When I'm safe onboard, we'll pitch the cage over and you can fish it out with a gaff we got for you. If you make a move to stop me, the dog gets thrown overboard and drowned. Got it?"

I got it, but I didn't like it. Nothing could stop them from drowning the dog. Or keeping it.

Trusting them made no sense. I had to do something. We had to have a new exchange. I got to my feet.

"You aren't goin' anywhere, Franco."

His eyes squinted in the darkness. "Who are you? How'd you know my name?"

"I met you this afternoon at the slaughterhouse. I put your colored pal to sleep. And now I'm gonna break your neck unless you tell me where Eddie Munroe is."

His gun was still pointed at my face like he was trying to hide behind it. He looked down the steps to the river.

Now he really *is* going to jump, I thought.

"Where's the kid, Franco? Last chance before I kill you with my bare hands."

His nice teeth ground together.

"You're the one who's gonna die!"

I was staring right at the dark hole of the barrel. Franco pulled the trigger and the hammer snapped down.

Nothing happened, just like I knew it would.

"You picked that one up at the slaughterhouse, didn't

you? I recognized it just now. It was Reddy's gun. He got it from his boss. And I happen to know Bunker doesn't keep his guns loaded.''

Franco snarled and squeezed the trigger again and again. I started laughing. Then he cursed in some language other than English and threw the gun at me. I sprang at him. He lost his balance when I plowed into him. We both fell down the stone steps, clasping each other like two drunken dancers. Before we reached the bottom I heard shots.

They weren't coming from the river. As I landed on Franco, I glanced above us. Bunker was there with his Winchester, taking potshots at the boat. He was a terrible marksman. There were some ricochets mighty close to where I was lying.

Franco's boot slammed into my neck. With a grunt I drove my elbow into his rib cage. We were flat on the cold stone, scrambling to get up.

From the boat I heard Glick holler, ''Jump, you damn fool!'' Then he was silenced for the moment by another shot from Bunker's rifle. Glick dropped down into the boat. I saw him haul up an anchor. I was too preoccupied with Franco to tell Bunker to stop firing. Why he was wasting his time with Glick was beyond me. Standing where he was, there was no chance he couldn't see us. I wondered why in hell he wasn't coming down to help me.

Franco and I didn't waste time or energy with words. All that came out of our mouths were bestial grunts of rage. While I clung to him with one arm I used the other to drive my fist into his kidneys. His boots lashed out at my shins and knees. I had to dodge his hands once or twice. His sharp nails were going for my eyes.

While I protected my peepers, his boot drove into my stomach. I let him go long enough to catch a painful breath. In the meantime he squirmed onto his knees. He was about to stand up when I grabbed his shoulders. Just before I dragged him back down, he leaned with all his weight over the ledge. His duster ripped apart in my grasp as he slipped into the river. It swallowed him in its silvery maw.

Glick was already rowing like mad to the west bank. A small rectangular object was barely afloat in his wake. It was swirling out to the center of the river.

I knew it was Jocko even before his terrified whimpers reached my ears.

Bunker kept firing at the boat intermittently. I started screaming at him.

"Stop firing, you idiot! I want them alive!"

By this time Nolan had joined him. He scrambled down the steps and said, "I'm sorry, Mack. I got here as fast as I could after the shots. Where are they?"

"One jumped into the river. The other's in that boat there. Go back up and get that rifle away from Bunker. I'm going after the dog and I don't want to get shot."

I dived into the Schuylkill.

It was so cold I cried out when I went under, swallowing water. I kicked to the surface and burst into the open air, hacking and spitting.

Nolan and Bunker were firing at a figure swimming toward the boat, way ahead of me. Both Glick and Franco were too far away for me to reach. They had the money sure enough, but I couldn't ignore the piteous yelping of the drowning dog.

It was bobbing just a few yards ahead of me. I swam a crude crawl toward it, keeping my head above the water so I didn't lose my sense of direction.

Kicking furiously I made the distance in a minute, just as the box dipped below the surface completely. My hand caught one of the wooden bars and hoisted it above water.

I took hold of the other side of the cage and held it in front of me while I kicked toward the gazebo. I had to fight against the tide. Once I nearly lost my grip on the cage as I tried to take a breath. The dog made no response. As soon as my knees brushed against the rocky surface of the ledge, I took the cage and threw it over. The first time I missed and Jocko fell back into the water, almost right on top of me. The second time I landed the cage at the foot of the stone steps. I clawed my way out of the water, my fingers and toes digging into the crevices of the wall. When I got to the ledge, I stood up and turned toward the west bank. I could no longer see the boat in which Glick and Franco were making their escape.

A wooden pin held the door of the cage in place. I unfastened it and lifted the wet furry object outside. He was heavier than I expected.

At first I thought the dog was dead. It lay on the earth without moving. The white of its eye showed.

But then I saw its midsection moving with the rhythm of breath. I patted its dark head and muzzle. The tail moved weakly. Jocko gave my hand a lick or two before Bunker got to us.

"Didya get 'em, McCleary?"

"Franco? No, he and Glick got away. Thanks to you, you bloody bastard. Why in hell were you firing at the boat? I told you we wanted them alive!"

"I'm sorry, McCleary. I guess I just lost my cool. I was thinkin' of what they done to Reddy. I wanted to make them pay."

"We could've gotten Franco, at least, we were fighting right under your damn nose!"

I was ready to kill him. But then I realized my anger was more for me than for him. It had been my fault that things had gone wrong. I could've gotten help from the Central Office. But I thought I could fight this one alone. I was wrong. Now it might cost a child his life.

Bunker stuttered a weak apology as Nolan clambered down the steps again. "They're all the way on the other side now, Mack. No chance of getting them. Boy, did we fuck this up!"

I ground my teeth together for a moment. Then I said, "Not completely. I did get someone back for you, Bunker."

I picked up Jocko and put him back in his master's arms.

Bunker collapsed to the ground and held the dog close to him, baby-talking it.

I almost laughed at the spectacle he made.

Leaning against the gazebo, I watched their happy reunion, partaking vicariously in their joy. For the first time in a few days I felt satisfied with something I'd done.

Then the excitement wore off and all the pain came back to me. My shins and neck hurt like mad. A massive headache pounded at my eyeballs. I wanted to just sit where I was for the next week or so.

Nolan said, "They headed under the Wire Bridge, last I saw of them. Could be anywhere."

"Forget it. They'll be hell and gone after to-night. They have more money than they know what to do with."

"You say they got a lot of money after to-night?" Bunker asked, still cradling his dog in his arms.

"Sure," I said. "Franco dropped the carpetbag right off there where the steps are." I made a gesture toward where I'd been fighting. "Glick fetched it from the boat. They're probably thinking of ways to spend it right now."

I was gloomy. I didn't know how they'd react, now that they had ten thousand dollars. Would they even bother trying to collect the ransom for Eddie Munroe? Or would they leave the city till things cooled down for them?

Would they get rid of Eddie? Giving him back to his parents was unthinkable. Most likely they would kill him.

Would they do it? Would it be my fault?

The anguish I felt about Eddie adumbrated my bodily pain.

"I don't think they'll get more than a side dish of oysters with what they got to-night," Bunker said. "Maybe a main dish, if they pawn the carpetbag."

"Huh?" I said.

"They didn't get no money to-night, McCleary. I didn't pay 'em no ransom."

"Whatta ya mean? I saw the carpetbag. I looked inside it. There were stacks of money there. Tons of them!"

"How well did you look, McCleary, huh?"

I admitted that I'd just glanced over the surface of the pile. But I was sure I saw stacks of crisp bills.

"Did you flip through those stacks?"

"No. Why bother?"

"Let me ask you a question. How well did that son of a bitch look at the money himself? Did he count it? Play with it?"

"No. The light was lousy and he probably didn't want to risk lighting a match or carrying a lantern. He just opened the bag and shut it."

"So he was satisfied with the surface, a few bills attached to a heap of stacks of what he thought were like bills. Just like you were satisfied, hmm?"

I was almost defensive. "Why wouldn't I be? It wasn't my money, Bunker."

"That's so. But it wasn't my money, either."

Nolan and I were dumbstruck.

"You ever hear of the ring drop, McCleary?"

"Sure. A confidence game. What does that have to do with anything?"

"That's what I did to-night. You ever fall for it? 'Course not. You're a copper. You been around. But I know some people who have. The variation I seen done is where two fellas drop a leather on the street and wait until somebody notices it and's about to pick it up. Then they make their move and say they'll split whatever's in there with the chump. They open the wallet and see this big roll of bills. The one confidence man asks the chump to give him whatever money he has on him already. This is for his pal who's supposed to be a lawyer and needs a deposit to go make things legal. They both tell the chump to wait while they get the papers filled out. The chump keeps the roll. Only after the two sharks have dusted out of there with a nice bit of real change does the chump examine the roll. Sees there's nothing under the top bill but cheap sheets of paper.''

"Why, you son of a bitch," I said. "You fleeced them."

Bunker's moustache curled under his cheeks as he smiled. " 'Course. You think I'm gonna be on the up-and-up with two pieces of shit who stole my dog and somebody else's boy? Plus killed Reddy? Ha!''

All this meant that they were more than likely to stick around and try to collect the money from Munroe. They weren't going to leave until that ten thousand dollars was in their pockets. And something told me they would play it for keeps this time. The boy was going to die unless they got their money.

"What do we do now, Mack?" Nolan asked me.

"Let's go back to my place and freshen up," Bunker said. "Y'all can sleep it off there if you like. Then we can go to City Hall in the morning and tell Heins all about it. McCleary, you done good to-night. You saved my dog and I'm ever grateful to ya. Believe me, Joe Bunker doesn't forget favors. And our deal still stands. For to-morrow night, I mean.''

"The classic?''

"You bet. I'll give you the ticket to-morrow morning. Wait'll you see what this sucker can do in a pit!''

As we climbed the stairs back toward the mount, I scanned the west bank for any sign of Glick and Franco. They had vanished, swallowed up in the night. And with them, my chance to get Eddie back.

Before we got to the carriage, I stopped to look at the stars again and listen to the mice scrambling beneath the grass. Something made me shiver, perhaps my wet clothes.

EARLY THE NEXT morning all three of us showed up on Chestnut Street. Cap was waiting for us in his office. As Nolan and I walked in, his mouth opened to bellow a curse. When Bunker followed us in, his trap shut with surprise.

"What brings you here this bright and early, Joe?"

"I came to thank you personally, William, for assigning this man to my case. We had quite a night. But the tall and short of it is, Jocko's back and your McCleary's the one who got him."

He told the whole story, making me look mighty good. I didn't let his praise get to my head. Encomiums from someone as powerful as he was always had a price.

I barely listened to what he was saying anyway. The memory of last night unsettled me. Not because we'd lost the kidnappers. That was my own bungling and I could accept that. But I wondered why Bunker had spent all his energy shooting at Glick and not helping me out with Franco. When Bunker finished his speech and smiled at me, I was almost afraid to meet his eyes. He might see the suspicion there.

Now it was my turn to talk and I realized I would have to come clean about the whole investigation. Before I could embarass myself more than the previous day, Cap asked, "This business at the waterworks have anything to do with Reddy getting shot at a Front Street slaughterhouse yesterday afternoon?''

He wanted to surprise us. Bunker merely bowed his head. We remained silent. Cap got impatient and filled the silence with another question, ''Or with some harness thief with a sprained arm in the Pennsylvania Hospital?''

For the first time that morning I looked into his eyes. They were hard to read. Cap's whole face was placid, bland. He was waiting for me to speak my piece.

''It does. And it doesn't.'' I hesitated, not wanting Bunker to hear the truth about Reddy.

''Go on, you're among friends,'' Cap said.

''Reddy knew the men who kidnapped Jocko. Knew what they looked like, where they lounged about when they weren't peddling Rat-Oh, all that. He kept quiet because he wanted to blackmail them, get a piece of the pie from the ransom.''

I stopped and looked at Bunker. His face wore a curious expression, like someone who'd just had to swat a cockroach with his hand.

''But then Reddy heard something in the paper that made him send for me.''

''What was that?''

''Reddy heard the description of the men who'd kidnapped Eddie Munroe. They were the same men.''

Cap fumbled in his desk drawer. He pulled out a long segar, chewed the bit off, and spat it in his cuspidor. With a match he lit it and started puffing. Then he leaned back in his seat and said, ''All right. Let's hear it, McCleary. All of it this time.''

He listened for a good fifteen minutes, interrupting every now and then to clarify a point or to ask a question. But I still hadn't told him everything. For some reason, I'd left out Leah Munroe.

When the story was told, Cap said, ''Joe, you ever heard of these men?''

''Never.''

''Well, how you think they know who you are?''

"I'm a politician, William. People are supposed to know who I am."

"They weren't interested in Bunker the politician. They knew you as a ratter. How do you figure that?"

"I been ratting in this city since I was a lad. And I get around with the dogs, you know. Jersey, York, Delaware. Plus all the matches we fight right here in the Quaker City. Reddy, God rest his soul, and I been building up a reputation for years."

"I know. You done mighty well with the dogs. Enough to make people jealous. Different kinds of people. Owners, trainers, breeders, any sport who lost a pile betting against Jocko or Cindy."

"Hell, that ain't my fault."

"I'm not sayin' it is. All I'm sayin' is I think it's people who are in the sporting world. This Glick and Franco."

"But I told you already, I don't know 'em!"

"That doesn't matter. They know you. They also know you played them for fools. And from the way they've been acting ... well, anything could still happen."

"You trying to say my life's in danger?"

"Could be. They might not take too kindly to what you pulled last night."

I saw a new emotion on Bunker's face. Fear.

"We gotta find these men," he said, after nearly choking on his chewing tobacco.

"Last night McCleary almost had 'em."

He looked at me like I was one of the many flies buzzing around the windows.

"Then he let 'em go. Now, if he'd taken the time to brief me on the status of his investigation, we might have had men all over the waterworks last night. Plus the Harbor police. He would've collared them for sure."

After a pause he said, "Boys would you mind if I talked with Detective McCleary in private?"

They shuffled out of there. I remained standing. Cap came up right to my face.

''You think you're one fly cop, don't you?''

I said nothing. There was no time. His fist slammed into my bread basket with no warning. Then it lifted my jaw.

I fell back on the table. My eyes were getting watery.

Words came seething out of Cap's taut lips. ''One fly cop, my ass. You blew the whole fucking thing to smithereens last night. You and that pighead of yours. We coulda had 'em!''

His fingers clutched at the air like talons.

''And you thought you could handle it by yourself, didn't ya? Why tell Heins, huh? Why tell anyone? General U.S. McCleary to the rescue! Huh?

''Listen, I trusted you. I thought you trusted me. I don't give a shit about your problems with Diefenderfer or anybody else. When I tell you to do something, you do it. You got information you don't wanna give to him, you give it to me. Understand? I always liked your pride, McCleary. Ever since you were a bluebelly back in sixty-six I liked your pride. And your pluck.

''But I'm not gonna let that pride mess things up with the Munroe kid. And the department. And me. I got the mayor breathing down my neck, the press yapping at me whenever I leave this office to go to the latrine, and I even got my own wife saying every night, 'When are you gonna get the Munroe kid back?'

''Plus I have to worry about these scamps going after Joe now.''

He threw up his arms in supplication.

''No wonder you made a lousy soldier. You think you can fight alone.''

That hurt. It was meant to. Cap knew all about my prison experience.

I wanted to kill him right then. Crush his old bones to powder. The way I was gritting my teeth, I thought I might snap them in two.

Then the anger abated and my fists unclenched. After a few deep breaths I knew why.

Cap was right.

I didn't want to admit it to myself, but there it was, in my head.

And the worst part was that even though I knew he was right, I still wanted to fight alone.

There was no way for me to help it. That need was like a scar on my soul, burned in there years ago.

I couldn't give him what he wanted. Or what he thought I needed. But I asked him, ''What do you want me to do?''

Cap sat on the edge of his desk scrutinizing me, his arms folded across his vest. He took a few deep breaths himself and said, ''Come with me to Germantown. Something's happened.''

''What? Is anybody hurt?''

''Not yet. Munroe got another letter. Just arrived this morning. The Germantown Station House wired us. The mayor and just about everybody else agrees he should refuse to pay. So we're going over there to make him see our point of view.''

''You're going?''

''I'm representing the mayor. Let's go get Nolan.''

''What about Bunker?''

''Forget about Bunker. He can take care of himself. Anyway, he's got a lot of work to do to get that dog of his in shape for to-night.''

''You think Jocko will be able to fight?''

''He damn well better. I got a few cans bet on him. Oh, he wanted me to give this to you.''

Cap slipped me a piece of paper with a steamer's name on it and where it would depart from that night. It was an invitation to the rat classic, signed *From Joe, with my heartfelt thanks*.

We left Cap's office. I was confused. I went over the past few days and examined my motives for each action. They were as confused as I was.

My mind was still reeling when we got to the street and climbed in a carriage.

*   *   *

The Munroe house looked like a fort on the frontier. Men in blue stood guard at every portal.

The sheep dog was off the porch steps. I heard him out back, barking up a storm. From the street I saw Stephen there, too, throwing something for the dog to catch.

Franco had gone right over that stone wall there. I could see in my mind's eye the stolen carriage from Bucks County parked on the street, waiting like a patient predator. I looked behind me at the lot where the boys were playing when the abduction occurred. In my imagination it happened again. And I was powerless to stop it this time as well.

A few days ago Glick and Franco were right where I was standing. Very close. Irrationally, I kept expecting them to show up while I waited there.

The other coppers followed us when we went inside. The rest of the detectives were waiting in the parlor. Leah was seated at the parlor organ bench. In her mourning dress, trimmed in crêpe, she looked ready to play a dirge. A few of the detectives watched her askance. She took no notice of them or anything. Her index finger tapped at the organ keys but no sound came out. She went on tapping.

Archibald was watching Stephen from the window. The sunlight streaming through the lace curtains didn't detract from the somber atmosphere.

Cap said, "Everyone here?"

Archibald turned at his voice. A halfhearted smile creased his face when he saw me. He approached us, shaking first Cap's hand, then my own.

Leah turned when her husband called my name. Our eyes met. Then hers shifted from me to her husband and back to me.

The way her eyes flickered told me Archibald didn't know about what had happened at the slaughterhouse, or afterward. And she wanted to keep it that way. I saw no reason to go against her wishes—at least for now. There were still a lot of questions I needed to ask her. But they could wait. I wanted to ask them when we were alone. If she had secrets, I wanted to be the one to hear them.

Our silent communication ended abruptly when her gaze strayed behind me. Whatever she saw there made her get up and leave the parlor. I watched her skirt trail over the carpeted stairs leading to the upper floor. Looking back all I saw was Nolan and another dick just coming in, talking up a storm.

Cap began the briefing.

"Before I get started I want to present to you, Mr. Munroe, the full amount of the ransom, donated by an anonymous citizen. He told me he wished he could do more for you and your son."

Archibald, stunned, looked at the carpetbag full of money. Then his gaze turned inward. Something like loathing appeared on his sallow face. The rest of the detectives didn't catch it. They tried to encourage him by saying, "Well, now, no more worrying about that."

But Archibald didn't seem to hear them. Cap went on.

"We've been at this for two days now and turned up nothing but a lot of false pointers and cranks. According to the reports, Eddie Munroe's shown his face in two hundred forty-three different places, from San Francisco to Saskatchewan, always with shady-looking Eye-talian characters who barely meet our descriptions. A few of the sightings in our city Mr. Munroe here has had to sort out. We can only imagine his heartbreak when, on arriving downtown, he finds yet again it's a false alarm.

"Two days and we've got nothing. I was about ready to start a full-scale search of every building in the entire city. Until some intelligence reached me to-day about the identity of the kidnappers."

Chattering erupted among the dicks. They threw all kinds of questions and speculations at each other and at Cap. I kept mum, hoping Cap wouldn't bring my name into it.

Sure enough, he did.

"Detective McCleary's the one who gets the credit here. While working on another case he came across witnesses who saw the men in a vehicle identical to the one used to abduct the children.''

I sighed with relief when he ended my involvement with that. No need to tell them I let Glick and Franco escape. Twice.

"Their names are Glick and Franco. They peddle stuff called Rat-Oh, for poisoning rats. They're also sneak thieves. Ring a bell with anyone?''

The dicks started chattering again. The housekeeper Minnie had to shout above the din they made.

"You say Rat-Oh?''

"That's right. Why?''

" 'Cause I bought some o' that stuff a few weeks ago.'' The woman looked scared, like she was about to confess complicity.

Everybody got quiet then.

"Who'd you buy it from?'' Cap asked her.

"There was two men. One colored, the other white.''

"Was the white man swarthy? Curly hair, short beard, nice teeth?''

Her eyes lit up on the last detail. "That's the one! He and this colored fella axed me whether we had a rat problem. I told 'em most do, out these ways. If not rats, some other kinda critter.''

"They ask you anything else?''

"Not that I can recall. Just sold me the stuff and left.''

"Did you ask them inside?''

"No, I kept 'em on the porch. Missus don't like peddlers comin' inside, disturbin' her. I told 'em to unload the stuff out by the shed. In fact, Stephen was playin' out there. He mighta helped them.''

"Was Eddie also by the shed that day?'' I asked.

"No, I don't think so. He and the missus was to the doctor.''

"How long were they out back?''

"Coulda been a while. I was busy with dustin'.''

Cap asked her, "When did this all occur?''

"Musta been about three weeks ago. I didn't think nothin' of it, they was so polite and all. I never seen 'em round here before, but I figured they's just out makin' a livin'. That Rat-Oh stuff worked, too.'' She seemed on the defensive.

Diefenderfer shouted at her, "Why didn't you tell me this two days ago?"

"Like I said," she whined, "I didn't think nothin' of it. Just two peddlers. We gets 'em all the time."

"So now we have a third kidnapper to look for," Diefenderfer said, exasperated.

"No, you don't. I shot him yesterday."

He looked at me like I was a talking gorilla. Then he turned to Cap. "What's he talkin' about? And what's he doin' here? I thought we had an agreement!"

"He's been put back on. By me. McCleary's the one who got the names and everything else we have. While working on another case, like I said. This colored fella, one Albert Johnson, was a part of that case."

"That's swell. Did it occur to you to question the man before you killed him?"

I was ready to take a swipe at him. Cap held me back and said, "McCleary was defending his life. That's settled, as far as I'm concerned. We won't get any further bellyaching about it. All that matters is we know now the men were here. Well before the kidnapping."

"Maybe Stephen can tell us some more about it," one of the other detectives said.

"That's a good idea," Cap said. "Mr. Munroe, why don't you have the boy brought in here while you read the letter?"

"Certainly, Captain. Minnie, go fetch Stephen."

The woman departed, downcast. I felt sorry for her. There was no way any of us could have known Johnson was a part of it until yesterday. Glick had been absent or sneaking around the house while they'd distracted her. If he had come to the door she'd have remembered it well.

"Now," Cap said, addressing everyone in the room. "Mr. Munroe received this letter in yesterday's mail. It was postmarked from the city again. The handwriting's as queer as the last one, almost like a child's. Mr. Munroe, you go ahead.''

Archibald cleared his throat and started reading.

Phil., July 2—Munroe: yur actions this day desides Eddie's fate—it is left with you alone wether he shall live or die. You are to take the 12 a.m. train to-night from West Phila for New York it arrives New York 5 A.M. take a cab at Cortland or Disbrosser Sts New York, an ride directly to the Grand Central Station at 4 ave and 42d streets. take the 8 A.M. northern express by way of Hudson River (take notice) you are to stand on the rear car and the rear plat form, from the time you leave west phila depot until you arrive at Jersey City—you are then to stand on the rear plat form of Hudson River car from the time you leave the Grand Centeral at New York until you arrive at Albany. You may not go one mile before our agent meets you or you may go 250. These are the signals: the moment the rear car passes him he wil exhibit a bright torch in one hand an a white flag in the other. The instant you see this signal drop the money on the track and you may get out at the next station. If the cars continue on their course we consider you have kept your word an yur child shal be returned you safe but if they stop to arrest our agent then yur childs fate is sealed.

Torture. That was what it sounded like to me. Archibald would ride all through the night, never knowing when the signal might come. That kind of suspense would break him. And there was no guarantee they would return the boy. I knew the kind of men Glick and Franco were.

"So this is it," Cap said. "If we don't get 'em tonight then we've lost the battle *and* the war. I want all of you on that train. One whole car of policemen, in plainclothes. I'm coming with you. The instant anybody sees a torch anywhere, we stop the car and give chase.''

''But the letter says explicitly . . .'' Archibald protested.

''Hang the letter! You don't make deals with men like this! I know they got your boy, Mr. Munroe, and we're gonna do everything in our power to get him back to you safe and sound. But the best way to do that is to collar these men. We have no way of knowing the boy will come out of it alive, even if you do pay the money.''

The skin of Archibald's cheeks was drawn in, like he was biting the inside. He was fighting hard to keep back the tears.

''The first we see of this 'agent' we grab him and make him talk. And he will talk. Won't he?''

The more sadistic detectives smiled.

''We're gonna be at the depot to-night well beforehand. I want all of you there, working the crowds. It might be these men'll show up to make sure things are square. Might even go on the train if we're really lucky.''

It wasn't much of a way to spend Independence Day. A few of the dicks grumbled about the extra duty.

Cap drew me aside for a moment and said, ''All of us are goin' to-night except you, McCleary. You stick close to Joe. Just in case one of them shows up on that end. And if he does, you make sure you get him alive this time, understand me?''

I promised I would.

I felt let down. The main action was going to take place on the way to New York. I would not be a part of that, after all I had been through.

The end of the case. I wanted to be there for it, wanted to put my fists to Franco's pretty teeth.

But I was back to where I'd started. With Jocko. In the rat pit.

Maybe it was what I deserved. For not telling what I knew when it might have helped.

At least Bunker's offer still stood. The extra money

would come in handy. And I wouldn't lose anything if the dog lost.

Despite the consolation, I was depressed. I had come to like Archibald and wanted to be there with him, especially to-night. He would need someone to talk to.

The crowd of detectives had split into little factions by now. All of them were discussing plans for to-night and what they would do when they caught Glick or Franco. Nolan whistled to himself in a corner by the photograph-littered mantel. That was a sure sign he was puzzling something out. He hit a wrong note and said, "Hey, Captain. What did you say the names of those men were? Not the colored one, but the other two?"

"Franco. And Glick. Why, you heard of them?"

"The first one, yeah. Not the second one. At least, I think so."

"Tell me."

We surrounded him, breathless.

"This was a while ago, when I was still on the beat. There was this gagger I ran up against once or twice. Used his wife in a badger game but rented her out other nights. Spent all the money she made him on the dog and rat fights they had in the saloon back of the station house. I pinched him one time. He was smacking his wife around, right on the street in broad daylight. Kicked me in the nuts on the way to the station house. Had a headache for hours."

"What's this have to do with anything?" I said to him.

"I'm gettin' to that. I just wanted you to understand why I might remember this fella. This gagger was known around the neighborhood as Dago Frank. That name Franco sounds foreign to me. And the descriptions match. It could be the same man."

"Why didn't you tell me this last night?" I said.

"I didn't have much time to think about it. But just this morning . . . I don't know, something musta jarred my memory."

"This is very good, Nolan. What I want you to do is

get off your tail and head back into the city to the Central Office. We must have records of this Dago Frank. Find them. Find out where he holes up, or used to. How long ago did you say you knew him?''

"Oh, boy. This was when I was with the Reserves. Year before the War ended. Sixty-four.''

"Go find him,'' Cap said.

Dago Frank and Franco. The man I'd seen at the waterworks the previous night had had the look of a gagger, a man who lived off whoring his wife. Plus Franco was a Spanish name.

Nolan left us, excited, humming an Irish ballad. As he was going out the front door, Minnie came through the kitchen into the parlor. She told Archibald, "That boy. He don't pay me no mind. I think you're gonna hafta fetch him.''

"I'll go with you,'' I told him.

As we walked outside Archibald said to me, "You're not coming with us to-night.''

"No. You talked to Cap?''

"Yes. I asked for you to come especially. I don't see why we need to have every detective in Philadelphia on that train. It might scare them off.''

"We already have one man who may be able to recognize Franco. Your chances of getting whoever collects the money are much better this way.''

"They still might be recognized by the kidnappers. Isn't that possible?''

"Sure it is. But right now I don't think you have much choice but to go along with Captain Heins. I think he's right. You don't know that they'll ever give Eddie back to you. Remember, Eddie can identify them.''

I didn't want to go on from there. Archibald looked piqued enough as it was.

"These crazy directions they've given me. I could be waiting all night for them to flash that torch, at any point from Philadelphia to New York! How much anguish do they want to put me through?''

I shook my head. The directions sounded well thought

out. There was no way to plan ahead. They had complete
control. Archibald and all the detectives would be well
out of the city for the whole night. All except me. I'd
be on a riverboat watching rats get chomped to pieces.

Just as I was thinking on Jocko, I heard the Munroes'
sheepdog. What started as a bark turned into a yelp, the
kind dogs make when they're afraid or in pain. Archibald and I hurried outside to see what was the matter.

The first thing I saw was Stephen. He had a stick in
his hand, the same stick the sheepdog was fetching when
I pulled up. But he wasn't throwing it anymore. He was
beating the dog with it, viciously.

The animal kept yelping with every lick it got. It was
trapped, tied to a clothesline stretching between two
trees. The sheepdog ran back and forth, trying to elude
its tormentor. Stephen followed, lashing out whenever
he could.

Archibald hollered at him, "Stephen! Stop that! Stop
it this instant!"

The boy turned to us, laughing. For a moment he
looked like an idiot child, with glazed eyes and a mirthless smile.

His father snatched the stick from his hands and broke
it across his knees.

"What do you think you're doing? What kind of a
way is that to behave?"

The boy's first reaction was to cower like the dog at
his feet. Then he straightened his posture and said, "We
were only playing."

"You call beating a dumb animal senseless *playing*?"

"He doesn't mind, do you, Freddy?" The dog backed
away from Stephen's hand, tail between its legs.

"Stephen, how many times do I have to tell you to
leave that dog be? He never did you any harm. You can't
just hit him for no reason."

"Why not?"

"Because it's wrong. Now, tell Freddy you're sorry."

Stephen mumbled an apology. The idiotic smile
faded. Other expressions and emotions to match them

flashed across his face. As if aware that I was watching, he lowered his head.

"Stephen, do you remember Detective McCleary? The man who pulled you out of the fire?"

His head bobbed up and down.

"Well, he'd like to ask you a few questions. So listen to him carefully."

"Stephen," I said, "do you remember two peddlers coming to the house about three weeks ago? One was colored and the other white. They were selling rat poison, called Rat-Oh. Minnie told them to bring the Rat-Oh to the shed. She thought you might be playing there. Were you?"

"Yes. Freddy and I were playing. When he saw the men, he ran up sniffing them like they were the best of friends. He's a terrible guard dog."

The boy petted the dog with real affection now, gently stroking his furry ears.

"So you spoke to these men?"

"No. I didn't see them."

"But you just told me you saw Freddy sniffing them."

"I mean, I didn't talk to them. They came up and put some sacks in the shed."

"And they said nothing to you?"

"No. They left us alone."

"How long were they there, unloading the sacks?"

"Not long. They just dumped the sacks and left."

"Did you overhear any conversation between them? Did they talk about your dad, or mom, or Eddie?"

The boy shook his head. "Is that all you wanted to ask me?" he asked breathlessly.

"I guess so."

"Can I go inside now? I've got my lesson with Mommy."

"Mommy has to go into the city this morning, Stephen. Why don't you help me with weeding those flowerbeds?"

"I don't wanna."

Archibald took the rejection hard. His whole expression sagged.

"Why don't you go ahead, Stephen?" I said. I put a hand on his shoulder, turning him toward the flowerbeds behind the house. He stiffened at my touch. I let go of him automatically. The boy walked to the flowerbeds and silently began to rip dandelions and crab grass out of the dirt.

His father watched him, shaking his head.

"I'm sorry about that, McCleary. Stephen has been acting this way ever since Eddie was taken. He's hurt and frightened more than any of us, I think."

As I made to go back inside, he said to me, "I suppose I'll go to the city well before midnight, maybe six or so. My place of business isn't too far from the depot. Might even have dinner at the oyster bar there. I know you're not coming with us, but I'd appreciate your company, if you can manage it. We can share some oysters."

The poor man needed someone to take his mind off what he had to do, and what he might or might not get out of it. I said, "I'll see you there at seven."

I gave him a pat on the back and walked into his house. Minnie was fussing about the kitchen.

"Might as well forget about dinner for to-night," I said.

"I know. Here I made a roast and there won't be no one to eat it."

"Even if they were here, they probably wouldn't have much of an appetite."

I was just about to step out of the kitchen when I remembered something that was in the back of my mind.

"By the way, Minnie, how long did you say Franco and Johnson were out back unloading the sacks of poison?"

"Well, I don't know, exactly. Like I said, I was dustin' the parlor."

The way she avoided my eyes told me she was hiding something. I decided to press for it.

"You don't know exactly," I repeated. "But I don't

think it's because you were dusting the parlor.''

Her eyes darted to the room where the rest of the men were still mulling over the case. Behind my back I heard the front door open and close, very softly. Leah's back was turned to me as she stepped out, with a parcel in her hands. I wondered where she was going in such a hurry. And whether or not it had to do with overhearing us just now.

"I can't say, Mister. I *can't*."

"Can't say what?"

My hands gripped her arms, pressing them into her sides.

"Please, you're hurting me."

For an instant I wanted to press harder, break the information out of her. But I let go of her and said, "You're trying to protect someone? Look what comes of it. You want Eddie back or not?"

Minnie was sobbing. "I didn't do nothin'. I just promised to keep my mouth shut about it. I shoulda never said nothin'. But I had to, understand? When I heard you men talk about them peddlers I just had to say somethin'!"

"Tell me the rest, Minnie. You can trust me. I want Eddie back as much as anybody."

I projected every ounce of sincerity in me at her watery brown eyes. It made the desired impression.

Drawing me even further from the parlor, she whispered to me, "I was dustin' the parlor, like I said. But it was mighty hot that day. So I sat down on the sofa for a rest. This was right after I sent the men back to the shed where Stephen was. I know he was there, I saw him. In fact, I told him to help those men put the sacks in the shed. Then I guess I must've dozed off. The clock there woke me up, strikin' the half hour. When those men called it was strikin' three, just as I went to the door.

"I got up quick 'cause Missus was comin' back soon and I had a lot of things to do. I went to the window and saw that one of the men, the white one, was still there. He was just comin' out of the shed and walkin' fast around the side of the house. The colored man was waitin' in the wagon. I was too worried about gettin' everything in order to wonder what took them so long with their unloadin'. I did make sure he wasn't takin' none of Mr. Munroe's tools.

"They were gone by the time Missus come home. She asked me where was Stephen, and I told her last I saw of him he was in the shed, helpin' the men unload the sacks of poison."

"Did you tell her what kind of poison?"

"I mentioned the name. Said I bought some out of her purse for the pantry."

"Then what happened?"

"She went out to the shed. She was there for a mighty long time. Maybe fifteen minutes. When she come back in with Stephen, she sent him right up to his room. Then she said to me, Minnie, don't you be tellin' no one 'bout them men who came to-day. You just forget about them. Made me swear on the Good Book, too. And now I done broke my promise."

I took her gnarled hand and squeezed it.

"I think you'll be forgiven. Now I want you to promise me something. Forget we ever had this conversation. At least for a while. Okay?"

"I'd like to, that's for sure."

"Good. Would you mind telling Captain Heins and Mr. Munroe I'm leaving?"

"Sure. Can I get your hat?"

"I'll get it, thanks. Can you tell me where Mrs. Munroe went?"

"Don't know where she gone to."

I thanked her and ran out the door. Down the street I saw one of our carriages heading south, toward Philadelphia. I asked the driver of the other one, "Where'd they go?"

"Went back to the Central Office, I think. Took the lady with them."

"Listen, how about taking me back in, too? Right behind them?"

"What am I gonna do about the rest of the men inside?"

I didn't think Cap'd take too kindly to my stranding him in Germantown.

I ran to the back of the house where Munroe's phaeton was hitched up. I grabbed the reins and headed for the street.

"Tell Munroe I borrowed his phaeton. Very important business."

I left the driver coughing in a cloud of dust.

Ahead of me the police carriage was barely visible. I urged the horse on, trying to shorten the distance.

I was shadowing Leah Munroe. She and that parcel weren't going to leave my sights.

I had an idea where they would lead me.

Right to Franco and Glick. And Eddie.

14

TRAFFIC GOING INTO the city was heavy and slow. I saw two accidents happen when drivers tried making a new lane and failed. The first time, a wagon tipped over on the sidewalk and sent bottles of milk flying everywhere. The second time, a buggy made the mistake of cutting in front of a streetcar. The streetcar driver pulled the brake, descended from his seat, and, with the usual prelude of oaths, held an amateur pugilism match with the buggy driver.

The open phaeton didn't give me any cover so I had to lag behind, watching the carriage navigate through the huddled streets. It didn't seem to be in any particular hurry. Each time it paused at an intersection I waited for Leah to get off. But she didn't. Not until we reached the corner of Eighth and Market.

I left the phaeton at the corner, showing the bull directing traffic my star and telling him to keep an eye on the horse and carriage.

She was going up Eighth Street. There was a horde of morning shoppers out, wandering beneath the awnings hung from every storefront. Above the awnings wooden animals perched like gargoyles over signs advertising every kind of business under the sun. An ostrich drew your eye to the drapery store it guarded, while its neighbor, a beautifully painted elephant, boosted a

printing office. Furniture company eagles presided over
the thoroughfare from the other side of the street, like
figureheads on a permanently beached ship.

I pretended to absorb myself in a shop window, ob-
serving Leah's reflection in the glass. A boy tugged at
my coat and asked me if I wanted to buy a chocolate
bar. I figured he'd probably stolen the box from a wagon
or the back of a store. But I gave him the exorbitant
nickel he was asking for.

Leah herself did not stop until she reached a haber-
dashery, where she glanced up at the address and stood
for a moment, immobile. Then she headed south, back
toward where we came from. For a moment I watched
her step through the crowds. Her back was arched and
she leaned slightly forward in that fashionable Grecian
curve brought on by her bustle and corset. The posture
ornamented her stride, drawing attention to the movement of her hips. I wasn't the only one staring at her as
she made her way toward Market Street.

When she got there, she passed right by the seductive
shop windows of the new Strawbridge and Clothier store
and braved the intersection. I passed the traffic cop and
he gave me a nod. The phaeton was still where I'd left
it.

It was easy to lose myself in the crowds at this time
of day. But Leah wasn't looking. She stared ahead of
her, moving swiftly. The parcel was still in her hands.

She stopped in front of a small tavern, wedged between two taller and more modern buildings. It was a
grimy old half house, the first story extending just short
of the insurance company beside it. There was enough
space between them for a tiny alley. A gutter ran from
underneath the alley door to the street. Water trickled
through it, with a tincture of blood. Beneath the wood-
shingled roof was a tiny attic window. For an instant I
thought I saw something move, a child's face. At least,
that was what I wanted to see.

The sign beneath the ground floor window read, JAS.
BOYLEN'S BOTTLEING CELLAR. FOR PORTER ALE & CIDER

OF THE BEST QUALITY. EMPTY BOTTLES BOUGHT HERE.

The place where Reddy had delivered messages to the kidnappers. I had planned to visit it anyway during the course of the day. And here was Leah Munroe, leading me right to the front door.

It was no coincidence.

Peering through the window, I saw a few men clustered around two long tables, eating oysters and drinking. Leah walked right to the bar stand and handed the parcel to the beerslinger there. He shook his head and pointed toward a side door. She stepped into the alley. I waited for a few minutes on the doorstep of the neighboring patent office, hoping there wasn't another exit from the alley. Finally she came out, sans parcel.

I watched her go back toward Market. I was torn between shadowing her to see if she went anywhere else and staying with the parcel. I was too interested in its contents to follow Leah. That was the excuse I gave myself.

A lady didn't go calling on a tavern like Boylen's. It was a politician's place. One of the centers of the sporting world in Philadelphia. Faro tables were out every night and dog fights were held each Thursday. Ratting matches, too.

I walked inside, catching stares from the seated men. I recognized one of them from a political rally I was forced to attend several months before. I assumed his cohorts were politicians like he was. They were telling a joke to one of their number as I passed them. The punchline had something to do with a biological function. They thought it quite funny.

The beerslinger said to me, "What can I get ya?"

"You Boylen?"

"Nah. He's out back with the dogs. What can I do for ya?"

"Business. I'm a friend of Joe Bunker's."

The name meant something to him. He said respectfully, "Just take that door there."

I stepped into the alley, slipping in the gutter leading

to the street. When I got back behind the tavern, a dog smell hit me like a slung shot.

The odor came from a dozen wooden pits set along the back of the alley. A man and a young boy stood in front of them. The boy had a fox terrier pup in his arms. From its size, the animal was maybe half a year old. At their feet was a large pit, its four wooden planks clamped together with metal clasps. Something was scraping at them from the inside.

The man said, "Okay. Now watch. I'm going to put 'em in now."

He lifted a sack over the wooden walls and tipped it. As he did so, I noticed Leah's parcel set on an empty kennel to his side.

"Okay. Drop him in!"

They waited for a moment. The dog barked from behind the walls. His owners urged him on.

"Good boy! Go get 'im! Get 'im, boy!"

After a snarl there was silence.

"Get the tongs."

The boy took up a pair of tongs much like those Reddy had made for the Edgerton boys. He drew a rat from the pit. It was dead, leaking a little blood.

"Toss it on the pile there."

The tongs released their catch over a barrel. The rat fell in, making no sound against the wood. There must have been a lot more in there to cushion the fall. Blood leaked out from the bottom, flowing through the drain to the street.

Both man and boy leaned over the walls and petted the dog. Then the man reached over and picked it up. As he held him in his arms, stroking his ears, he turned around. When he saw me there staring at him, he said, "What can I do for ya?"

"I'm a friend of Joe Bunker's."

I tried to keep my eyes off the parcel and on him. When he smiled at me, I noticed a couple of teeth were missing. He put the dog down and told the boy, "Go put the muzzle on him and take him out. Don't bring him back till he goes, hear?''

"Okay, Pa.''

The man scratched his scant red hair and extended a hand.

"Pleased to meet ya. I'm Boylen. So Joe told you to come over here, huh? Well, you ain't the first he steered my way. Let me tell ya, I got the best damn dogs you can hope for. At reasonable prices, too. That one there, Buddy? He's a real hellion. I bet he'll be takin' ten rats out within a week.''

"Well, can I take a look at the ones you got back there?''

"Sure! Sure! I was just about to feed 'em.''

We moved over to the wooden pits. It was hard to ignore the smell. I tried breathing through my mouth. I couldn't help coughing.

Boylen said, "Smell gets to you, huh? You haven't done any ratting before, have ya?''

It sounded like an accusation. I admitted I hadn't.

"Well, I understand. See, the smell doesn't bother me. Like the smell of my Pa's farm didn't bother him none. He had a big farm in Chester County.'' He added inconsequentially, "My brother got it now.

"These are all from the same litter. My dog Daisy's. Y'ever heard of her? What am I talkin' about? If you know Bunker, he musta told you about Daisy. Gave Jocko a run for his money a few months ago. I was mighty proud of her.''

Beside some stacks of old bottles a very small pit was erected, with a tiny pup inside.

"This is how we feed 'em.''

Boylen took a fleshy bone and dropped it in the pit. The dog attacked it with aplomb.

"They gotta gnaw the meat right off that bone. Helps strengthen their teeth.''

I nodded. I was trying to figure out how to bring the parcel into the conversation. For the moment I decided to keep pretending I wanted to buy a ratting dog.

I noticed there was a rat scurrying around in the pit with the puppy.

"Why doesn't it attack that rat?"

"I haven't trained him to yet. The rat's there just so he gets used to 'em. Some dogs are more scared of rats than the other way around."

"Doesn't it bite the dog?"

"Naw. I knocked its teeth out. You do that with every pup's first rat. Otherwise the pup'd get scared of the bite. That's one thing it can't be afraid of, cause they get bit up plenty in the pit. Now, look at this one here. See, he's a little older, so I gotta do this."

Boylen withdrew the lone rat from the pit. The dog started barking.

"He wants his food, see? He knows the rat has to go before he gets his food."

Then we moved to a third pit and lowered a rat to the dog there.

"This one's two months old. That rat there's got his upper jaw. So he bites. And Bud knows it. He won't get too close to it. Will ya, Bud?"

Bud snapped his teeth on the rodent's head and squeezed. The thing twittered and died after the dog shook it a few times. Boylen threw the dog a large fleshy bone and took out the carcass.

"My dogs get the best victuals. Gives 'em fighting spirit! You gotta give them fresh, raw meat, so they get the taste for flesh. Rat flesh. You ever try it?"

"Try what?"

"Rat."

"No. Can't say I have."

"Tastes like chicken."

"No kidding."

"At least, that's what I hear."

"All these dogs are novices." He waved his hands at the dozen miniature rat pits. "They stay that way until they're about two years old. Now I got a few two-year-olds back at the homestead. You wanna come over and take a look at them this afternoon?"

I mumbled something and changed the subject.

"You do a good business, training ratting dogs?"

"Yessir. As if I didn't do well enough with the tavern. But every man has his passion."

"Bunker is certainly passionate about that Jocko of his."

Boylen agreed without emphasizing the point. Then he said, "Can't wait to see him to-night."

I said, "Some of my other friends are just as excited by ratting as Bunker. Maybe you heard of them—Glick and Franco?"

"I know a lot of ratters," he said noncommitally.

"Oh, really? You know Glick? He's a swell fella."

"Don't think I know him."

"Or Franco?" I was looking at that parcel now.

Boylen's eyes twitched when I said Franco's name. He tried to stifle it but did a messy job.

"That name sounds familiar. I don't know." He was getting pretty suspicious. He'd been around dogs so long he had gained their acute sense of smell. I smelled like the law through and through. Boylen caught the scent.

"Hey, listen—I'm busy right now. Got a lot of things to do. Why don't you come back tomorrow?"

"I thought you wanted to sell me a dog."

"I changed my mind. Now beat it."

He was holding the tongs tightly. The muscles in his arm were standing out.

"Go on, you heard me."

When I didn't move, he made the mistake of taking a swipe at me.

I sidestepped and kicked him in the gut. He dropped the tongs and fell to his knees, gasping.

I was getting mighty tired of people threatening me. Anger had been building in me for quite some time. Boylen was unlucky enough to be around when I finally lost my cool.

While he was still on his knees I picked up the tongs and stepped behind him. I wedged his neck between the metal rods and put on the pressure. Boylen kept gasping.

"Franco. Or a broken neck. Your choice."

When the gargling noises he made started to approximate words I let up, just a bit.

Then, just when he thought a little relief was coming, I squeezed even harder.

His face was turning blue when I released him. He put his head to the ground like a Mohammedan, coughing and wheezing.

I wanted to hit him for making me do it. The anger was gone now. I felt a little sick at the way I'd purged it.

"All right, Boylen. Talk to me."

I brought him a bottle of his own cider. He gulped it down and started.

"I'll tell ya, I swear. Just lay off me, please. For Christ's sake."

He took another drink and said, "You're not gonna kill me, are ya?"

"Why would I do that?"

"You Bunker's man?"

"No. I want Franco. That's it. Now tell me what you know."

"First time I saw him was last week. He came out back while I was feeding the pups and introduced himself. Said he came to me first cause he knew my reputation."

"Came to you for what?"

"With an offer. First he tried to sell me this rat poison stuff he and his pal were peddling. I told him I didn't have any use for it. Then he asked me if I'd heard about Bunker's dog Jocko. I said no. He said Bunker'd lost his dog. And he knew where it was. Bunker ain't gonna hear this, is he?"

"I might forget about it if you tell me everything. Keep going."

"So this fella says how would I like to breed Jocko with one of my bitches? Well, I didn't know what to say. Everybody knows Jocko's the best. I think every ratter from here to Boston would like a few pups from him. Bunker'll let you do it, too. For a charge. A very expensive charge.''

''You agreed to Franco's proposal?''

''Whatta ya think? Of course I did. How many times do ya think Bunker's beaten my dogs in the pit? And everybody else's, too? I lost a lot of money to him over the years. So I saw my chance to get a little of it back. And it didn't hurt no one, did it?''

''Two men are dead.''

He wiped his hands on his apron like he was absolving himself. Then he said, ''Who?''

''Reddy the Blacksmith and Albert Johnson.''

''Bunker's man? Oh boy. Look, I had nothin' to do with that.''

''Then why are you sweating like a pig?''

''All I done was let Jocko and my bitch Heidi do their thing.''

''You saw Jocko?''

'' 'Course I did. You didn't think I'd give 'em any money right there, did ya? Not without first seeing what they got?''

''They brought the dog with them?''

''Yeah. They had him in a cage in the back of their wagon. This other fella went an got 'im. With a banged-up nose and a withered arm.''

Glick.

''They never took you anywhere with them? It all took place right here?''

''Yeah. We watched 'em go at it for a while. When we could separate 'em, they took Jocko back where they came from.''

''How much did you pay them for the privilege?''

''A hundred. And it was a bargain. Bunker charges three times that,'' he said bitterly.

''That was all you had to do with them?''

''Just that one time, I swear.''

''You're still in it up to your neck.''

''All I wanted was a chance to get back at that bastard. I lost a lot of money to him once. A *lot* of money.

I asked him for a break and he turned me down flat. So I had ta sell my share of Pa's farm. I never forgot that.''

"I sympathize with you, Boylen. But I'm still gonna have to break your neck.''

I moved toward him with the tongs open wide.

"No! No! Why you doin' that?''

"'Cause you lied to me. You said you only saw them that one time. Why'd you deliver messages for them?''

"What're ya talkin' about?''

"I'm talkin' about the message Reddy gave to you to give them.''

He winced like I was about to hit him.

"I had to.''

"Why?''

"They made some threats. I was scared.''

"So scared you're holding onto this parcel for them?''

"That parcel? Oh, that.''

"Yeah. That. What's it doing here?''

"There's some boarders upstairs. It's for them.''

"Boarders? Would they happen to be Franco and his pal?''

Garrotting him was beginning to appeal to me.

"Keep that thing away from me! No! They ain't there! Just a lady and her brat.''

"Who are they?''

"Her name's . . . Catherine something.''

"And what about the child?''

I was gripping his apron with both hands, thrusting my face into his.

"I never seen the kid.''

"They rented the place from you? When?''

"No, they didn't. That pal of Franco's gave me the money. Told me to keep them out of sight and keep my mouth shut.''

"Or what?''

"Or they'd make sure Bunker found out about what I'd done with his dog. And do some other things . . . to my kid.''

"When was this?''

"A day or so after they came to me with the dog."

"Have you seen him since then?"

"Who?"

I smacked him in the head. "Who do you think?"

"No, I ain't seen him or anybody with him."

"Haven't you been reading the papers for the past couple of days?"

"I don't read. Anyway, I been out of town since Sunday. Listen, Mister, whatta ya want me to do? I'll get rid of them. Would that make you happy, make you leave me alone? I'll do anything you want! You want some money? I got money! Let's pretend we never met up with each other. How does that sound?"

"Give me the parcel."

"Sure, take it!"

He handed it to me. There was no name or address or any other marking on it.

"What'd the lady who delivered this say to you?"

"Just told me it was a package for the boarders upstairs. I was gonna have my boy send it up when he came back from walking the dog."

"I'll take it up myself."

"Look, Mister, be careful with that bull-dozer of yours."

I hadn't noticed until then that I was gripping the handle of the revolver at my waist.

"I don't want anyone to get hurt," Boylen said, cracking his gap-toothed grin.

"If anyone gets hurt around here it's going to be you."

His boy came in just then. He helped his father off the ground and stared at me with hatred. The man was too beaten to look me in the eye. Guilt welled up in me from nowhere. It was misplaced, I know. But it was hard to get rid of once it had surfaced.

Boylen didn't look too threatening now, or evil. Just pathetic and dumb. I left him where he was, went back into the tavern, and climbed the stairs to the attic. My revolver was out.

THE STAIRCASE WAS steep and narrow, as if to discourage visitors from ascending to the rooms above. The smell of hops funneled up the stairway from the kitchen to mingle with other older smells, caught in the murky passage.

My boots made the wooden planks groan beneath them. When I got to the top, I was facing a single door with a rusted knob. I stopped to listen for the sound of a child, for Eddie. But I heard nothing.

Despite this I knew there was someone behind the door. It was an instinct.

I knocked with my left hand, keeping a firm grip on the barker with my right.

From behind the door came a faint shuffling as someone approached it.

"Who's there?"

The female voice was faint, like it was coming to me from across an ocean.

"Package for you," I mumbled.

The door came open just a crack. I didn't wait for an invitation. Throwing my shoulder against the flimsy panels, I flung myself inside the room, tripping over something human in my way.

I spilled to the floor and rolled in a crouch. In an

instant I was standing up against a wall with my revolver out, ready for anything.

Almost anything. I expected at least one of the kidnappers to be aiming a gun at me. I was hoping to find the boy.

Instead I saw a woman asleep or dead in a bed by the tiny window that overlooked Eighth Street. The child Boylen spoke of was at my feet. It was a little girl of about eight or nine years. She was the one I'd tripped over when I'd come barreling in.

I picked her off the floor and asked, "Who are you?"

"I'm Nilda," she mumbled, trying to keep back a sob, "Please don't hurt me, Mister."

A frowsy ready-made dress clung to her emaciated body. It was way too large and made her more frail looking than she actually was. She wore her long brown hair in a ponytail, tied by a purple bow, the only colorful thing in the room. Her tiny body stood rigid, as if she were expecting me to strike her, or something worse.

"Relax. I won't hurt you."

Large brown eyes stared into mine, weighing the sincerity of my words. Despite her thinness and poor clothes she was a beautiful child. That beauty was tarnished by an ugly bruise on her cheek.

"I'm looking for some men."

"Are you a policeman?"

I put the gun back in its holster and said, "Yes, I am."

"Then you're looking for Papa."

"What makes you say that?"

"Papa doesn't like the police. They're always after him."

"Who's your papa?"

The question seemed imbecilic to her.

"Papa's . . . Papa."

I gestured to the woman on the bed.

"Is that your mommy?"

"Yes," Nilda sighed. "I'm taking care of her."

"Is she sick?"

The girl nodded. I saw her lower lip quivering. Then tears started coming.

"I think she's gonna die," she said. "And you're gonna take Papa."

I went to the door and checked to see if anybody was coming. Then I shut it and went to the child. Kneeling before her, I put both hands on her shoulders and said, "Now, stop crying. Maybe I can help your mommy."

"You a doctor, too?"

"No. But I know a little bit about medicine. Let's take a look at her."

Beside her bed were two chamberpots. One held watery excrement in it, the other vomit. The open window helped with the smell, but not much.

I felt the woman's head. It was cold and clammy. Her eyes were sunken and her feet and hands darkly colored, as though blood was beginning to clog. I checked her pulse. It was feeble.

"How long has your mommy been like this?"

"For a day."

"Can't keep water down? Thirsty all the time? Cramps?"

"Yes."

"Your mommy has to get to a hospital right away."

The girl started weeping again.

"Don't worry, she'll be all right," I said, though I didn't quite believe it. Cholera could be and often was lethal.

It was as hot as a greenhouse in the room. Sweat was streaming off my face. The stench from the chamberpots couldn't be doing the girl any good. Miasmas like that were dangerous. It was just the time of year for cholera to strike. If I didn't get her out of there, she might be next.

"Is your father coming back anytime soon?"

"You know Papa?"

"I think so." I described Franco.

"That's him, all right."

Any pity I had for the child quadrupled with those words.

"And his friend Glick. You know him?" I asked.

Nilda made a face. "I don't like that man."

"Why not?"

"He's mean to me. So is Papa. The only one who's nice is Mommy."

"When was the last time you saw your papa, or Mr. Glick?"

"I haven't seen Papa for a long time. Maybe three days. The last time he was here he told me a secret."

"What kind of secret?"

"I can't tell you. It's a *secret*."

"Well, maybe I can guess."

"Okay!" That seemed to excite her. The girl was starved for human company. I was fairly sure I could get her talking if I stayed awhile and got her confidence.

"All right. First guess. Papa was gonna buy you a new dress."

"No! Try again!"

I decided to be less subtle. "He was going to make a whole lot of money."

"No! That was last time."

"The last time he saw you before that?"

"Uh-huh. He told Mommy and me he was gonna make a lot of money and buy us a house! And I'd get a dog, too!"

"Really? Did he say how he was going to make the money?"

"No. Not to me. But he told Mommy. I heard him, even though I was supposed to be sleeping. He said he found a lot of money in Germantown."

"That's all he said?"

"No. He said one more thing. He promised me we would go fly a kite. But he broke his promise."

Her little lip began to quiver.

"Now, guess what he told me this time."

"How many more guesses do I get?"

"Two more."

The child's game was getting me impatient. I blurted out, "He told you he stole a boy."

Her eyes widened with surprise. "No! Nothing like that! But you're close."

"I am?"

"Uh-huh."

"What's close about it?"

"The boy."

"He told you about a boy?"

"Yes." Then she could no longer contain her excitement. "He told me I had a brother, and he was going to come live with us!"

Sweat trickled into my eyes. I wiped it off and said, "Have you seen your brother, Nilda?"

She shook her head. "Not yet. Mr. Glick said I'd see him to-night."

"To-night? So your father and Mr. Glick are going to come and get you here to-night sometime?"

"I hope so. Mommy's really sick. They left us all alone and I don't like it here. They won't let me leave the room. When Papa found out I'd gone down the street to the confectioner, he gave me a lickin'." She pointed to her cheek. "He told me never to step out of this room until he came for us."

"Does your father give you a licking often?"

"I don't think so. Every now and then."

"What about your mother? Her, too?"

The girl changed the subject. "You're not really a policeman, are you?"

"I'm someone who wants to find your father. And Mr. Glick. When was the last time you saw him?"

"Mr. Glick called on us last night. He gave me a chocolate bar."

"That was nice of him."

"He only gave it to me 'cause I wrote a letter for him. He can't write so good."

"Has he made you write some other letters?"

"Uh-huh. Just one other."

Then they *had* gone to fly a kite—in the flash language that meant sending a letter. Glick or Franco must've written the barely legible ransom notes to Munroe. That was why I hadn't been able to link the two sets of letters together at first.

"You had to write some funny things, huh?"

"Sure did. Mr. Glick said it was a game. He wanted to see how much schoolin' I had. But I'm not stupid. I asked him why he made me write such crazy things."

"And what did he tell you?"

"Nothin'. Papa was there the first time. He just told me to shut up and write. Then Mr. Glick said they were kind of secret codes. I didn't understand half the words anyway."

"Like 'signal his instant annihilation'?"

"You read them! Were they for you?"

If she wanted to think so, that was fine with me. I nodded and said, "I read them, all right."

"Did *you* understand them?"

"Most of the time. Listen, Nilda, did Mr. Glick say anything about last night's letter?"

"Mommy asked him about it. She heard Mr. Glick telling me what to write and asked him if he was really going to New York. He said they were going for a trip but they would be back."

So both of them were going to pick up Munroe's sack of money. I had to get this news to Cap right away. But before I could go, there was more information I needed.

"Did Mr. Glick say anything about your brother? Where he was?"

"No. I asked him why Papa didn't come visit us. He said Papa couldn't. The police were looking for him. He and Mr. Glick were hiding somewhere else. He came really late last night. I don't think he wanted anybody to recognize him downstairs."

"Would anybody down there know who he was?"

"Maybe. He and Papa used to come here with their dogs. That's what Mommy told me. She said they used to make a lot of money at the ratting matches."

"When was that?"

"Oh, when I was a baby. Before they went to prison again."

"The second time?"

She nodded, unashamed. "I didn't see Papa for a year."

"Was the jail here in Philadelphia?"

"No, back in New Jersey, where I was born. They stole a boat and some other things from a man. The police caught them."

"And they just got out of another prison a few months ago?"

"Uh-huh. This was the third time Papa went to jail. So he made us move up here to the city. He promised Mommy he'd go to work. He and Mr. Glick found jobs at a meatpacking place. I think they still work there now."

"Have they ever mentioned the names Munroe or Bunker to you?"

"No. What are we gonna do about Mommy? She looks awful sick."

"I'll tell you what. Why don't I go get an ambulance to come here? Would you like to ride in the back of an ambulance?"

"Only if they ring their bells real loud!"

"Oh, they will. They always do."

I started walking toward the door. "You stay here, Nilda. Don't move out of this room until you hear those bells."

My hand was just about to turn the knob when someone yanked the door open from the other side.

Glick looked surprised to see me.

But not half as surprised as I was when his foot landed in my crotch, kicking me out of his way.

I fell back against the wall while he made it across the room to Nilda. As I pulled myself together, shaking my head to get the pain out, Glick stuck a carving knife to the girl's throat. His withered hand clutched her hair, pulling it back until she screamed.

"Out the door and down the stairs. Or I do her up

right now.'' His misshapen face contorted itself in a grin. He seemed to want to slit her throat anyway, just for the hell of it.

I thought of the choices I'd just given Boylen. These were about the same in quality.

"Where's the fucking money?" he shouted at the girl. She tried making words, but nothing came out.

"You looking for the parcel, Glick? It's right where I left it." I pointed to the table where Nilda had composed the ransom letters.

"Don't spend it all in one place," I said, walking out of the room.

"Back down the stairs!" he called to me, as I shut the door. I stayed where I was, with my gun out now. When the girl started screaming again, I decided to risk entering the room.

She was alone, collapsed in a little heap on the wooden floor. Glick and the parcel were gone.

The attic window was still open by the sick woman's bed. I jumped over the bed and leaned outside. Below, the roof of the ground floor extension was just a ten-foot drop. From there it was another ten-foot drop to the alley, where I saw Glick scurrying past the miniature rat pits.

I didn't bother hollering at him. I just took aim and shot. My ear drums took a beating. The ball missed him and thudded into a creaky partition behind Boylen's kennels.

I told Franco's daughter, "Stay here! I'll be back for you and your mother!"

Then I jumped out the window.

My ankles nearly twisted off when I landed on the wood-shingled roof. I kept hold of my revolver and ran till I was above the dogs and their pits. When I jumped down, my heel caught on a barrel rim and sent me sprawling.

It was the barrel with the dead rats in it. A score of them spilled all over me. Flies buzzed in my face, chastising me for disturbing their luncheon. My knee scraped against the cobbles and was bleeding some. There was going to be one ugly bruise on it, but that didn't bother me. I picked myself up and ran after Glick, hoping I hadn't lost him.

Straight ahead I saw him, emerging from the alley onto the street.

There was a lot of distance to make up. I was afraid to run too fast because someone had poured water over the cobbles to clean off some filth leaking out of a backhouse. My knee didn't need another spill.

The alley was narrow and cluttered on both sides with barrels, some full of refuse, the others empty. As I ran by, I checked to see if he'd thrown the parcel in any of them to retrieve later, but there was no sign of it. Glick wasn't letting go of Leah Munroe's money.

I emerged onto Ninth Street. Glick was nowhere in sight. There was a wallpaper store to my left, a newstand to my right. Across the street was a hat store. There were no other alleys or open doorways he could've crawled into in time.

The newstand was too small to afford him any concealment. I stuck my nose up to the wallpaper shop's window, scanning the inside. A salesman was busy flipping through a book of samples, trying to interest a female customer whose old-fashioned hoop skirt swung like a pendulum when she leaned toward the counter. There was no one else in the store.

I walked across the street to see if he was trying on any hats.

The store was crowded, its walls honeycombed with storage spaces for various sizes of each of their display models. A young man was trying on the latest broad-brim while his friend slanted a top hat at a rakish angle. They looked in the mirror and laughed at themselves.

A few people saw me looking at them intently and ignored my stare. I was just about to give up on Glick when I saw something move in the glass.

That is, I saw a reflection. The movement came from

across the street. I kept my back turned and waited.

A pair of cellar doors had opened next to the newsstand. Glick was squeezing out. He didn't seem to recognize me from behind.

I kept waiting while he shut the doors and headed back toward Market Street. He glanced over his shoulder a few times.

His stride was close to frantic, but he didn't want to look too conspicuous. My eyes followed him, as did my gun. I held it up and took aim.

A woman walked by, strolling her infant. She looked up and saw me pointing the gun.

Her mouth opened with surprise. The little cry that came out of it was enough to warn Glick. He turned around for just an instant and then ran off toward Market for all he was worth.

"Get out of the way, damn it!" I hollered at the woman.

All she could do was clutch her baby to her, begging me not to shoot.

My chance at a clear shot was lost. I ran after him, pointing the barker before me like a compass.

Glick was about a half a square away, with no people to protect him anymore, just a brick wall to one side. I fired while I was still in the middle of the street. For a second the smoke made Glick invisible. When it cleared, I saw the parcel fall out of his hands. He stopped to pick it up. When he started running again he was limping.

As I ran past where he'd just been, I saw the ball lodged in the brick wall.

Cursing, I kept my speed up. My lungs were heaving. The hot, muggy air made it hard to breathe. I wanted to stop for just a minute to catch my breath. But then I would lose him. Market Street was just ahead.

He turned the corner, heading east, before I could get another shot off.

Ten seconds later I was turning the same corner.

I ran right into a mob gathered by the lamppost. The

crowd of people took up the whole sidewalk and flowed into the street, holding up traffic.

I heard someone say, "Go get a policeman. Quick!"

They had him!

I stopped to take a few breaths and wipe the sweat from my face. My chest felt like a boiler on the verge of exploding.

I steadied myself on one fella's shoulder. He turned around with a grimace that speedily vanished when he saw the revolver.

"I'm the police. Where's the man?"

"We got the police!" the man said to the mob.

Everyone started talking at once.

"We got him!"

"We got the kidnapper!"

"And the kid!"

"Ran right into us!"

"We're makin' sure he doesn't get away!"

"Call a patrol wagon!"

I couldn't believe what they were saying. They had Glick and Eddie, too?

"The boy from Germantown?" I asked, just to clarify things.

A few of them nodded.

"We saw this fella with the boy. They didn't look like they belonged together to us. He looked just like the descriptions in the *Ledger*, like that Eye-talian."

"Is there a reward for this?" one of them asked me.

"Could be," I said. "Let me see them."

The crowd moved out of my way except for two burly mechanics who were holding a man to the pavement.

A man who was not Glick.

I swore loud enough for them to hear it.

"What's the matter?" they said.

"Let him go. He's not the man."

Their captive got to his feet, wiping the dust off his sleeves. He was an Italian, dressed in a tattered suit, which was the worse for wear since his capture.

He resembled Glick not one bit. Nor Franco. But he

was an Italian, like Cap thought the kidnappers were, and that was good enough.

The boy was too old, though his blond hair was long and curled, like Eddie's.

The man was arguing with one of the mechanics.

"Dammelo!"

"What's he sayin'?" they asked me.

"How do I know? I look Italian to you?"

They had a small sack he was trying to take from them.

"Does that sack belong to him?"

"He dropped it."

"Then give it back to him."

"Okay. We just wanted to make sure there wasn't any evidence in it."

I opened the sack. The contents were a violin case and some oranges.

"Signore, io non ho fatto niente e questi stupidi . . ." the Italian said to me, as if, having saved him, I should naturally speak his language.

"He call us stupid?" the mechanics asked.

"Yeah, stupid," the boy said.

"You speak English?"

"Yeah," he told me. "He says he wasn't doing anything."

"That ain't true! We saw him take a swipe at the kid. It looked like he was taking him somewhere against his will!"

"Is that true?"

The boy was embarassed. "Papa was taking me to the dentist to have a tooth pulled."

"I see."

I gave the mechanics a withering look and put my revolver back in its holster.

"The Eddie Munroe kidnapping is solved. Good work, men."

I was bitter. There was no use going after Glick now. Too much time had passed.

Hoping against hope he might still be lingering

around, I started to look up and down Market. Seeing all the vehicles and people, I quickly gave up.

"All right, then," I said to the boy. "They made a mistake. You and your father go about your business."

I waved them out of my sight, hoping to chase away my disappointment, too. It didn't work.

"*Grazie tanto,*" the Italian said. "*Andiamo,*" he told the boy.

The Italian father and son went their way. The mob that remained gave me angry looks, like I'd cheated them out of their respective fortunes.

"All right, get lost. Nothing to see here. Beat it," I said, like a bluebelly dispersing crowds. It sounded funny coming out of my mouth now, the great detective.

If I'd had a billy club, I might've even shoved a few along, just to get some frustration out. As it was, all I did was kick the lamppost. I walked back toward Boylen's, my toes stinging with pain.

By the time I got the girl and her mother to the hospital, it was getting late in the afternoon. I had a roundsman stay to keep an eye on them. On the other side of the hospital, Pete Shields was still out cold. He wouldn't be giving me any more information for a while.

The day felt like a complete waste. Depression hung over me like a rain cloud. I had to keep telling myself that I had Franco's woman and daughter in custody. Something told me that didn't matter. He would drop them like a stone if he had to.

Demoralized and frustrated, I had only one thing to look forward to: seeing Jocko in action onboard the steamer to-night.

There was just enough time to talk to Archibald before the boat departed from the Delaware waterfront. On the way over to West Philadelphia, I kept my eye on the streets, hoping Glick and Franco would suddenly materialize, like ghosts.

Then I realized I was looking for someone else. The woman who'd led me to Glick. Leah Munroe.

With any luck she'd returned to Germantown after

delivering the parcel. There was plenty of time to have a nice, long talk with her before I was due at the steamer. I had the feeling she would have plenty of things to tell me.

16

ARCHIBALD MUNROE'S DRYGOODS store lay just on the other side of the Market Street Bridge. I walked the few squares from the stop, staring at the dwindling sunlight on the river through a copse defiantly growing next to a new square of row houses.

The neighborhood was quiet, almost desolate. Nobody answered when I knocked on the display case window or the front door. Peering inside, I could see no one. Munroe must've already left for the depot, I decided.

I headed for the depot myself, enjoying the leisurely walk. It gave me time to think about everything I'd done since Cap had dropped Jocko and Eddie Munroe in my lap. I was not happy with more than one or two things.

I felt responsible for the failure of the whole investigation. If I had gone to Cap and Diefenderfer when I was supposed to, I could have avoided the censures and Reddy's death, and maybe caught Glick and Franco. Especially if I'd followed Leah Munroe.

For some reason I was avoiding what had to be done. I didn't want to know why.

Dwelling on my stupidity did nothing but sink me into despair. There was no way I could stop the descent. Once I got sucked into the maelstrom, I couldn't help but plunge further into it.

That was the way I felt as I drew near the depot. For a brief moment I thought of quitting the police department. I wanted to be punished for what I'd done. Then I got angry. At Glick and Franco. At myself. At Diefenderfer. At Cap. At Bunker. At Leah Munroe.

What did it matter, anyway? I asked myself. Munroe pays the money and either gets his boy back or not. Maybe his wife has something to do with it. What can I do to stop it now?

The answer for me was, a lot. When I first heard of Eddie Munroe I was thrilled. I knew nothing of the boy or his family. All he was to me was a problem to be solved, a break in the monotony.

Though I'd never seen him in the flesh, I realized now that it didn't matter if I ever saw him. Because I had already imagined him many times, as I was doing now. I saw him lying huddled in a dark place, lonely, desperate, and in pain. He could not escape. People had taken him to a strange place and held him like an animal in a cage. A grotesque image floated before my mind's eye: Eddie Munroe in a tall wooden pit surrounded by hordes of rats, their lower jaws empty, gaping. The wooden pit was not a pit at all, really. It looked like another kind of place where I had been. The Rebel prisons where I'd spent almost two years.

I tried shaking it out of my head, but the image kept going like a magic lantern show. I saw Glick and Franco leering into my face like I was the boy. Their lower jaws hung open, slobbering. Like Boylens' rats, their teeth had been knocked out. They tore at the brass buttons of my uniform.

The image broke as my hand clutched for those buttons. But they had all been stolen from me within a few days of entering the prison. Along with a lot of other things.

I had been in that same dark place. Lonely and desperate.

I had to get Eddie out of there, get us both out of there. There was only one person who could help me.

Leah Munroe.

I walked into the depot's oyster house, went to the bar, and got a plate of oysters and two rolls. I sat down at a table. There was plenty of space. A train had just blown its whistle and the whole crowd inside the restaurant got up as one and dashed out toward the tracks. A few stragglers ran in, scarfed down their oysters, and ran out again in the space of a minute. It was no wonder the stand next to the restaurant sold a host of nostrums for dyspepsia.

I ate my meal nice and slow. Munroe hadn't shown up yet. I stared at the gilded clock outside. It was seven. I wondered what was taking him so long. After half my plate was gone, Archibald walked in.

He stepped to the bar and got his food. Then he joined me at my table.

"Where've you been?" I asked a little querulously.

"Out for a walk. I couldn't stay in the store. I had to get some fresh air. I don't know how long I've been walking. Could've gone forever. But I heard a church bell toll the hour and realized how late I was. I'm sorry about that."

"Were you walking in the opposite direction of the depot?" I asked him.

"Yes. How did you know?"

"Just a guess. You don't look like you want to be here."

"Would you?"

I shook my head.

When he sat down with his plate, I smelled the whiskey on his breath right away. His eyes were slightly bloodshot. He'd been drinking for some time.

"So . . . are you ready for to-night?"

"Yes. No. I can't believe it's come to this. I kept hoping over the past few days that something would turn up. That you would bring one of the men in, find Eddie—I don't know. That I could have a chance to do something to get my boy back. Something other than buy him back with strangers' money."

"I wish I could have done more. I really do." It was better not to tell him about losing Glick this afternoon. I wanted to forget it myself.

"So do I."

It sounded like a reproach, but when I looked at his downcast face, he said to me, "Please don't feel bad about it. I don't hold anything against you or any of the detectives. I know you did your best."

"There still may be a chance of catching them after to-night," I said, unconvincingly.

"No. I don't think so. As a matter of fact, I don't think there's a chance of getting my boy back, either."

"How can you say that? Especially now? Why bother to go through with this, then?"

"Because I have to! I have no other choice! I have to take advantage of any opportunity I have left to get him back. Every time they get a report of a boy resembling Eddie being found, I go downtown. I've been there for the past two days, running around with Captain Heins. Even before I get there I know it isn't Eddie. But I go just in case, by some miracle, it might be him."

"The way you talk, you'd think he's dead already."

Archibald said nothing. His weakness enraged me.

"So you're just going to sit there and let your son get snatched out of his house? Let him go without fighting one bit?"

"There's nothing I can do. Or you. Those men don't care a hang about me or my boy. I can't do anything to stop them from doing what they're going to do. Neither can the whole Philadelphia police force."

I wondered what had caused such a deep-seated pessimism in him. It reminded me of the way I'd been feeling on my walk to the depot. Somehow it disgusted me. I hated what I saw reflected in his cringing, beaten face. Half of it was the booze. The other half was my own self, staring back at me.

"First my business goes. Now my son. And who knows? The other one might be on his way. My wife, too . . ."

His words had become slurred and his bloodshot eyes brimmed with tears.

"What are you talking about?"

He looked at me as if he were seeing me for the first time. "What?"

"I said, what's this about losing Stephen and Leah?"

Tears started streaming down his cheeks. I was surprised and uncomfortable.

The words came out slowly. "I think she's going to leave me."

"What makes you say that?"

"Oh . . . I'm no fool. A beautiful girl like that, with someone like me. An old weakling."

"That's not how she described you to me."

I told him something of what Leah had related to me after the slaughterhouse. I kept out some of the circumstances. I didn't want him getting any ideas about her being at my house.

"Certainly. That's how it was. But it's all gone to pieces. First my business. Then my son. Now my wife." The repetition was annoying.

"Snap out of it. You're not going to lose your wife. She loves you."

I said it to make him feel better, not because I believed it. I was as suspicious of his wife as he was.

"That's what I used to think."

His head leaned toward the table. He pulled a hip flask out of his coat pocket and drank some more.

"I don't know if that'll do you any good now," I said.

"Can't be worse off than I am."

His mind wandering back to Leah, he said, "Thinks I don't notice anything. Thinks I don't have eyes."

A little guiltily, I realized it was the perfect time to talk to him. The liquor would keep up the conversation. There was just enough time before the train left for me to learn something important.

I thought about Leah's appearance at the slaughterhouse. The way she'd urged me not to go to the waterworks. The lie she'd told about Stephen keeping Minnie from talking. The way she avoided us this morning. The parcel she'd delivered to Boylen.

I said, "Tell me about Leah."

"She doesn't want me to touch her," he said. Then he whispered, embarassed, "Sleeps in the guestroom."

He was ashamed just enough not to look at me. But he wanted to tell someone. The liquor was making him talk, better than I ever could.

"Sleeps there ever since last month."

"Why last month?"

"I don't know." He stared at the table as if it would give him the answer.

"You know, Archibald, your wife had some bruises on her face the last time I saw her. You wouldn't be smacking her around, would you?"

"I? I wouldn't harm a hair on her head! I never lifted a finger to her!"

"But you've seen the bruises?"

"Oh, I've seen them, all right. She told me she fell from a streetcar. But you don't fall from a streetcar two times in one week, do you?"

"Not unless someone pushes you."

"Someone's been pushing her, then. The way they used to a long time ago."

"Who's 'they'?"

"She wouldn't tell me. But I knew who she was, where she came from. And I didn't care. But she doesn't know I know."

This didn't make any sense to me. I thought I was beginning to lose him. "How about another drink?" I said.

"Don't want another drink. Don't wanna talk anymore."

"Listen to me, Archibald. You want things to get better? You want your boy back? Then you'd better start talking some more. About Leah."

"What's she done?"

"You tell me."

"Nothing." He clasped both sides of his head and kneaded his sparse hair.

"Bullshit. You're lying, Archibald. Not just to me. You've been lying to yourself. You like it that way."

"Shut up!"

"It's better if you don't notice those bruises, or where she goes during the day, or how your son acts now. You have the equation set up right in front of you, but you're afraid to add it up. Aren't you?"

He stood up abruptly and headed for the train tracks. When I reached him, he was vomiting on the tracks. I dragged him into the toilet room and leaned him over a sink.

After a few minutes I splashed some water in his face.

"Now's your chance, Archibald. You want to do something to help? You want to get Eddie back? You told me you did. Now prove it."

"What do you want me to do?"

"Talk to me, damn it!"

I shook him against the dirty tiles beside the mirror. The impact jarred his skull.

He gave me a dazed look, like someone who's fought his first battle. Then he said, "You're absolutely right, McCleary. I haven't wanted to look. It's better to not notice things, things that could hurt you. Safer."

I gave him a moment to collect himself. His trembling hand wiped the water and tears from his eyes.

"But I can't believe Leah had anything to do with Eddie's . . ." He left it unfinished, afraid to describe or think about what had happened to his son.

"I saw her to-day in the city. She didn't see me. I shadowed her to a tavern on Eighth Street. Boylen's. You ever hear of it? I didn't think so. She delivered a parcel there. There was a lot of money in it."

I didn't tell him who the parcel was for. I wanted him to draw his own conclusions.

"Parcel? Lots of money? Yes. I see."

"What?"

"She's been pawning jewelry I bought for her. Ever since last month."

"How do you know that?"

"I noticed it gone from the dresser. And I found a pawn ticket last week. It fell out of her coat when I went to hang it up. Every piece I've ever bought her is gone. Not that I gave her a lot."

"Why would she be pawning jewelry? Does she have bills to pay?"

"No, no. I mean, my business hasn't been doing well ever since Seventy-two. The Panic and all that. I haven't had an easy time making payments. But I've always had enough to support her respectably."

"Then how do you explain what she's done?"

"I can't. And I don't want to try."

"When did you first notice the jewelry was missing?"

"A month ago. I didn't think much of it at first. Then I thought one of the boys might be pilfering them. But I went to the address printed on that ticket I found and there was the ring I'd given her for our fifth anniversary."

"How much money do you think she would have gotten from pawning all those baubles?"

The last word irked him. He drew in his lips and said, "Hundreds of dollars, certainly."

And those hundreds of dollars went right to Glick and Franco. But not for any ransom. Why would they collect ten thousand from the father *as well as* several hundred from the mother? I was beginning to have an idea.

"Where do you think those bruises on her face come from?" I asked him.

"I don't know."

"Do you think she's seeing another man? Is that why she's not sharing your bed?"

His silence was answer enough.

"But you have no idea who, do you?"

He shook his head.

It all made sense. Even at our first meeting it was

obvious he needed to prove himself to his wife. But I hadn't known where the need came from. Until now.

"How long do you think this has been going on?" I asked, a bit more gently.

He squeezed the sides of his eye sockets, as if to draw an answer from his brain.

"Since the beginning of June."

"The same time that she started pawning your jewelry?"

"Yes."

"How do you know?"

"First she left the house too often. She said she had to visit this or that person. Then I'd run into them on one of my walks and they'd tell me she'd never called on them. She lied to me like that several times, but I never confronted her about it. I was afraid. I thought if I kept quiet about it, maybe the trouble would go away."

"But it didn't?"

"No."

"Did she treat you any differently? Quarrel?"

"No, nothing like that. She was as gracious, pleasant, attentive as ever. But she started shrinking when I touched her."

"Just like Stephen."

"Yes, like Stephen. And then she wouldn't sleep in the same bed with me. She said I snored and kept her up all night. But that wasn't the reason. She hated the idea of sleeping beside me, I'm sure of it."

Pain contorted his face in a parody of a weeping child. I wanted the interrogation to end as quickly as possible. Torture was not my business.

"But you have no idea where she went, or who she was with?"

"No. I don't want to know. I told you that."

"Do you think Stephen knows anything about it?"

He stared past me like I wasn't there. His mouth opened like an imbecile's.

"I don't think so."

"But you told me he doesn't want you to touch him anymore, either."

"Just to-day I tried to give him a hug. And he jerked out of my arms and started shouting at me!"

"What did he say to you?"

"Terrible things. That I wasn't his father. That I was a liar. He hated me."

Tears were in his eyes again. "How could he say those things to me?"

I shook my head. "Has he done anything else like this before?"

"You were there when he was teasing Freddy, our sheepdog. He does it incessantly. This morning I caught him trying to set fire to the poor thing's tail. I sent him off right away to his grandmother's. She lives in Manayunk, not far away, but far enough. She'll keep an eye on him. When all this business is over, I was hoping I could have the chance to talk things over with Leah, alone. I'm worried about Stephen as much as anyone. To-day was the worst yet."

I didn't mention the lie Leah had told about Stephen and Franco at the shed. He would learn about it soon enough.

We walked out of the lavatory and headed back toward the oyster house. Most of Archibald's escort had arrived, including Diefenderfer.

"What brings you out here, McCleary?" he said to me. "I thought Heins ordered you off our little expedition."

I didn't have time for Diefenderfer. All I said to him was, "Take good care of Mr. Munroe. Understand me?"

I sat Archibald down, nodding to Nolan and Bowie as I left the depot. Then I commandeered one of the Central Office carriages and headed for Germantown.

17

I HAD TWO and a half hours to get to the steamer launch.
I hoped it was enough time. I urged the horse as fast as I
could. The pedestrians had to fend for themselves.

I kept picturing Archibald Munroe and the dicks back
at the depot. They were probably getting on the train
about now, excited, expectant. But I knew even then that
their trip to New York would come to nothing. What
they were looking for was waiting for me at 252 Rittenhouse Street.

We were a square away when I decided to stop, right
by Dr. Moyer's residence. It was better that I go the rest
of the way on foot.

Approaching the house from Rittenhouse Street, I
looked for the patrolman who should have been on duty.
I saw no sign of him.

From the street the Munroe house looked deserted,
except for a lantern hung in the kitchen window. I made
my way around the property to the back. About halfway
there, I nearly stumbled on something sticking out of the
hedge. At first I thought it was a tree root. But it was
far too pliant for that. On second glance I saw it was a
leg.

The patrolman was stuffed into the bushes. Pulling
him out, I got some of his blood on my hands. It came
from a gash in his forehead. Blood was still coursing

out of the recent wound. The man was alive but unconscious. I dragged him into the open air and left him like
that. I took my barker out of its holster, clutching it with
a sweaty palm.

When I got to the top of the hill, I climbed over the
stone wall, just as Franco had done a week ago. I stayed
in a crouch, advancing slowly through the backyard. I
hoped Freddy wasn't chained outside.

As I made my way to the back porch, I could see that
the door was ajar. A faint light streamed outside onto
the stoop. When I got to the shed I heard two people
screaming at each other inside the house. I was too far
away to hear what they were saying.

There was no cover between the shed and the back
door. I scurried toward the house, my gun arm aimed
like an arrow at the bull's-eye of the lighted doorway.
My eyes never strayed from that spot. I was waiting for
any sign of movement, hoping I could get in position to
hear what they were saying before I had to make another
move.

All I heard now was laughter.

Then the laughter was cut short by a deafening noise.
It sounded like all the crackers boys were setting off
across the city to celebrate Independence Day.

Except this was no cracker.

Just as I got to the back door a man stepped through
it, silhouetted for an instant against the orange light. He
stumbled down the stone stairs to the grass and made
for the shed. He was mumbling something. It sounded
like, "Damn, that hurts."

The man collapsed on the lawn and then got up again.
I watched him go, waiting for him to fall.

I should have been watching the back door. Another
figure came through with a revolver. The gun barked
again. A ball collided with the man's back, right below
the neck. He went down face first. Dogs all over the
neighborhood were howling like the gun spoke a language they understood.

Before Leah could fire again, I wrenched the gun from her. Her wild eyes didn't recognize me.

I left her where she was and ran to the prostrate body, turning it over.

The starlight fell on Franco's dead face. His mouth was twisted in a sneer of hatred. Blood trickled through his dark beard. His teeth weren't so pretty anymore.

My fingers ran through his pockets, hoping to find a key. Or an address. But there was nothing.

Leah stood on the doorstep, mumbling like a madwoman. I gestured with my revolver for her to go back inside the house.

She took no notice of me. I had to carry her. Her limbs were rigid, like they were foreshadowing what would shortly happen to Franco.

I took her to the parlor and laid her on the sofa. As soon as I did it, she fell off and stayed the way she was, drooling on the Persian carpet. It was an ugly sight. I went to find some liquor.

When I came back with a bottle of spirits, she was still lying on the floor. Her whole body was wracked with sobs. Between them she gasped for air and coughed. I wished she would faint, but she kept on going.

After a while the sobs turned into words. She kept saying the same ones over and over again: "Help me. Help me. Help me." It didn't sound like she was talking to me. I went over to her anyway and gave her a stiff drink, half a tumblerful. Then I gave her another. She winced as the alcohol burned down her throat.

I hated seeing her, seeing anyone, that miserable. I wanted to comfort her but I stopped myself, merely standing before her in the darkness.

We had stayed there for about ten minutes when I asked her, "Why did you do it, Leah? What did he say to you?"

"He said . . . he said he was going to take . . . Stephen."

"His son?"

She nodded and covered her face with her hands.

I knelt beside her, running my hand over her tangled hair soothingly. Then I whispered, ''Tell me now.''

Her first few words were hesitant. Then the dam burst. A cataract of pain flowed into the room, nearly drowning her. And me.

''I told you about the War. And the hospital. I left everything out I wanted to. Everything I hated about myself and my life. But they won't go away just because I don't want to think about them. No.''

She took a breath, pursing her lips, and said, ''I came here from New York when I was a child. A woman promised me work in the city, cleaning and such. I was hungry, so I went. Only when I got to Philadelphia did I find out I wasn't going to be doing any cleaning. Frank was working at her house then. He broke me in. And I started servicing all the soldiers. This was during the War, in sixty-one. I was very young, about thirteen or fourteen. There were so many soldiers. Night after night.''

''You call him Frank.''

''Yes. That's what they called him in those days. Dago Frank.''

''I see. How long were you in the house?''

''For years. Frank walked up and down the streets, steering the soldiers and anybody else our way. A few times he saved me from getting beaten. Other times he beat me up himself. After a few years a funny thing happened. Frank fell in love with me. He decided he wanted to marry me. I laughed at him. But he said if I did it we'd leave the house and I'd never have to do what I did again. I was always stupid. I believed him.

''So we were married in a Methodist church. He had a flat near a marbleworks, where he worked for a few months. We lived there. I had hopes that things might get better. But they went to hell right after the ceremony.

''He didn't like the way I slept with him. I didn't put any feeling into it, he said. It was like sleeping with a whore. I said, 'That's what I am. That's what you made me.' He didn't like that. He beat me up that time. He was always doing that.

"One day a policeman saw him beating me on the street and arrested him."

That explained why she'd left the room in a hurry when Nolan had walked in. I was amazed I hadn't put it together sooner.

"I ran away. They must've wanted him inside, because they came up with some other things to charge him with. I stayed in his flat. I was getting hungry and had no money. The hospital wasn't far away. I started going there for the food. Then, the more I went, the more I liked it. Finally, I left Franco's flat and never went back."

"When you met Archibald?"

"Yes. The first day I met Archibald." She spoke his name like it was the symbol of her childhood innocence.

"And what about Franco?"

"He couldn't find me when he came out. I was in Germantown by then. I never went back into the city if I could help it. Then Stephen was born. I stayed with him constantly."

"How long was Stephen born after Franco went inside?"

"You know already."

"Does Archibald?"

"No. Two weeks he was in the hospital and then we left, together. And then that very night it happened. It was beautiful with him."

I blushed in spite of myself.

"When Stephen came, we all knew who the father was. Archibald. The one who should have been the father. We named him after his grandfather. Stephen arrived a little prematurely, we all decided. That was all."

"Did Franco know?"

"Not until . . . last month."

"When he found you here?"

"Yes."

"Let me try to fill in the blanks. You can stop me if

I go wrong. Franco met up with his deformed pal Glick this last time inside. They decided to go into the sneak business. Peddling Rat-Oh was a good way to size up neighborhoods without looking too suspicious. And everybody knows Germantown has some pretty fancy neighborhoods. It's surprising they didn't come sooner.''

I paused and looked at her. Her nod made me continue.

"So they came peddling Rat-Oh and sizing up your house. And then they saw you.''

"Frank saw me walk out the front door with Eddie. We had an appointment with Dr. Moyer that day.''

"And that's when they talked to Minnie? And Stephen?''

"Yes.''

"What went on in the shed, Leah? Why did you lie about it? What did Franco do to Stephen?''

I was shouting at her. Stephen's name echoed through the empty house.

She flinched like I was going to hit her. When I made no move, she said, "He told him the truth. That he was Stephen's father.''

"How could he know that?''

"Frank questioned him. Asked him how old he was, things like that. And he has his eyes. Stephen doesn't look like Archibald, anyone can see that. I always said he took after my father's side of the family. His curly hair, dark complexion. But Frank knew right away.''

"How is it Archibald didn't?''

"He never wanted to see it, understand? He never looked for it. So it wasn't there.''

"And that's all Frank did in the shed?''

"That's what Stephen told me. I promised him not to tell anyone. We pretended like it never happened.''

"Why would they take Eddie instead of Stephen? Why take both and let the other one go free?''

"Frank was coming to get Stephen to-night. He said Stephen belonged to him, was his flesh and blood, and he was going to take him away. And he laughed at me.''

"Then you shot him."

"Yes. And it felt good. I want to go out there and dance in his blood right now."

"Where did the money go to, Leah? The money from all the jewelry you pawned?"

"It went to him and Glick. And Frank's family. Some other girl was stupid enough to marry him, God help her."

"What made you give them any money? Wasn't one ransom enough?"

"It wasn't a ransom. It was blackmail. Frank sent me a message the day after the ransom letter came. It said I'd better give him a little something extra. Or he might let it out that I was a whore. And a bigamist. When I gave him the first bit of money, he wanted more. He hit me. And threatened Eddie."

"Did you say bigamist?" I asked incredulously.

"I never told anyone about my marriage to Franco. I never got a divorce. I pretended like it never happened."

"You've been doing that a lot. It doesn't work too well."

"Who are you to judge me? You have no idea what my life has been like! I was filth until I met Archibald! He made me clean. He made me want to live. I love him more than anything in the world. How do you think I've felt, watching this destroy him, knowing it was all my fault? How do you think *I* feel? Like filth again! He wants to hold me, comfort me, and when he touches me I feel how filthy I am and how clean and good he is! I can't stand it. I can't bear to let him touch me. I don't want him to touch someone like me! He doesn't deserve this! Why did I do this to him? How could I?"

Her sobbing gasps, without tears, were hard to take. Especially because I knew that all her anguish was a waste. Archibald already knew. He had told me himself at the depot, though I hadn't known what he was talking about. He had known all along but had never let that truth come between them. Part of me cursed Archibald for keeping silent.

"He loves you very much, Leah."

"Oh, thank you. That makes me feel so much better. How long do you think he could love a whore like me? A whore who passes off her gagger's son as his own? Would he love me if he found out I've known who stole Eddie all along?"

I felt betrayed as much as Archibald. "Why didn't you tell me the truth yesterday? I could've ended it all. I could've saved you both from all this. Why didn't you trust me?"

"I was afraid! Afraid of losing the only good thing in my life! If Archibald knew who I was, knew about Stephen, he'd leave me. And I'd be right back where I came from. I won't let him go! Never!"

"Even if it means losing Eddie?"

"Frank doesn't want Eddie. He never did. He just wanted to bleed Archibald dry. That was his way of getting revenge, see? He's been stabbing at me for weeks, twisting the dagger around and around. If I talked, he'd kill Eddie and tell Archibald everything. If I kept my mouth shut, Archibald would lose his money, but we'd get Eddie back and we'd be together again. Did I have a choice?"

"What about Eddie? How can you trust Franco to give him back?"

It was the one question she wasn't able to bear, the one fact that she couldn't pretend away.

"He promised me," she said, like the words were memorized, but meaningless to her.

"I'd trust a man who beats me and steals my children," I said sarcastically. "And now you've shot him. We have no way of knowing where Eddie might be."

"Glick knows."

"What else did he tell you about Glick? Did he mention stealing Bunker's dog?"

"Yes, I knew about that. Frank bragged. He liked telling me all about what they were doing. He knew I couldn't say anything or Eddie would die."

"You tried to keep me from going to the waterworks last night."

"I knew they were going to try something. They told me they wanted to kill Bunker. I didn't want you dying in his place."

"Why would you care?"

"I didn't . . . not at first. Oh, how can I explain it to you? You were good to him, and to me. You could've . . . when we were at your home . . . but you didn't. After that I didn't want you getting hurt . . . all right?"

I let it go, afraid to explore it any more. I asked, "Why would they want to kill Bunker?"

"Glick told Frank all about it when they were in prison, years ago. And I got to hear it from Glick one night when I met them in the city. They were drunk and so proud of themselves they needed to boast about it to someone. I guess Glick and Bunker go way back."

"How far back?"

"Years, he said. Around the end of the War."

"Was Glick still a sneak thief back then?"

"Yes. But he was protected."

It was easy to guess the rest.

"By Bunker?" I said.

"Yes. He knew Bunker from the rat fights they both went to, knew his reputation as a fixer. He offered Bunker a percentage of his take in exchange for protection from the police. He even did Bunker favors."

"What kinds of favors?"

"Some people wound up drowned in the Schuylkill. People Bunker didn't like."

"I see."

This was not what I wanted to hear about a man whose life I was supposed to protect that night. A friend of Cap's.

Now his behavior at the waterworks made sense.

"And Glick fell out of favor?" I asked.

"Yes. He kept borrowing money to cover bets at the rat fights. When Bunker came to collect, Glick couldn't pay his debts. So Bunker had him arrested on some trumped-up charge. He sat in prison for a few years. That's when he met Frank. Frank told me all Glick talked about was Bunker and getting back at him.''

"When did they get out?''

"Around sixty-seven.''

"What took them so long to get around to it?''

"They had to leave Philadelphia. They worked in Jersey, York, and Long Island until seventy-one.''

"Worked, meaning 'robbed'?''

"Yes. Then Frank was arrested again and Glick waited a year for him to get out. Then they came back to Philadelphia early last year.''

A year was plenty of time to set the stage for revenge. They were slow about it. They must have delighted in each little step, each little jab.

And for Glick, it had all been for nothing. I hoped the same would go where Eddie was concerned.

"So Glick is out collecting the ransom to-night?''

"No. Frank was supposed to go. But he came here instead to get Stephen.''

"Wait a minute—are you telling me that no one is going to collect that ransom on the train to-night?''

"Not now. Glick is on some steamer and Frank is . . .''

I took her chin and tilted it upward. Our eyes met for the first time that night.

"Steamer? What are you talking about?''

"Frank said Glick was going on a steamer to watch a rat fight to-night.''

"Did he mention anything about Bunker?''

"Not to me, he didn't. All he told me was how much money they were going to make for themselves with what I'd given them to-day. Betting on how long it takes a dog to kill some rats. Everything Archibald gave me for that . . .''

She was sniffling again.

"Stop it. I may be able to get the money back for you. And get the boy. Now that you've ruined our only other chance of finding him.''

It was a cruel thing to say. Leah began to wail.

"What have I done? My baby . . ."

"You haven't done anything that you can undo. But I'm going to make sure I bring back Glick before the night is out."

"You know where he is?"

"Oh, yes. And this time I'm not going to lose him." It was a promise to myself. And Eddie.

"What will happen? To me?"

I stood up again and looked down at her shaking, crumpled form.

"You're going to find out if Archibald really loves you. Or not."

As I left the parlor I told her, "I'll send Dr. Moyer over. He can summon the police. Don't do anything stupid in the meantime."

I ran back to where the carriage was parked and woke up the doctor. He promised to get the police and wait at the Munroe house till they arrived. I thanked him and headed for the river. Far off, coming from the city, I heard the sound of crackers exploding, and pistols being shot into the air. A burst of red light scattered above the treetops for a moment. Someone was having a private fireworks display, even though it was against the law.

The steamer's whistle was blowing when I reached the landing stage. As I walked up the gangplank there was a pop. Then, above me, red and white fire streaked through the sky like a comet. Or an omen.

18

THE LONE STEAMER cabled to the pier was named *General Hooker*. It was a sidewheeler with a long and sharp bow, its white paint gleaming beneath the fading fireworks. The rigging glimmered with golden light as the ship lanterns flickered in the breeze. This craft wasn't for little excursions up and down the river. It was a full-blown night boat, with two stories of berths rising above the deck. I whistled when I thought of all the money it took to charter the thing.

I stepped onto the quarterdeck, toward the stern. A stench of hot oil came from the engine room. The massive paddlewheel was to my side. Swells and their mabs littered the decks, ruffling through each other's hair, tickling, laughing, drinking from huge goblets. A few of the men were ward heelers and city councilmen I knew. The women with them were not their wives. I knew a few of them, too, the ones I had arrested over the years. Their cheap perfume hung in the air like smoke clouds.

A negro in livery offered me a glass of champagne on a silver tray before I took two steps. I declined and headed for the purser's office, proceeding up a staircase that looked like it had been transplanted from Versailles. I asked the man at the office where Bunker's berth was. The man checked a list and the various slots for keys and told me room number 52.

At the top of the stairs I went forward into the grand saloon. It was two decks high and ran practically the whole length of the boat. Most of the doors to the berths were wide open. Peering into a few, I noticed men and women lying on their bunks in various stages of undress. A few of the more conservative souls had closed their doors.

Two enormous glass chandeliers dangled from the ceiling, gas aflame. Below them, on the lower deck, men and women mingled around faro tables and roulette wheels or danced a quadrille in little clusters to the gay sound of a colored band. In the center of the saloon, taking up most of the space, was a large wooden structure consisting of four boards joined together by metal clamps. It was about four and a half feet high and eight feet long. The inside was lined with metal, tin or zinc. Wire was strung around the rim, making it escape proof.

The rat pit.

For now it was empty. Bunker told me the festivities would commence when the steamer got under way. Then I would have my chance to see what Jocko was made of.

I scanned the crowds for Glick or Bunker. Without meaning to, I caught the eye of a girl decked in muslin and lace. She cocked the feathered cap perched on her curls and glided over the plush wine-colored carpet to me. Her bustle, trimmed with flowers and tassels, trailed behind her a few feet.

"Hello, Blondie." She smiled. "Care to buck the tiger with me?"

"No faro for me to-night, Sweetheart."

"Then how about taking me to your berth? We have twenty minutes until everything starts."

She fanned her flushed cheeks daintily. I figured her at about fourteen. Her hands wrapped around my waist, deftly going for my pockets. I stopped them just before my watch vanished down her sleeve. I held her hand in mine and squeezed, hard.

"Stop it! You're hurting me!"

"Go find someone drunk. And richer than I am."

I laughed when she stuck out her tongue at me.

I went back outside to the main deck. The gangplank was up now. They were casting off the lines. When the engine room gong sounded, everyone cheered. Steam started pouring out the stacks. The *General Hooker* moved onto the Delaware.

The paddlewheel near me was churning up water, trailing foam back to the launch. I gripped a part of the hog frame, cables streaming past it, and remembered the excitement I'd felt the first time I rode a steamer as a boy.

Then I went back to the grand saloon. It already reeked of whores' perfume, segar smoke, and sweat. Liquor was spilled liberally on the carpet.

I made my way to berth 52 but found it empty. Bunker must've been milling. I wasn't too eager to find him. After what Leah had told me, I wouldn't know what to say.

Slowly I made another round of the gallery, getting a good look at everything that was going on around me. When I recognized someone, I made sure to note who they were with. The information might come in handy someday. I could cause a lot of embarassment if I gave that information to the right people. If I ever ran up against these men, I'd let them know that.

Referees were starting to make preparations for the ratting. I saw them clearing the area of gamblers and drinkers. I decided to go outside and look for Bunker.

I found him with some friends, drinking near a dozen kennels on the quarterdeck.

He was dressed in a top hat and long tailcoat. His polished shoes gleamed as brightly as his black curly hair and oiled moustache. He cracked a wide smile when he saw me and rubbed the protruding gut beneath his expensive vest.

"McCleary! My boy!" He gave me a bear hug, like I was his prodigal son.

"Nice night for a cruise," I said.

"You got that right. So glad you could make it. Wait'll you see Jocko. You're gonna see the service you done for me. He's in prime shape! Game as all hell!"

"Where is he, anyway?"

"Right beneath my rump!" He patted the kennel where his girth rested.

"Mrs. Bunker make it to-night?"

He slapped me on the shoulder, laughing. "That's a good one!"

"I got something else that'll make you laugh."

He waited expectantly.

"Glick's onboard. And I'll bet he's got a gun he'll be wanting to use on you."

Bunker's smile disappeared.

"I happen to know why. It wasn't just because you stiffed him last night. He's got a bigger grudge against you. Isn't that right?"

He took out a monogrammed handkerchief and wiped his moist lips.

"What are you saying, boy?"

"I'm saying I know about you and Glick. The jobs he did for you ten years ago."

"Well, now. What are we going to do about that?"

"I won't say anything. But Glick will. And I don't think I'll stop him."

"That might not be such a good idea. You wouldn't like to see me go down."

"After the way you lied, I might at that. You let his name slide right by like you'd never heard it before. You tried to kill him at the waterworks. And you knew he was the same one who stole Eddie Munroe. But you didn't say anything." I stepped up to him and tapped his chest with each word. "You could have helped me get that kid back. But you were more worried about your own hide. And now it's about to be skinned. I kind of like that."

Only after I'd finished did I realize I was as guilty as Bunker. There was plenty I'd found out and kept to myself. Till it was almost too late.

I couldn't hate him without hating myself for the same weakness. So I did both.

"Listen, McCleary, we can still be pals. The deal with Jocko is one hundred percent square, and I'll add something extra. Let's say you see Glick to-night. If he doesn't make it back to the city, I'll be very grateful. Ten thousand dollars grateful."

I wondered if he settled on that figure out of the blue. Or did he remember that was how much Jocko's ransom was? And Eddie's?

I laughed and said, "I'll see you inside."

Then I tapped Jocko's kennel and told him, "Good luck."

Mastiffs were already fighting each other in the pit. People were taking places in the gallery and on the floor, to get good views of the action. I perambulated my way through the crowds, keeping an eye out for Glick. For some reason I kept expecting to see Eddie along with him.

There was no sign of Glick after nearly an hour of dog fights. A few men were still gambling or dallying with their whores by then, but not many. The crowd around the pit rippled like sharks in a feeding frenzy. Greenbacks flashed from hand to hand like lightning, enough to pay my salary till the twentieth century.

After the last dog's bloody carcass was lifted out of the pit and fresh sand poured in, the referee started shouting, "This is it! Jocko's coming!"

Bunker walked into the saloon, cheered by the horde. They poured champagne on his head and threw coins at him. In his arms was the little fox terrier, his ears perked up. Jocko looked nervous, like he was about to jump out of his master's clutches.

Another man waited, cradling another dog. He was announced as Billy Fagan, from Secaucus, New Jersey. His dog Jack Underhill was the challenger.

The referee waited for everybody to shut up. He was enjoying himself immensely. When the crowd got as quiet as it was going to get, he said, "Are the enumerators ready?"

Two men, representing the rival owners, nodded their heads. They advanced to opposite sides of the pit.

"Then let in the rats!"

A youth brought a low, flat wooden cage to the wiry rim and thrust it over. Then he lifted the door.

Albino rats came out squealing, scraping their claws against the cage's metal lining. Some people clapped with approval. Albinos were bred for the sole purpose of better showing their own spilled blood.

A few of the women in the audience squealed themselves at the sight of the rodents pouring into the pit. The creatures huddled in corners, clambering on top of each other. Spectators jeered at them between gulps of liquor. At the uproar, the few closed berths flew open and men and women came out, some in little more than bed sheets.

Now the heavy betting commenced. I heard people call five hundred on Jocko, three hundred on Jack Underhill. The pot was five thousand dollars, equivalent to my pay for half a decade. Even if Bunker lost, he would get a third of it, according to custom.

The enumerators mouthed a count as each rat spilled out of the cage. When the youth was finished shaking it, the referee asked, "How many gentlemen?"

Bunker's man said, "One hundred."

Fagan's enumerator said the same.

Then the referee turned to us and said, "The count is correct. One hundred rats."

The inside of the pit was a seething mass of white furry lumps, twitching their worm-like tails. I thought of my night with the Edgerton boys and shivered.

For the next five minutes the vermin provided our entertainment. As they frantically tried to claw their way out of the pit, the spectators laughed and mocked them. It was like some grotesque parody of a Roman death match. The cackle of whores resounded through the room as a few of the rodents, reaching the top of the pit, were thrown back by the protective flange and wire. Their tiny claws made futile scrapes against the smooth metal lining. Each time they managed to climb above their fellows, they inevitably slid back to the bottom.

The referee again summoned the youth, who now had a pair of tongs. One rat had managed to get himself caught in the wire. As it was twisting viciously, the wire bit into its flesh. Drops of blood speckled the sand beneath. The youth snatched up the rat with his tongs, depositing it in the wooden cage. In a few moments he returned with a fresh, healthy rat.

Only perfect specimens were allowed in the pit.

Jocko and his rival were straining in their masters' grips at the sight of the rats. They looked ready to pounce on them straightaway. Jocko barked and wagged his tail at them like they were long-lost friends.

By now the rats had got their ease and were moving away from the corners of the pit.

Bunker and Fagan tossed a coin. Then Bunker approached the pit, stroking Jocko's ears and neck, whispering to him. The crowd got very quiet.

"One!" the referee shouted.

Bunker shifted his hold on the terrier, aiming him like a cannon at the sandy arena.

"Two!" Most of the audience picked up the count. Jocko was straining to go, wriggling in Bunker's grasp.

The referee waited an inordinate time. All you could hear was Jocko's whimper and the sound of the rats squeaking to each other.

Then the whole crowd screamed, "Three!" and the referee cried, "Drop!"

As Bunker dropped Jocko lightly in the middle of the pit, the timekeeper rang his bell. Then the room exploded.

Within two seconds Jocko had a rat between his jaws. He shook it back and forth viciously. Then, with a snap of his neck, he sent it flying into the air. The crowd went wild with delight. Thunderous applause broke out before the dead rat hit the sand.

Usually it took the average pit dog about thirty to forty-five minutes to kill a hundred rats. But Jocko'd cut that time in half in the last match he'd fought, finishing at nineteen minutes. Men betted on not just which dog would be quicker, but also on how long each dog would take to kill his hundred.

Jocko was game. He attacked the rats with aplomb, plunging himself into dense packs of the terrified creatures. As he ripped one rat out, three or four more attached themselves to his face, their jaws holding on tenaciously as their comrade's neck snapped.

After five minutes it was impossible to see the dog at all. Jocko was completely covered with rats sinking their fangs into his wiry body. They clung to his legs, back, head, muzzle, and ears. But their hold was weak and the dog ignored them, concentrating all his energy on the creature in his maw. With another whiplash jerk of his neck, he sent the rat sailing into the metal wall. Once again the audience cheered.

Bunker looked like he was having the time of his life. He beamed with more pride than a First Lady on Inauguration Day.

I looked up from the pit and watched the crowd. Their leering faces were flushed with liquor and excitement, perspiring and guffawing. They moved about, groping their painted women and slapping money into each other's hands with the same frantic energy of the rats below me. The whole grand saloon seemed like an enormous rat pit, with hideous gigantic vermin laughing, spitting, sweating all around. It was hard for me to breathe. I felt just like I was back under that beached schooner, in the rat nest.

I put my hands to my face to blot out the image. I removed them in time to see Jocko savage half a dozen rats in less than a minute. Bunker was watching him, too, laughing with the crowd. Then his laughter ceased, cut short by something he saw. His eyes were averted from the pit. It couldn't be Jocko's plight that had caused that pallor, that gaping mouth quivering with fear.

Leaning over the railing, I tried to see what it was. I followed the path of his gaze past the pit and over to one of the large pillars supporting the ornamented ceiling. Men and women clustered around it, jumping up and down to catch a view. One and only one of them stood still, returning Bunker's stare. His withered arm started parting the crowd in front of him.

Glick's mouth opened in a snarl as he made for the pit. I could see a pistol in his hand. So could Bunker.

I stayed where I was, frozen, watching them like the rest of the people watched the rat pit, with fascination and disgust.

Bunker stood his ground beside the pit where his dog was busy finishing up the last two dozen rats that remained alive. Glick pushed his way through the drunken revelers until he stood directly opposite Bunker. The two men faced each other silently. I tried shouting Glick's name, but the sound didn't carry over the torrent of cheering and clapping.

Meanwhile, Jocko was finishing up with his last kill. His ears were torn to shreds and blood streaked from a dozen wounds. It seeped into the sand with the rat's gore. The dog tossed his final kill into the wire and the thing stayed there, twisted and nearly bitten in half. The timekeeper rang his bell to signal the end of the bout. Jocko barked with triumph.

The referee shouted, "Eleven and a half minutes! A new record!"

In the ensuing pandemonium, no one noticed the two men, locked in their own death match. Glick's arm rose, his pistol aimed at Bunker's head. Before he could get a shot off, I stepped onto the railing and dived into space.

I landed on a group of men a few feet behind Glick. They were pressed hard against him. When I landed, the force threw them to the floor. It wasn't a soft landing. I felt my leg twist and snap. I cried out with pain.

Glick fell forward, pushed right onto the pit itself. His gun flew out of his hand as he scrambled to avoid the wiry rim and the rats caught in it.

While he was trapped beneath the men I'd toppled, Bunker advanced into the pit. At first I thought he was going for Jocko. But he kicked his dog out of the way and stepped over the heaps of dead rats and right up to Glick. As I pushed my way toward them, I saw something gleam in Bunker's upraised hand. Glick desperately tried to avoid the downward thrust of the knife. But he was trapped in the wire and the men on top of him. Before I could get to him I saw Bunker's knife sink into Glick's chest.

Screaming, I trampled one or two men before I reached the pit, dragging my broken leg all the way. When Bunker saw me, he dropped the knife with a smile and raised his hands. Glick turned to me, groaning. A thick red ooze was beginning to stain his shirt.

"You bastard!" I screamed at Bunker, whipping my revolver into his teeth. He fell back into the pit unconscious.

The crowd had noticed us by now. I heard screams and felt hands on my shoulders. I discharged the revolver at the ceiling. The hands released me.

"Police!" I shouted. "Out of my way!"

I shot again and again. The crowd was dashing for the protection of their berths. A huge space widened around me.

I took the dying Glick and untangled him from the wires. Blood drooled down his chin and into his beard.

"You," he gasped. Then he coughed some. I took hold of him as the life drained out.

"Franco's dead, Glick."

"God help his wife and poor family," came the weak reply.

"God help you if you don't tell me where Eddie is!"

"You want to know, policeman? You really want to know?"

He told me, whispering between coughs and groans.

Then he said, ''Tell Bunker I'll be seeing him. Soon.''

Glick managed one last smile. Then he died.

I remembered I had a broken leg and cried out with pain. It took awhile for the crew of the steamer to reach me. Meanwhile I rested against the wall of the rat pit. Jocko, completely ignored now, came over and licked my hand. I liked to think he remembered me. I thought about what Glick had just told me. Then, stroking Jocko's bloody head, I started crying.

19

I WAS IN the hospital for two weeks before they let me
go home. After that it was another four weeks before
the leg healed well enough for me to go back to active
duty at the Central Office. A lot of things happened in
the meantime.

Alderman Joseph Bunker was arraigned for Glick's
murder. I didn't think much would come of it. Bunker
still had plenty of friends and money. Glick was a deformed sneak thief. Most people would agree that Bunker had done the world a service in killing him. But I
didn't want to let it go at that. I met up with a newspaper
acquaintance of mine and told him about Bunker's deal-
ings with Glick. He promised to pass the information on
to the right people in time for the trial. I hoped it would
hurt Bunker enough to get him into Moyamensing on
manslaughter. A two-year vacation would do him good.

The money I found in Glick's pockets had gone into
mine before anyone had looked. It was most of Leah's
blackmail payment. I had it with me when I visited Nilda
in the Orphan's Asylum. Her mother had died a few
weeks before, of cholera. When she saw me, her face lit
up. I wanted to take her home myself. But I had promised her to two childless neighbors of mine, good Christian people. I showed the money to Nilda as we rode
back to South Philadelphia. It would be in a trust, I told

her, until she reached maturity. She took it all silently, still mourning for her lost parents. I delivered the girl to her new home and watched her dolefully climb the steps to the waiting arms of her foster family.

I checked up on Nilda a week later and barely recognized her. More than the new clothes or groomed hair or doll she clutched like it was the first thing that was ever hers, I noticed the smile on her face. I sat in their parlor and watched her play with another child from the neighborhood. Their innocent joy was the one spark of happiness in my life that month.

That, and the companionship of my new friend. A certain fellow with a pitch-black head and white body and four legs. I'd kept Jocko since the night on the *General Hooker*. He was a good guard dog and kept the place rodent free. Every time we went for walks, the ladies of the neighborhood fawned on him. And me.

Naturally, I'd been keeping up on the status of the Eddie Munroe investigation. When Cap first called on me at the hospital, I told him nothing of Glick's dying words. I kept the ugly secret in me like a festering sore. He told me that Leah Munroe was exonerated completely of Franco's death. Indeed, no one knew it was Franco. Everyone agreed she'd acted in self-defense against an unknown maniac threatening to outrage her. No one ever came forth to identify the body. For all Cap knew, Franco was still at large. When Cap asked me about Glick's last words, all I told him was, "He said, 'Ask Franco. He's the one that knows.'"

Eddie Munroe had not yet been found. Archibald was in the papers every other day, called in by the Central Office again and again to look at children suspected to be his. But they never were. He vowed to search for Eddie "as long as it takes. Even if I spend my whole life searching."

Leah had not tried to contact me since the night she'd murdered Franco. Maybe she was hoping I'd vanish, too, like all her other nightmares.

The press was stirring up the public with stories about

police inefficiency and incompetence. Diefenderfer bore the brunt of most of these attacks. His investigation was going nowhere. Detectives were looking for Eddie from Canada to California. But nothing was turned up. Not a single clue. The other Ds scrambled to get off the sinking ship. They rushed to make various other arrests to restore their tarnished reputation. I was the only one who remained free of the mudslinging. Nobody linked me to anything but the recovery of a stolen dog. That merited two lines in the Police Intelligence column.

While everyone was out chasing leads on Eddie Munroe's mysterious kidnappers, I had the chance to break up a horse-thieving ring Pete Shields had told me about in the hospital. It restored me to Cap's good graces, especially after I split the reward money with the rest of the detective officers. I didn't exactly give it to them. Instead I chartered a boat and we went out on the Delaware, fishing. I made a lot of new friends that day. Even Diefenderfer started sneering at me a little less.

It was exactly a week after the fishing trip that I revisited Germantown for the first time since July. Now August was ebbing into September and fall was in the air. There had been a lot of rain and the leaves gave off a rich scent as I walked past the forests bordering the Wissahickon. Chickadees and cardinals twittered in the branches above me while insects swirled before my eyes like dancing sparks. The country air felt good going into my lungs. I stopped now and then to watch a squirrel scuttle up and down a tree, or a teeming mass of tiny ants go about their business at my feet. I liked being away from people and surrounded by nature. There was so much life all around me.

Then the wind ruffled my hair and made the leaves whisper. And I knew all that life would fade, like the green in the leaves, going wherever the wind went.

My mood vacillated between high and low all the way to Dr. Forrest Moyer's house. He was examining a young girl's ear as I walked in. Moyer recognized me right away, smiling.

"Do you have some time to spare to go for a walk?"
I asked him.

"As soon as I finish with Cynthia here," he said.

In a few minutes he had extracted a tick from Cynthia's ear. He placed it in a phial and held it to her face.

"Want to take it home with you? For a souvenir?"

All the girl could say was, "Yuck!"

We followed Cynthia and her mother outside.

"Where would you like to go?" Dr. Moyer asked me.

I recounted the story he'd told me way back in July. About the carriage and the men he'd seen driving it.

"You said there was a path to a quarry you used to take. That you saw them somewhere off the path, in the woods. You wondered what they were doing there."

"Yes, I remember. Do you want me to show you the spot?"

I nodded. For the rest of the way we talked about the weather, how bad ticks were in the woods, and about a new trip the doctor was taking out west.

Where Harvey Street ended, the path began.

"Better check yourself when you come out of here," he told me. "Especially your legs. Ticks."

I thanked him for the advice. We walked for a couple hundred yards when Moyer stopped.

"See up there? That's where they were, set back about . . . fifty, sixty feet from the path. Where that fallen tree is."

"Okay. Thanks. Now, go on home."

"Wait! Is it something about Eddie? A clue?"

I looked away from his eyes when I shook my head. "I just want to look around. You go on home."

We shook hands and I was left alone in the middle of the woods. The trees arched over me, blotting out the sky. Sun rays pierced their web in thin rivulets of light. The only sounds I could hear were squirrels running around, stirring up fallen leaves.

I walked toward the clearing Moyer had pointed out. Thorny vines barred my way, twisting around my legs. After two or three minutes I reached the spot.

There was nothing to distinguish it at all from any other part of the woods, except a path, wide enough to accommodate a wagon, that led down to the quarry and a large fallen tree barring the way. The path was almost completely overgrown.

I paused for just a moment and listened. Not far off I heard the Wissahickon, and it made me want to run there as fast as I could. I wanted to be away from this place.

With my boot I disturbed the cover of leaves on the ground, revealing moss-covered stones and patches of grass. Brush grew over most of the tiny clearing, except for right around the old path. There grass struggled toward the dim sunlight that the trees leaked downward.

The fallen tree looked like it had been there for quite some time. Fungi-covered bark hung off it in strips, with all kinds of insects scurrying in and out of the irregular grooves. When I put my hands on the bark to push it away, the wood crumbled like wet powder. I heaved at it again, trying to roll it. My muscles knotted up. I broke into a sweat. The dead tree started moving. I succeeded in lifting up one end but had to drop it.

I got down on my knees and pushed as hard as I could. My boots dug into the moist soil. I felt the veins in my head about to burst.

Suddenly the tree rolled away, but only slightly. Beneath it was nothing but soft earth.

I had nothing to dig with but my hands. They clawed through the dirt like twin plows. I didn't have far to go.

Eddie Munroe lay in the ground, on his side. The child's linen suit, laced shoes, and short skirt were all there. They remained intact around a thoroughly corrupted body. It was curled up, on its side, as if in sleep. His broad-brim hat dangled around what used to be a neck. My fingers untied its purple ribbon. I stuffed it in my pocket.

Then I replaced the log over the grave, fighting back the acid boiling into my mouth.

I wasn't thinking too clearly when I stepped off the

overgrown path. The Wissahickon was beckoning me. It was a calm, peaceful sound. I needed that peace. I needed to be away from this clearing.

All the regrets I'd had back in July for what I'd done and not done didn't seem to matter anymore. Maybe if I went down to the creek and stared at it long enough I would forget everything. This day would be just a trip in the country and nothing more.

The woods made it hard for me. Instead of taking the path, I waded through the brambles and vines adjacent to the clearing. Ahead, through the trees, I thought I saw the opposite bank of the Wissahickon. I started hurrying, to distance myself from the fallen tree and what lay beneath it.

Then I stumbled over something. It was not a rock, or even a thick branch. The way it rolled under my foot made me look down. Half of it was concealed beneath wet leaves and thorns. I yanked it out, feeling the thorns lash across my hand.

It was a miniature base-ball bat, in good condition. I wiped the dirt off it and carried it with me to the creek.

I sat down on the bank, resting my head against a warm, dry bole. The water slipped over the rocky bed, made clear by a brilliant afternoon sun. The murmur it made was the closest thing to eternity I could imagine. Eternity was on my mind. I felt the bat in my hands, felt the dirt which had covered it cake on my skin.

My eyes were closed, but I still heard him approach. He came by way of the quarry. I listened to him carefully make his way over the slippery rocks bordering the water. I waited until he was just beneath me.

Then I called to him. "Stephen."

The boy whipped around, startled.

"You remember me?"

He nodded very quickly. I stood up and walked toward him, swinging the base-ball bat.

Stephen saw the object in my hand. His expression changed from surprise to horror.

"This was his birthday present," I said aloud.

The boy said nothing, standing completely still. His shoulders were hunched. His hands tensed like he was choking two invisible creatures.

To me he looked very young and fragile. His neck was like the wick of a candle. If I took it between my two fingers, I could extinguish the brain above it, dull those fear-glazed eyes forever. That seemed like a good thing to do at the moment.

When I got within a few feet of him, Stephen began to back away. I kept advancing until his heels were up against the water. There was nowhere else he could go now.

My voice was surprisingly calm when I told him everything Glick had said to me on the steamer. Like I was talking to an elderly victim of dementia, telling him the story of a life which he'd forgotten.

"They never took you, Stephen. Or Eddie. But you saw them before. That's how you could give such a good description. The first time was at the shed. When you met your father. The second time was back there," I gestured toward the clearing from which I'd come, "where they saw you murder your brother."

"Glick and Franco, that's your father, Stephen, were hiding out in the woods there, planning to rob Munroe's house. That's all they were after. Then they saw you and Eddie run by on your way to play at the quarry. Glick said they could hear you hollering at each other. The little one, he said, was bawling. You were laughing at him. What were you saying to Eddie? Do you remember? Stephen?"

I reached out and grabbed him with one hand, while the other grasped the miniature bat. He didn't try to wriggle out of my grasp. His face looked dead, asleep with eyes open. That mirthless smile I'd seen before creased his placid, soulless expression. I'd seen the same look in padded rooms. And on the gallows.

"Why'd you have the bat with you?"

Surprisingly, he answered me. "I wanted to show it to him."

"Why? So you could tease him? So he would know you had it? And he could never get it?"

His legs twisted from the pressure I put on him. He sank down to the rock. I kept gripping his shirt, pushing him backward. The muscles in his neck strained against me.

"But he tried to get it, didn't he? He tried. And then you hit him. You hit him in the arm. Then he started wailing. Right? Did he say he was going to tell on you then?"

Stephen said nothing. He was grinding his teeth now, and squirming.

"So you hit him again. And he fell down this time. He didn't say anything else. He just kept on wailing. You could've let him go with that. But you didn't. Why not, Stephen?"

The child squirmed, kicking wildly. I was hurting him. I couldn't help it. Rage had entered me like a fever. The bat dropped out of my hand as I shoved him backward. His head dipped into the creek. I took a handful of hair and kept him under for about ten seconds. Then I let him up. He spat water in my face.

Somewhere along the way I had started screaming.

"Why did you hit him again? Why did you hit him in the head?"

I dunked him again for a few seconds. Bubbles leaked out of his mouth. He thrashed about like a turtle on its back.

Once again I let him up for air.

"Not just once! Three times in the head! Why?"

My hands plunged him back under. There was nothing left to say. No more questions. I didn't know why he'd answered me that one time, or why he hadn't denied everything else I'd said. I didn't know anything except that I wanted to hold him under some more.

I watched the small hands of the drowning boy scrape the wet stone. As if for the first time I looked at them, and my hands, too. And I became confused. The small hands were like mine as a child's, or another boy I had known but never seen. *Eddie*.

Then I saw my leering face reflected in the creek, with that same vacant, soulless stare I'd seen on Stephen.

There was the answer to my question, Why? It was the only answer I was going to get. The only one that would mean anything.

I let the boy out of the water. He flung himself forward and lay there, his chest heaving.

I stretched myself on the rock and looked at the sky. The sun was going down, darkening the clouds. The Wissahickon flowed on like it didn't notice. I washed my face in it.

Then I took the boy back home to his mother.

Leah was waiting for him in the backyard. When she saw me, her look of concern deteriorated to dread. She held the boy to her as I advanced, pushing his head into her bosom as if to close him off from the rest of the world.

"Is Archibald around?" I asked her.

"He's . . . gone to New York to talk with the police chief there. Someone says they saw Eddie in Long Island."

"What about Minnie?"

"She's doing the wash."

"Have her look after Stephen."

It wasn't a request. She told the boy to go get the clothesline. We watched him stumble toward the house.

"Look at him sulk. He misses his father."

"Who? Franco?"

"You know who I mean."

"How long is he up there for?"

"A few days. He keeps looking and looking."

"Let's hope for his sake that he never finds anything."

She cocked her head and squinted at me.

My hand dipped into my pocket. I took her hand and put the purple ribbon in·it.

Leah held it in front of her like it was the finest of gems.

"This . . . this was Eddie's," she told me.

"I know."

"Where did you get it?" Each word came out like a sigh.

"Stephen can tell you."

The fingers stroking the ribbon began to tremble. So did her jaw. She looked on the brink of a fit.

"What do you mean?" she cried.

"I mean there was never any kidnapping, Leah. There was never any child for them to steal. He'd already been stolen from you. And you didn't know it."

She looked back at Stephen, who was walking around the side of the house. Then she fell to her knees. At first I thought she would cry out. But she just sat there with her palms outstretched. The purple ribbon trailed to the grass and blew away. Her eyes went inward. The questions she was asking herself destroyed the beauty in her face.

Then she said, "Yes, I did."

Now it was my turn to stare at her, mouth agape.

"That's why I killed him, don't you understand?"

"Who?"

"Franco! I killed him because he told me the truth. He told me how he and Glick had watched Stephen beat Eddie to death. How they'd watched him run away. They buried the body because they didn't want to be blamed for killing him. They knew they'd been seen by Dr. Moyer near the same spot. They were afraid." She laughed a joyless laugh and went on.

"Then they read the newspaper stories about the disappearance. They realized they were the only ones who knew Eddie was . . ." It was impossible for her to finish the sentence. "Frank got the idea of writing a ransom letter to Archibald. Let him think Eddie was still alive. And me, too. He thought that was so funny. He was laughing about it when I shot him."

She was laughing and crying at the same time now.

Her hysterical eyes looked straight into mine.

"Show me where he is."

"No. You'll have to ask Stephen."

"But I can't. No, I won't. I won't kill him, too. I'll take him away. Send him away," she promised herself.

"You'll have to. He set that fire in the shed on purpose. And he would have stayed inside if I hadn't gone in after him."

"I know that."

"He has to stay for a long time wherever you send him. He might never be able to leave."

"But maybe not. Maybe someday he can come back to us."

It didn't sound like a futile dream, coming from her lips.

I stood up to leave her. When I turned my back and headed for the street, she cried, "Wait!"

I let her approach me.

"You're not going to . . . say anything. Are you?" It was a statement, not a question.

I shook my head and left her there as dusk started transforming the sky and casting shadows.

Leah had wanted a reason for my silence. I had been afraid to answer her. It had nothing to do with a concern for her happiness, nor Stephen's, really. Nor Archibald's, though I liked him and knew, as Leah did, that the truth would kill him.

No. The silence came from remembering my reflection in the Wissahickon. And how I had washed it away by letting a killer live.

I wanted to believe in some kind of redemption.

Afterword

ON JULY 1 , 1874, Charley Ross was kidnapped from his home in Germantown, Pennsylvania. Not long afterward a ransom letter written in a nearly illegible scrawl was delivered to the grief-stricken family. What followed, the whole tragedy of the Charley Ross case, became a national obsession. Letter after letter was sent to the Ross family while the police searched in vain for the child and his abductors. Police departments all across the nation were on the alert. False alarms were habitual, as any strange man or men with a child were suspected and often savagely attacked by mobs of irate citizens.

The child was never brought back to his family. The kidnappers were shot dead while trying to burglarize a Brooklyn cottage months after the police had shown themselves incapable of bringing them to justice. To this day no one knows whatever became of little Charley Ross.

For those interested in reading more on this factual crime, I recommend *Little Charley Ross, The Shocking Story of America's First Kidnapping for Ransom*, by Norman Zierold (Little, Brown, 1967). This book gives a detailed account of the whole case, including reproductions of the myriad ransom letters received by Mr. Ross.

Decades later the impact of the case was still being felt. In 1899 Mark Twain used an expedition in search of Charley Ross as a metaphor for uselessness. The boy figured in a popular Australian song. Tramps and vagrants, who in the popular imagination were responsible for the crime, were dealt with more harshly by the authorities. One stranger was even killed in a town for talking to children on the streets.

While we tend to think of the good old days as a time of innocence, it is apparent that by 1874 that paradise was already lost.

For most people, this period in American history is an enigma. The Civil and Spanish–American wars tend to envelop it and drown out its voice. Yet it was during this ''gilded age'' that America as we know it was born. All the meretricious emblems of capitalism, the widescale urban blight, the narcotics trade, the alienation—all these things blossomed in the stifling mill smoke. The urban jungle is nothing new.

My quest for this world stems from a more private and personal search for my own past, and the inherent frustration in that search, for my ancestors left little trace of themselves. When I started, all I knew about them was that they had appeared in Philadelphia sometime in the 1870s. In the absence of their own records, I decided to create one for them.

They were working-class people, not upper-crust ''Victorians.'' They built row houses and canals, shoveled coal into locomotive furnaces, and stitched shoes together in giant mills.

And, a fact I learned only after I wrote this book, they were policemen.

McCleary steps forth to give these silent ones a voice—the ones who worked, loved, and died in anonymity. But their humble silence disguises the profundity of their lives. The more they speak, the more fascinating they become. McCleary talks as they would—not with the crisp and formal diction of the bourgeoisie, but with the slang and contractions of the laborers. Not everyone in the nineteenth century spoke like the prose of Thomas Hardy. McCleary's world is not one of croquet matches, eclectic manses staffed by liveried servants, and lackadaisical frolics in brougham carriages. He, like my ancestors, is of the streets, the concrete and clay.

In assembling a facsimile of my nineteenth century ancestors' world, I am also recreating my lost identity, thus the need for historical authenticity and the avoidance of anachronism. I want to know not just what happened, but also how it looked, how it felt and smelled. I made sure to find out exactly what the colors of the omnibuses were and exactly how much their fare was. I wanted to know what odors were in the air and how the woolen clothes felt against the skin. I needed to know what the weather was like on July 1, 1874, and who won which ballgame that week.

All these minor details make me feel more a part of that time. And the more I feel in step with the nineteenth century, the easier and more tempting it is to explore alleys and back courts so long lost from view. New destinations in that world creep into my subconscious the more time I spend surrounded by dusty and forgotten manuscripts and journals. Recently, as I meandered through the stacks of the Historical Society of Pennsylvania, I found a true tale of racism and grave-robbing that told so much and yet left so much more untold. It didn't take me long to decide that it will be the next destination in this search for a forgotten world and its people.

Wilton McCleary will meet you there again, very soon.

Dangerous Excursions
Into the Mysterious Ireland of
Bartholomew Gill's
Chief Inspector Peter McGarr

"Simply astonishing."
New York Times Book Review

THE DEATH OF AN IRISH LOVER
0-380-80863-3/$6.50 US/$8.99 Can

Chief Inspector Peter McGarr has been called out from Dublin to investigate a troubling double homicide. The nude body of a young, pretty, and recently married policewoman has been discovered in the bed of a hot-sheet inn—wrapped around the equally unclothed corpse of her much older boss.

THE DEATH OF AN IRISH POLITICIAN
0-380-73273-4/$5.99 US/$7.99 Can

THE DEATH OF AN IRISH TINKER
0-380-72579-7/$5.99 US/$7.99 Can

THE DEATH OF AN IRISH SEA WOLF
0-380-72578-9/$5.99 US/$7.99 Can